DIESEL

By
Piper Malone

Published by Piper Malone
Copyright © 2013 by Piper Malone

All Rights Reserved

ISBN: 978-0-9913201-1-0
Print Edition

Edited by Seraph Editing

Cover Art by Dee Allen
www.deeallencoverart.com

Formatting by BB eBooks
www.bbebooksthailand.com

Dedication

Michele, I knew this secret would be safe with you despite my apprehension about sharing it. Thank you for your unfailing support, your passion for this story, for forgetting I was the one writing, and never hesitating to tell me "I told you so." A few sentences would never be enough to express my gratitude, so I give you an entire book. This work is lovingly dedicated to you, my friend.

Acknowledgements

Thank you to my beautiful betas, Ashlee, Shweta, and Heidi. Your dedication and enthusiasm around this book kept me focused on the goal. I am a lucky woman to have such caring and loving friends.

To the guru of Seraph Editing, your support, guidance and insights have been immeasurable. You have helped to make this dream a reality, and for that I am eternally grateful. Thank you for taking me under your wing.

Thank you to my parents who have kept my confidence, offered positive encouragements and have always instilled in me the knowledge that I can do anything I put my mind to.

Finally, to the love of my life, thank you for allowing me the freedom and flexibility to take these steps. I am especially grateful for your instance on changing my mantra from "if" I publish, to "when" I publish.

Prologue

THEY CALL ME Diesel.

I'm not sure why or where exactly the name came from, but it's stuck for years.

Old and new know me only as Diesel.

This is the way it is.

This is the way it will always be.

Chapter One
ELLIOT

STAFF MEETING ON Monday morning could not be more frustrating. We huddle around coffee cups and banter to each other about how spring has not yet sprung in Boston. I listen to the stories of the parties, girls, guys, drugs, and insanity that have corrupted my colleagues' time away from work. And me? I can do nothing but weave my pen back and forth between my fingers and wish this meeting would end. I'm bored wondering if taking this job was a mistake. Leaving home to work for a blog overseas sounded like a great opportunity, but now, I'm not so sure. How did I go from majoring in journalism and jump into a mediocre blogging job? Professional blogging for an entertainment site but blogging nonetheless. I can't believe I landed at this godforsaken place under the ruse I would amount to something. My peers just float through and appear happy and content with their vocation, while I sit here and actively plan my escape. *Could this garbage take any longer to sort through? What is taking so damn long for this mind-numbing meeting to start!*

I shift in my seat, looking around for Miss Alison, our boss whose only other vocation could be a fire-breathing lady in some demonic circus. She's a brute. Sheer callousness.

She's frightening and fucking sexy. I spend the majority of my days fantasizing about her rather than coming up with a story pitch that could be of any consequence. I imagine her walking down the hall toward the conference room. The *clack, clack, clack* of her heels sets the staccato for her hunt. Her skirt pulls taut against each leg as she pushes down the hall, toward me. Her advance pushes her hips from side to side as her black hair bobs in wavy curls round her –

"Elliot! What the hell are you doing?"

My arch back to check the hallway has lingered for too long and the venomous eyes of my prying colleagues have caught me mid daydream.

"Oh, I uh..."

The conference room door swings open with a force that would knock over a grown man. The Dragon Lady has entered. She's ten minutes late but anyone who has noticed is smart enough to not say anything. The busy chatter is silenced as she stands at the head of the table and surveys her minions. I am grateful for being saved from explaining my awkward stare by the one person who encompasses numerous personal fantasies and scares the everloving shit out of me.

"Okay, we need stories, people. Who has ideas?" Miss Alison snaps. *She would look good in leather...with a whip...*

Everyone stares at the Dragon Lady, afraid to speak first. I see her rolling her jaw, which I am entirely certain she has the ability to unhinge and eat someone whole. She's picking her victim. Two colleagues offer minor, worthless stories. The Dragon looks more and more pissed.

"I have an assignment," the Dragon sighs after a moment, "it's going to be more of an in-depth job. Our funders want us to take on some newer, longer term stories. Who's up for it?"

Again, no one answers.

"Fine. No one wants it?" She begins to pace the conference room, heels clicking against the floor. "I don't think I'm being clear here, kids. There's a job that needs doing. The bigwigs are coming down on us to make some serious cash in the next year, so that means you need to get your asses out there and find some stories. Who has done that lately?" She stares down each one of us. "Have you?" She points to Victor. "Or you?" Sam flinches under her pointed finger as if she's sent a bolt of lightning though him. "No one has come up with anything of consequence, so we need to go after what they want or it's the unemployment line."

Silence hangs in the room like a heavy cloak. The Dragon has won no awards for her motivational skills. *Maybe she was a drill instructor in a past life, or hell, this life...*

"What's the job?" I take the bait and immediately regret the step out of line. She turns toward me and glares. It's official. I'm going to die.

"There is a club or some kind of social hall in New York that is gathering underground chatter. I want you to go there, find out what it is all about, come back and we'll see what you've got."

I have to travel to New York for an underground club. Seriously?

"We'll pay for your expenses over there and get you a suite close to the club. I think you'll be there for about six months. What's required is an in-depth monthly post telling about how you infiltrate the club, the culture, and the staff. I want you to get in close with the people who run the place and share them with the world via our site. This place is gaining momentum and I want to know about it. I want us to break it open. The operation is heavily guarded. Their people don't talk too much, but from what I hear, they put on a hell of a show."

"What's the show?"

"It depends on the night. It's mostly a DJ club but I've heard they have an eclectic style. It has been running for some time and they have the same clientele at most shows. It's run by someone named Diesel. Apparently he's a guy who always wanted big in the entertainment industry, but, that's all we know. You will find out the rest. Get in with Diesel and figure out what he's all about. You leave on Monday."

"And if I can't get in?"

She squints her eyes at me with a devilish delight. "You don't come back." The Dragon doesn't flinch when the audible gasps of Kim and Sarah mingle with the uncomfortable shifting of some of the guys. There's no change in her at all, she only continues to bore through me with her stare.

"Any other questions?" I shake my head. "Good. Then we're done." She pushes out of the room.

I wonder if this is what sex with her is like. She ravages you so severely, you have no idea she's done with you until she's gone.

I exhale and look around the room at my colleagues, nodding lightly before pushing away from the table.

I guess I'm going to New York.

✧   ✧   ✧

BACK AT MY desk, I rifle through some papers, attempting to organize my mess of a cubicle.

"Elliot, here's the stuff for your assignment." Megan, the Dragon's number one assistant, drops a thin folder on my desk. "It's some background information on Eden and directions to the hotel where you'll be staying."

"Eden? What is that?" I pick up the folder, thumbing through the scant pages.

"The club, Elliot," she huffs in irritation. "In New York. Your plane ticket will be at the airport."

"I don't need a plane ticket; I can ride down on my bike. Can you guys just ship my stuff instead?" The spring weather has me eager to get my Superlow out of storage and on the road. It would also be practical to have my own means of transportation back to Boston.

She looks at me with a vapid stare that can only mean *fuck off*. "Yeah," she huffs, "we can do that."

"Thanks." I try to offer her a placating smile before she turns on her heel and stomps out the door. I look at the information she's given me.

This place is called Eden? Like...paradise?

I CALL MY father in London and friends around town to tell them about my assignment out of the state. During my last few days in the office, I try to do some research with the background information Megan shoved my way. Unfortunately, it's a dead end. There's really nothing out there about Eden, only a nondescript, odd Facebook page. Eden has thousands of Likes and pictures partygoers have posted, but there is nothing about Diesel. No website. No "About Us" or "Contact" page. Nothing at all.

The profile picture is a black background with white lettering that holds a single word:

When I look through the pictures posted by fans, it rivals that of an orgy. People kissing, sweaty bodies writhing together on the dance floor, girls on suspended catwalks frozen in unmistakably stripper-esque movements. *What the hell is this place?*

Before I leave, I make sure to stop the mail and clean out the fridge. One last night of debauchery before I leave is all I can really muster. Sunday is more of a recoup day, truly a day of rest.

Monday I drop my essentials at FedEx for shipping, load my pack, and head south to New York.

Chapter Two

ELLIOT

TWO HOURS LATER, I park outside what appears to be a massive abandoned warehouse. Clearly a historic building from an industrial era, the steel girders holding the building together are brown and rusted. The windows are caked with a permanent film of dirt and gravel, giving them a smoky appearance. Mother Nature has definitely made this place her bitch. It has that eerie look as though it might be haunted with the souls of those who have entered before. I pull myself off the bike and roust a cloud of dust and gravel from the open lot in front of the massive steel entrance. *This is Eden?* The location is desolate and utilitarian. Walking up to a steel ramp, I have no choice but to pound unceremoniously on the steel doors. Muffled sounds from the inside, possibly music but definitely chatter, stop after a second round of my fist hitting the door.

I pound again, making sure whomever is in there knows there's someone at the door. From inside, a disembodied voice yells, "Yeah, hold on a minute."

The heavy door creaks open to reveal a man in his early twenties. He's sweated through his undershirt and looks like he could go several rounds with any opponent. I immediately feel self-conscious next to this guy. Essentially, he's a stud. Good looking. Great shape. I would be no match for him in any and all competitions. I may be taller and leaner, but he's pure power.

"Can I help you?" His questioning tone is calm but direct.

"I need to see Diesel," I say with more power than I anticipated.

He scoffs and crosses his arms across his chest. "Why?" he asks with a slight smirk.

"I'd like to interview him for the entertainment blog I work for. We hear he's running a tight ship that is blowing up the nightlife. We'd like to be the first to showcase what you have going on."

He stares at me, his eyes assessing and taking me in. He's made no move to let me in the door.

He breathes in audibly and looks over his shoulder. "Look dude, I don't know what your deal is but we really don't do stuff like this. Thanks for your time but we've got to pass." He rocks backwards and moves to begin shutting the door.

"Can we just talk about it?" I put my hand on the door, trying to stop its progression. The guy looks at me as if I've lost my mind.

"Look," I blurt, "it could be good for you guys." *You've got to sell this shit and sell it now!* "More exposure means more people, which ultimately means more revenue."

I hold my breath as he stares at me, hand stroking his chin in contemplation.

"I can see you are one of the people vested in this endeavor. How about I take you and Diesel to dinner so we can talk about this a little more?"

After what feels like twenty minutes of contemplative thought, he speaks. "Where are you from?"

"I drove down from Boston today." I can't tell if he's asking about my accent or location. "I'm originally from London."

"Hmm." He considers this confession with raised eyebrows. "How long are you in town?"

"As long as it takes."

He smiles wryly and sighs. "Okay, we'll meet you for dinner and continue this discussion. Eight o'clock at Rosie's on Seventh."

"Excellent. See you then. Here's my card. If you need me, you can text or call me in the meantime." I start to back down the ramp and remember myself. "Will Diesel be joining us as well?"

He looks up from my business card and smiles. "Of course."

"Brilliant. Eight o'clock, then."

I hear the metal doors close behind me with a deafening sound of old metal as I walk down the ramp to my bike.

That was easy.

Maybe a little too easy.

Chapter Three
DIESEL

I AM FURIOUS.

"You did *what* today?"

"I talked to some guy from a blog. He wants to talk to us about doing a spot for his site." Bain looks at me with nothing but blinding amusement at the knot he's deftly tied me in.

I can't hide my disgust or my anger. Being anything but transparent when righteously pissed has never been my strong suit.

"I can't believe you! What the hell are we supposed to do! And what does this guy want?" I yell. The ability to be calm or even slightly normal has abruptly left my toolbox for managing this stress.

"What's the big deal? We talk to him and see what it's all about. What harm could come from dinner?" His tone is calm, as if he's trying to keep me from jumping off the ledge. He knows this is not something we do. We don't willingly expose ourselves. How could he just do this, especially without talking to me first!

I look at Mike, who's seated on the couch in my office. He's been quiet during this entire interlude. He has always been the yin to Bain's yang. He holds his hands up to me. "I have to agree with Bain on this one. I know you aren't happy about it, but it could mean good exposure and revenue for us." The words pour from his mouth and I immediately hate him for it. He's my number one when it comes to being rational and making financial choices for our little enterprise and now he's conspiring with Bain, our wild child.

He stares passively at my scowl as I try to manage my breath. With his green eyes imploring me to be calm, as he sits like Buddha. *Damn it! I hate these men!*

I roll my eyes to the ceiling, focusing on the highest point in the room, and cross my arms tightly across my chest. "Fine," I acquiesce, "what do we have to do?"

"Dinner at eight at Rosie's. He's meeting us there," Bain says, and sinks into the couch next to Mike.

As we stare each other down, I hate them. Almost. Obviously anxious for me to agree to this ridiculous event, Bain drums his fingers on the arm of the sofa while Mike waits patiently. *Ying and Yang.* Mike's lean muscular frame is relaxed and calm. His sandy blonde hair is the perfect complement to his lightly bronzed skin. To me, he always looks sun-kissed. He is my cool surfer boy. My strong, mostly silent, business partner. My quiet respite against Hurricane Bain. If Mike is my surfer boy, Bain in my Bronx brawler. He is more muscular than Mike, with pecs and a six-pack that I've actually seen women lick on certain evenings. Bain's dark brown hair, deep blue eyes, and strong jaw make him a venerable Adonis.

They are discreet with their relationship and have been for years. I know it's Bain's decision more than Mike's but I can't say I disagree with the motivation to stay private.

However, in public they pass as straight without a second glance. I know they only have eyes for each other despite the fact they are never without female companionship when we're out. They are a dynamic duo, gorgeous and talented in their own rights. They are a lethal cocktail that have unsuspecting women everywhere bending to their will. Including me.

"Fine," I huff.

"Darling," Mike offers, "I know you're mad but this really may be good for us."

Despite agreeing to this, I'm still in full-blown defiance mode and there is no way it's going to end during this conversation. I glare at both of them before I begin stalking out of the room. *Bastards in my office! I was working so nicely until you come in here and shit up the place!*

"Um, sweetheart?" Bain calls after me, his sweet tone instantly putting me on the alert to be even more pissed off. "Clean it up for this guy. He's a good-looking piece and we want to make a nice impression, don't we?"

My eyes widen at him before my jaw clenches shut and I storm out the door, slamming it hard behind me.

Now I have to get dressed up for some creep I don't even know? Ugh!

I storm to my apartment and pray the hours until dinner drag on.

✧   ✧   ✧

I AM ROUSTED from my nap by the ping of a text message.

You know we have to leave in an hour and I've not heard you get in the shower.

Bain, you son of a bitch!

Tell me why you are monitoring my water usage?
Because you're mad and you'll take a stand by being childish and not get ready for this meeting.

You ARE a son of a bitch.

This was not my idea and I don't see why I should have to participate in your bullshit schemes.
Because you are you. You know this. Come on. Get dressed. This will be ok.
And if it's not?
You have the ultimate decision. Set limits if you must (you do with everything else). I won't strong-arm it if you don't like what he has to say. Just hear him out. Please sweetheart, this may be what we need to really get the Eden out there.
You act as if we are falling on hard times. We're doing really well.
This is an opportunity to grow. I know you like opportunities to grow…

Ugh! He's hitting below the belt. I flop back on the bed with a frustrated sigh. I get to make the final decision? This battle is not going to be won over text messaging. I drop my arm over my head. Fine...

Let me meet you there. I'll text you when I'm close.
That's my girl! See you soon.
I hate you.
I know and I love that you do

I sigh in defeat. *Bain...if it weren't for you...* I shake my dark thoughts away and walk into my bathroom thinking how pleased he will be to hear the water running.

Chapter Four
ELLIOT

I AM SITTING in Rosie O'Grady's, alone at a table reserved by the man I met this afternoon. About an hour after I left, he shot me a text stating that he had made the reservation for four under my name. The table is great, essentially. Despite being tucked in the back corner, I'm able to see all the action of the restaurant, the patrons who enter or leave as well as those who pick up takeout, in addition to the servers bustling around the crowded tables. The restaurant is fully active but calm and quiet. It's a dimmed den of warmth and fluidity scented with the aromas of freshly cooked dishes accenting the air. Despite the beautiful surrounding, my nervousness is clear. I fiddle incessantly with the placemat and look around again. Meeting three unknown people in the middle of a city I'm not familiar with for an assignment that has the ability to render me unemployed is less than settling. I'd feel more confident waiting on a Craig's List blind date.

Where the hell is my drink? At least with a drink in my hand, I can stop acting like a bored child. When I twist to look for the waiter, I see the man I met this morning pushing though the crowded restaurant.

Simply dressed in jeans, white shirt, and jacket, he looks

like a runway model. He's all muscle, strong jaw, and smooth canter. He smiles at me and extends his hand as he approaches me.

"Elliot, good to see you," he says, shaking my hand. "Sorry I didn't introduce myself earlier. My name is Bain McAully. This is Mike Weston." He gestures to the equally well-primped man behind him. His level of civility shocks me, especially after this afternoon. He's gone from pushing me off to seemingly cool customer in a couple of hours.

Before I can respond, Bain continues. "Sorry we're late. You know how women can be when they are getting ready. She'll be along soon. She got a separate cab."

She? Who is she? "Understandable. I have sisters. We had more than one family event run behind schedule for the sake of proper outfitting and makeup," I offer.

Mike and Bain order drinks and we begin small talk about where I'm staying and my trip into New York. As if not listening to the casual conversation, Mike abruptly changes the topic. "So tell us, Elliot," he says, leaning in on his elbows, "what is your ultimate goal for your story?"

Bain snorts lightly into his bourbon and raises his hand in protest. "Do we have to do the dirty work right away? Can't we enjoy dinner?"

Mike and Bain exchange a look; however, Mike ignores the comment. "Look," he says, turning to me, "I'm sure you're a great guy who comes from a wonderful family, but the bottom line is, we need to figure out what your end point is. I'm not having dinner with a one night stand." He's calm but intense. Bain looks slightly annoyed at Mike's immediate attack.

I huff at this obvious game of good cop, bad cop. "Well, I'm scheduled to be here for six months or more, depending on how long this takes. That's a pretty long one night stand."

Mike shrugs and appears slightly satisfied with my answer. *This is your chance...start talking.*

I begin to discuss the project, observing the development and execution of a night in Eden, one of the hottest underground clubs currently entertaining New York City. As I ramble on about the actual blog postings and what I hope to accomplish, both men seem to be interested. I feel the need to keep pressing the goals of this project to them; more exposure means more money. The lure of more money for them also means I'll get to keep my job. They don't need to know it's a win/win situation but that looming fact has never been far from my mind. I am interrupted only by Bain's phone receiving a text.

He looks relieved. "Ah, she's a block away. Wonderful! I'm starving." He looks at me. "She'll want to hear your spiel also, so hold that thought." He picks up the menu and without further explanation, the conversation ends.

We continue to talk lightly while perusing dinner choices until Bain says quietly, "Here she is."

I look up to see a woman walking lithely toward the table on heels that only magnify her statuesque figure. Her chocolate brown hair is long, softly curled and balances her fair skin, which seems to glow in the reflection of the table candles. Her coral halter dress shows off her soft shoulders. She is stunning. I have lost all my faculties on her except the engrained politeness to stand as she approaches the table. She looks at me, smiles slightly, and drops her gaze.

"I apologize for being late. I was tied up with other tasks before I realized what time it was," she offers with a cool and confident smile.

"No worries. Now we can eat," Bain says, looking up at her with an enormous smile before finishing his drink. She smiles back at him warmly as she sits directly across from me. I find it odd that neither Bain nor Mike make any move to greet her more than that casual interaction. Is this a girlfriend or wife? She's not wearing a ring. Would it matter if she was wearing a ring? It shouldn't. It doesn't. This is a business meeting for a job, not a dating service. *Focus, Elliot, and not on her.* However, it would be nice to know how they know each other.

Too late, I realize I am staring at her. She lifts her gaze and pins me with her beautiful eyes. Deep golden tones splash out from behind the black of her iris, sending flecks of light across a sea of deep green hazel. I have the ability to do nothing but look away quickly and hope the dimly lit restaurant hides my embarrassment.

Bain clears his throat and taps the menu on the table. As I look at him, he is smiling slyly. "Well, I know what I want. What have you decided you would like, Elliot?"

His question is pointed and I see from the corner of my eye that she shifts her glance from Bain to the busy restaurant. Mike looks up, only to flick his gaze between the brunette and myself. Holy shit! This guy totally just caught me gawking at his girl. This is going down. I'm totally fucked.

"I'm having the mushroom ravioli," she offers to the table as she gestures to the waiter. She's ignored Bain's question and completely disregarded any answer I may have offered.

"Hello," she offers politely as the seasoned waiter approaches our table with a genuine smile of interest, "we're ready to order. Before we go around though, I'd like a martini, dirty."

"Of course, Miss." The waiter smiles at her, holding her gaze for a little too long. At least I'm not the only one.

She smiles softly at him. "Thank you." Her voice is a purr, sexy and polite. The waiter's presence shifted the uncomfortable moment. Did she just save me?

As we wait for dinner, Bain asks me to again begin my pitch, telling them about my start as a blogger and how I got to where I am now. I discuss my ultimate goal for the blog: six pieces over the course of six months, each exploring the process for how the individual shows are set up and how Eden functions.

Throughout the evening, Bain and Mike ask pointed questions, not only about the blog but about me. The woman just sits and listens, taking it all in.

After dessert is done and we are all enjoying a cup of coffee, I decide it's my time to strike.

"So, you've heard my purpose. What do you think?"

Mike, for the first time during the entire meal, smiles as he pulls his napkin from his lap and throws it on the table. "Well, I like what I hear. However, we have to make a collective decision. I think we need Diesel's input before we make a final decision."

"I would have to agree with Mike on all counts," Bain seconds with an exuberance I would not have expected.

"Great! When do we meet with him?" I counter. *Victory is mine!*

Bain and Mike smile in unison. Bain laughs lightly and looks at the silent woman at our table.

"Well I think now is a good time, don't you, sweetheart?"

"Yes, I agree," she says quietly as she puts down her coffee cup. "Gentlemen, will you excuse us?" she asks, looking at Mike and Bain. Despite her initial introduction and ordering her food, this is the only time during the entire meal that she has uttered a word.

Without hesitation, Mike and Bain exit the booth. The woman and Mike exchange a nod. Bain leans over and kisses her on the cheek, lingering to whisper something in her ear. They exchange a glance before he turns to shake my hand.

"Good night, Elliot. It was a pleasure." Bain walks out of the restaurant with the cool pace of a man on the prowl.

I look at her with confusion. "I'm sorry, I don't think I understand."

"I can understand that. It should be very clear very short-ly." Folding her hands on the table, she leans toward me. "Tell me Elliot, what is your true purpose here?"

I scoff slightly before leaning back in the booth. *Where the hell have you been for the past two hours?* "I explained all of that." I try to hide the exasperation in my voice. "It's an assign-ment. I'd like to document the proceedings of Eden."

She looks at me intently and I am pulled into her stare.

Bloody hell, her eyes are unbelievable.

"Excuse me." A voice from beside the table shakes us loose from the other's stare.

"Yes?" she asks a young woman who is now standing nervously next to her.

"I just wanted to say hello and ask for an autograph. I'm

sorry to interrupt, but I've been coming to the Eden for years. I've never see you out before."

She laughs lightly. "Well, we don't really go out a whole lot. Sure, darling; what do you have for me to sign?"

The girl quickly shoves a napkin in front of her then holds up her phone. "Can we get a quick picture? No one is going to believe me!"

"Of course," she replies. The girl shoves the phone at me and scoots into the chair next to her. The phone snaps and she checks the picture before showing it to the brunette, who smiles in approval. The girl hops up and down in pure excitement.

"Thank you, Diesel! We'll see you on Friday!"

Wait....what?

"You're welcome. See you then." She looks back at me and offers a slight smile.

"Hold on. You're Diesel?"

She laughs with a wicked smirk. "I am."

"So this whole time you've just been here?"

"Yes."

"I thought Diesel was a man."

"Many do. I can assure you, I've never been a man. However, I can see how you would be confused. I was going to tell you eventually, but she broke in."

"But your shows. They're sort of...well, they're hot. Right?"

"Yes, the shows possess a healthy level of debauchery." She gives me a look I can only categorize as lustful. "Just because I'm a woman doesn't mean I don't know what people like, Elliot." She pauses; her lower lip is caught momentarily by her teeth before continuing. "Look, we do a lot of stuff, different shows have different flavors. You'll see." The side of her mouth curls ever so slightly.

"I'll see? Right...so does that mean you'll let me do this?"

"Here are my stipulations. You stick to Bain, Mike, and myself. What we want off the record is off the record. I review everything you want to publish before it's submitted. You come to the pre-show prep and attend the shows." Her demands are not questionable. They are clear, concise, and slightly too restrictive for my liking.

"Those are tough expectations. Do you really have to read everything? And I have to be there for everything?" I hope she is able to see some reason.

"Everything. If you want to have the full experience, you have to be there from conception to birth. Please don't fail to remember that Eden, and all the people in it, is my baby. I'll be damned if anyone is going to mess with my baby. If you do, I can assure you I am a far worse adversary than any man would be."

The seriousness of her tone shakes me for the moment. Without a doubt, she would be a handful pissed off. Now, she is not only amazingly beautiful but intriguing. Her stare is so intense I have no doubt she could level me, and after tonight, I think I want her to. I have to clear my throat to clear the raspiness I know has brewed during this turn in the discussion. "I wouldn't dream of messing with you or your baby. You have a deal."

"Very good." She leans back. "We'll see you tomorrow at Eden at 10 a.m."

"Okay," is all I can muster as we are locked eye-to-eye in the candlelit restaurant for what feels like the millionth time this evening. She is hot – all of her. Body, eyes, mouth, and voice. Her lips have a fullness that makes me think of nothing but laying my mouth over hers. We stare at each other in silence. I can feel her eyes bore into me with a curiosity I can't name. Desire thrums through my body, pulling blood from everywhere and pushing it directly into my cock. In this moment of weakness, I can't help myself, I need to see what she's made of.

"So, Miss Diesel, if you are in charge of Eden, does that make you Eve?"

"There's no 'Miss,' Elliot. It's only Diesel." She smiles at me, those lips curling slightly. "And no, I'm not Eve." She leans toward me. "I'm the snake."

The breathy sexuality of her voice registers everywhere in my body, which is worsened only by the slight bite of her lip after the words escape her mouth.

Without another word, she slides gracefully out of the booth and walks toward the door, glancing over her shoulder to look at me before she exits.

Chapter Five

DIESEL

I'M THE SNAKE.

What is wrong with me? Where do I come up with this shit, and why?

Trying to get my breath under control has become a cumbersome chore despite being sprawled in the back of the first cab I could hail. Panic. And what...lust? Is that was this is? My heart is pounding and I am unequivocally ramped up. The ache in my belly grew throughout dinner and quickly traveled south.

If sitting still when wanting to do nothing but squirm in your seat under the watchful eye of one Mr. Elliot Archer was an Olympic event, I'd be biting that gold metal atop the podium. Or, better yet, Mr. Archer would be biting parts of me. No!

I can't believe this! What have I done? I've agreed to this, that's what I've done. This man is going to be in our lives for the next six months and I handcuffed myself to him. And he's hot. Oh sweet baby Jesus, he's hot. He's, what, at least six two; he towered over me and I'm rocking these heels. What's even worse is he's got that slightly out of control hair that makes me was to mess it up even more. It's as if Ryan

Reynolds and Bradley Cooper had a love child and dumped him on my doorstep. Between his brown hair, those light blue eyes, and that jaw....damn it! And, of course, the accent. Fuck. This is bad. This is really bad!

And Bain left me alone with him. What an ass! What is his game, really? Was this a test? Let's see how far we can push Diesel? A blister of anger burns in the pit of my stomach. I can't believe he left me there alone, with a complete stranger.

I try to stabilize myself with a cleansing breath. Regardless of how sexy this man is, he's here on business. I'm here on business. This is business. He wants to do his little blog here, fine. He'll see what everyone else sees. The veneer we've worked so hard to develop and maintain is firmly in place and has been for years. There's no changing it now.

Put on the face and do your job.

That's what we do.

Chapter Six

ELLIOT

I PACKED EVERYTHING before going to bed last night in preparation for my first day at Eden. iPhone, iPad, laptop, camera, pens, paper, backup recorder, all ready for whatever I may experience. As I enter the warehouse that houses Eden, I marvel at the groundswell that this place has generated. Truly, it's nothing fancy or particularly ornate. It's just a shell of an industry that used to be, transformed into new industry. The steel girders lining the ceiling look as if they have been untouched since their original placement. A dingy skylight runs the length of the building, offering some sunlight to brighten the interior of the club. It's industrial and cool without trying to be.

Choosing a corner near one of the exits, I find the best spot to observe from afar during the first week. I've decided that getting the lay of the land and then exploring as time goes on is the best tactic for absorbing what Eden really is. I watch as the performance group practice different dance routines for the upcoming show. It is tiring and exhaustive but they all engage in playful banter and chatter. They are beautiful, sweaty, and smiling, and are focused on the task of developing a quality show. Bain and Mike are both present;

however, there's no Diesel. I look for her in the crowd but she is nowhere.

"She's not here yet," a voice says from behind. I turn to see a blonde woman drinking a bottle of water, sauntering toward me. Her hair is tousled from dancing and her cleavage is abundantly clear at it peeks out from under her white tank top. "Diesel usually doesn't come over until later when she's not actually in the show."

"Oh, uh, thanks..." I'm slightly embarrassed to realize my actions were so overt.

"Jessica." She extends her hand. "You must be Elliot, the journalist here to set us asunder."

"Well," I laugh, taking her hand in mine, "I'm not so sure about that but I'm here for meek attempts at journalistic integrity."

"Good," Jessica says, mildly distracted by someone calling her name from the stage. "Maybe we could get to know each other. You know, since you'll be around here for a while."

"Uh, sure, that would be nice," I reply.

"Okay, how about Thursday night. Dinner?"

"Right, um, okay. I'm staying at the Marriott. Eight o'clock? Can you meet me there?"

"Great, you got it." Jessica offers a quick wink before turning to return to the stage.

Watching her jog back to the stage, I notice Bain talking intently to Diesel. *When did she get here?* Bain, taller than Diesel, leans over her as if to keep their conversation private. Though responding to Bain with nods and what appear to be one-word answers, she flicks her eyes to me. Bain notices her distraction and mirrors her actions. I am caught by Bain again. I instantly feel like I'm in the market for a total ass kicking. I keep checking out his girl and he keeps catching me. Either I'm really slow or this guy is overly protective of what is his. I would be. I quickly look away at the stage and feign interest in writing something down. I peek up. Bain has his arm on her shoulder and has her pulled close, their faces inches from each other. He leans down and speaks directly into her ear. The interaction is quiet and intimate despite the music and movement around them.

Suddenly, the two break apart and move in opposite directions. Bain returns to the stage and Diesel walks toward me. My breath quickens as I rake my gaze over her, taking her in. She's casually dressed in jeans, linen tank top, and flip-flops. She's not as done up as she was for dinner, but equally as sexy. Her hair is soft and has an untamed quality to it. I'm relieved that she's looking at the stage so she can't see my visual assault. Thankfully, I am able to shift my stare to the stage before she focuses on me.

"Hey, have you been getting what you need so far?" Diesel's tone is direct, short. She's all business. The sexy vixen from the restaurant is gone.

"Um, yeah, I think so."

"Everyone's been good to you?" Again, to the point. No foreplay. No cuddle.

"Oh, yeah," I offer with a shrug.

"Jessica ask you out yet?" She smiles slightly. I see a humor in her eyes.

I am taken aback by her candor. "Uh, yeah." For some unnamed reason, I can't look at her.

"Okay." She smirks either at her knowledge of what Jessica is or at my embarrassment. "Well, have fun. But I just want you to bear something in mind." She leans into me and I can smell her, lavender and vanilla wafting around me, willing me to wrap my arms around her. "Be careful around her. She's all fur coat and no knickers."

I suck in a tight breath, shocked at her statement. "How do you know that?"

Again she smiles, but it's all Cheshire Cat. "You'd be amazed what I know, Elliot."

She turns and walks out as effortlessly as she walked in. As I watch her retreat, I force down the desire to have dinner with her instead.

FOR THE NEXT several days, I am immersed in the building of a night at Eden. The jovial nature of the group contrasts the hard work being done. No one fights, no one bickers, and everyone works toward the common goal.

Mike works to orchestrate everyone's movements throughout the night. At different places in the club there are raised platforms, open catwalks, and the stage. The dancers are placed and moved strategically to get and keep people dancing. Bain works to time and queue music to ensure a smooth flow of the evening. Everyone is everywhere at different points of the night, so, in effect, patrons in the club have a chance to see all the members of Eden. Diesel moves seamlessly from the front line to backstage. She is the matriarch and is in complete control of the proceedings. Her critiques of Bain's transitions are kind and encouraging. She gently pushes him to bring together sounds in a way that enhances the mood he's trying to create. They playfully banter but focus on the goal at hand. Their behavior is intimate at times but I can't tell if it's romantic or platonic. They seem to blur the lines even though I've never seen him touch anything but her shoulder.

Mike is an entirely different story. He and Diesel have no banter that I have seen. They are cool and collected business partners. There's never a glimpse of intimacy between them but they work flawlessly together. They trust each other, this fact is blazingly clear. He asks for her opinion and carefully considers her responses. They are polite and considerate to each other.

The two men exist in this universe where Diesel is the axis. They move together with the understanding that she has the ultimate say in what happens. She appears unfailingly supportive and encourages them to discuss their thoughts and ideas before offering her opinion. She is clearly respected by those who work at Eden and she has her hands in everything. The dancers chatter to her about the latest sales they've caught. The bartender laments about his ex and issues with custody arrangements as they inventory the bar. The electrician who comes to fix some broken lights is clearly taken with her warm smile and she does not seem to mind when he calls her *honey*.

I wonder how she got to be this way. How did she come here and become this – a leader of such a pack. How did she gain such command at such a young age? She seems so kind but she has this rough nickname. I am rapt by her. She is an enigma and I am so curious...

Writing about Eden will keep me employed and the Dragon happy. Learning who Diesel is? That's the mission I want to embark on.

✧   ✧   ✧

THIS IS JUST drinks. Only drinks and dinner.

I meet Jessica for dinner after a full day of observing prep. We look the part, a well-dressed couple having a couple of drinks, but her greeting is too familiar for my liking, a hug and a kiss on the cheek. She looks amazing but Diesel's warning rings in my head. *She's all fur coat and no knickers.* I will have to ask her how she knows Brit slang. Yesterday she called Bain's run-through for Friday night *pukka.* Twice now, she's needed to *ring* family.

Jessica questions me about living in England and makes me say various words to hear the full range of my accent. Once she's a little comfortable from her, what, third drink, I figure it's time to do some investigating.

"Okay, enough about me. How long have you been at Eden?"

"Three years. It's a good place to be," she offers before sucking back the last of her sour apple martini.

"Why did you decide Eden was what you wanted?"

"It's not that simple. Eden finds you, in a way. Diesel approached me and we started talking one day. I met Bain and they held this little audition for me. They asked me to stay and be a part of Eden. I was working at a strip club before coming here. When she offered me a job, I thought I would try it out. It's good money and I get to dance, which is what I've always wanted."

"So Diesel brought you in?"

"Yeah. She's the one who ultimately decides who stays or

who goes. She has this freaky intuitive way about her. It's like, she's around you and she knows something about you that you don't even know. Or you know it and you're trying to hide it. She's great at knowing if someone is lying."

"How long has she been with Eden?"

"I think from the beginning. All I know is Eden begins and ends with her."

"And what about Bain and Mike?"

"They are with Diesel. They've always worked together for as long as I've known." Jessica sips her latest drink and appears slightly annoyed.

"So are they together?"

"Who? Diesel? With Mike or Bain? I guess. They are always together..." She stares at me, clearly irritated. "I, uh, I thought this was about you and I getting to know each other. You can ask Diesel about Diesel, okay?"

"Right, sorry. I'm just curious."

"Yeah," says Jessica, clearly put off by my inquiry. After a moment, she appears to regain her focus. "Look," she coos, "you and I will be just fine; you just need to forget about her. She's all business. No one gets close to her except Bain and Mike. She's like ice."

I can only muster a half smile and raise my glass to her in cheers.

She's like ice.

Chapter Seven
DIESEL

"**A**RE YOU READY?"

"As ready as I'll ever be."

"Good. Let's go then. There's no reason to lament over me kicking your ass anymore."

How Bain can be competitive about a paced run we take on a daily basis, I'm not sure. Nevertheless, that's Bain. Everything is a game and that's how he likes it.

"Okay, enough with your incessant yammering. Let's go. We don't have all day." I have no desire to fight with him or encourage his chatter. We have a show tonight and I'm anxious to get back. I want to look really good tonight. Not that I don't look good on normal nights, but I want to put on a confident face for Elliot. This whole arrangement with him has got me nervous and I don't know quite how to handle it just yet.

I worry he's going to make us look like fools. I don't trust the fact that he's here but then I see him at Eden and he seems so genuine...

Bah! *No, stay focused.* He's here to expose what we are, not that we have anything to hide, really, but he has potential to do serious damage to our little haven.

He's good-looking, too....which I really don't like. I would have hoped his hotness would have reduced over the past couple of days but oh, no, it's worse. I think he's hotter. It makes trying to hate him that much harder. Athletic and tall, which I love...nothing like a tall drink of water to quench my thirst...

Bain pushes my shoulder and I realize I've not been participating in our pre-show prep run and chat.

"Helloooooo space cadet, where are you?" Bain's enthusiasm makes me crazy sometimes. He is a perpetual high school cheerleader.

"Sorry," I mutter. "I was just off on my own for a minute."

"Spill it," he commands. "What's on your mind?"

I've never had a problem being forthcoming with Bain. Well, maybe in the beginning, but once we got ourselves figured out and knew where each other was coming from, we were solid. I've had no reason to be shy with him. We have been through too much together. I don't think walls could be built between us if we tried.

"I'm nervous about Elliot." I'm sure he'll want me to articulate more, but it's a start.

"Nervous about what?"

"Everything. Bain, what if this turns out bad? What if he totally undermines us?"

"What is there for him to expose? We do everything by the books. We've never had anything unsafe or out of control happen. We are a reputable establishment for all intents and purposes."

He's right. We've worked very hard to maintain a level of sophistication to our little slice of the Earth. Quickly bouncing out overall aggressive, visibly intoxicated, or unsavory individuals has been our credo. Moreover, the regulars who attend Eden know the same. It's a brother's keeper mentality. Everyone at Eden is there to have a good time. If you come to Eden looking to have some fun, it is your responsibility to keep your pals in check.

"I guess you're right," I offer, wincing at my unconvincing and slightly whiney tone.

"Look, I really don't think he's going to take us down." Bain looks at me sideways as we push though the first leg of our run. "Besides, I don't think he's going to do anything to ruin any of us...especially you."

I look at Bain quickly. "What does that mean?" My curiosity is piqued.

"Diesel," Bain scoffs, "I know it's been a really long time for you but Elliot's got all his focus on you. A freight train could run though the main stage and he would just stare at you. He couldn't take his eyes off you at that first dinner, and that was before he knew who you were."

"I think he's just really interested in Eden. He knows our roles and he's keeping tabs."

Bain snorts at my dismissal. "Are you serious?" He looks at me without breaking stride. "He couldn't even have dinner with Jessica without asking about you."

How does he know this? "Look, it's curiosity. He does not feel comfortable asking me directly so he's trying to weasel dirt out of somewhere."

"Well, all I know is she was mighty pissed this morning because all he could talk about was you. Just thought you'd like to know."

"I don't really know what you want me to do with this newfound knowledge, Bain. For all intents and purposes, it's useless." I really don't know what else to say.

"Suit yourself, Diesel. This is your party," Bain offers as we round the last block. I realize all too late that I've completely missed the familiar burn of the midpoint or the joy of getting into the rhythm of the pace.

He can't take his eyes off me.

He was asking about me.

This is my party.

Friday night.

Eden's Facebook profile picture:

Chapter Eight
ELLIOT

I WATCH THE show. I am mesmerized. It's people everywhere laughing, dancing, and drinking. The music is nonstop. I watch Bain, Mike, Jessica and the entire Eden crew dance and move to different songs throughout the night.

But mostly, I watch Diesel. She's in the DJ booth. Then she's dancing on the stage. She's in the crowd. She is everywhere. Truly in her element. She looks relaxed and in control, not at all hampered by the pounding music or hundreds of people. At last call, she is in the main area dancing with Mike. Moving her body in time with the music, she is the pinnacle of sexy, dressed in badass black leather pants that hug every curve, softened by a tight shimmery tank top and killer heels. They appear to be having fun until they are abruptly interrupted by a tall muscular man with jet-black hair. Diesel looks slightly put off as Mike transitions to another woman and The Cutter wraps his arm around her waist.

He holds her close, grinding on her. A frisson of anger, followed by a jolt of jealousy, rips through me. Her hands are on his arms, attempting to keep him a distance. She is dancing for the sake of the music. I see clearly that she does not want to be anywhere near him. *Who the fuck is this guy?* My discomfort at watching them is remedied only by the song's ending and Eden sadly coming to a halt. The lights change and the music shifts. No more bone-rattling music, just the quiet din of background music encouraging everyone to head out into the night. Diesel pushes out of the man's arms and quickly paces off stage. He throws his head back, laughing at the ceiling, then rushes after her.

I rush through the throngs of people leaving the club and head backstage. Though anxious to see the aftermath of the night, I'm more focused on finding Diesel and the guy chasing her.

Everyone has congregated in the open backstage area. The people of Eden and friends lounge in a sea of plush couches and chairs, reminding me of old pictures of bands with groupies. Mike and Bain are sharing a drink around one of the high tables with Diesel. The Cutter walks over to them with a focused prowl and sidles between Bain and Diesel. Bain claps him on the back in a brotherly gesture. I am shocked that Bain would openly greet someone who was so aggressive toward Diesel. Did he not see this guy dancing with her? He must have. And Mike didn't say anything, either? Diesel turns away from them and catches my eye. She takes a drink of her water and moves toward me. The Cutter looks over his shoulder, obviously eyeing her ass.

We hold each other's gaze as she walks over. She looks amazing. Her hair is mussed and a little sweaty. She is still her in heels, which raises her overall height to a little closer to mine. Looking pleased and confident with the outcome of the show, she leans on the high table at which I am standing with her back to the room.

"Did you like it?" Her tone is light and happy despite her night ending with an unwanted guy pawing at her. It's a shift from the stoic Diesel of the past week. She appears sated, as if she was just thoroughly fucked and ready to curl into someone for a night of sleep.

"Yeah, I thought it was great," I stammer, slightly unnerved by her presentation. *Great conversation starter, you really wowed her with that one.*

"It was a fun night," she offers with a little smile.

"Hey! Diesel!" The Cutter yells from across the room. He's still looking at her back, with his head cocked to one side, dark eyes drilling into her as if she is something to eat. She breathes in audibly and rolls her eyes.

"Yes, Cass?" she replies without looking at him.

"When are you going to give me what I want?" I immediately realize from the slur of his voice that he is drunk.

"I don't have an extra set of balls to give you, Cass." Diesel says it with such a sharp and quick tone, I am taken aback. How she can radiate 'don't-fuck-with-me' and poise at the same time is beyond me.

He narrows his eyes. She's obviously struck a nerve.

"You know," Cass drawls as he moves toward us with a slow, slightly staggering pace, "I would think if you had someone like me interested in you, you'd take advantage." He holds his hands out to the side as if to encourage her to take a look.

She pivots, putting herself directly between Cass and myself. One hand is on her hip, the other stretched across the table as if shielding me. Across the room, Mike and Bain immediately stop their conversation and are at full attention.

"Well, I'm sorry to disappoint you, but I'm not interested," she says with an arctic tone. I watch Cass's dark eyes narrow on her. His face is a mask of frustration and hostility. He rakes his hands through his hair trying to gain some composure. It is clear she has been winning this match, much to his chagrin. From the look of him, he doesn't experience rejection often.

"What is your fucking problem?" he spits. The chatter in the room dies down instantly. All eyes are on them. Mike and Bain look at each other and silently move from their table. Bain eyes Cass as if he is the ultimate target in any war game.

Diesel looks at him impassively. "I don't have a problem, Cass. You obviously have a problem accepting the word *no*."

What the hell is going on? She's told him to fuck off and he's still after her!

"Ah," he mocks contemplation as he rubs his chin, "I know what your issue is." His features contort, looking slightly evil. "You must be one of those ancient legends, you know, those women that have teeth downstairs. You're a monster in the sack, all right." His tone is disturbing, caustic. I notice Bain and Mike moving closer to Diesel, who continues to stand stoic in front of me.

She smiles sweetly. "You know Cass, you might be very right. It might be possible that I have teeth downstairs." Her voice is soft and in control. He whoops with drunk laughter, clearly pleased with her response. She steps toward him and gently takes his face in her hands. He instantly calms at her touch, his shoulders softening as he looks her straight in the eyes. "Or....instead of teeth, it might be possible that it could be soft...and warm...and wet...and tight." Each word is enunciated in a slow, rhythm.

I can't believe what I'm seeing. I look to Mike and Bain, who seem equally shocked at the turn of events. Everyone in the room is still quiet, watching the interaction.

She strokes his cheek with her fingers. "But," she says, "instead of talking about the possibilities, we should focus on realities. You see, Cass," she pauses, "the reality is, you'll never know."

She drops her hands to her hips, popping them to one side, giving him a half smile as she cocks her head. Bain snorts a laugh and is quickly elbowed by Mike. The quiet room erupts with praise for Diesel and hoots of the oh-no-she-didn't variety. I watch Cass's delayed reaction. He blinks at her as if the alcohol has slowed his response time.

"Fuck you, bitch." He storms out of the room.

She watches him leave and then looks to Mike and Bain. Their unspoken conversation must speak volumes because Bain exhales loudly and runs his hand through is hair.

Mike shrugs. "At least he's gone."

"For now," she responds quickly before turning to me. "Sorry you had to see that."

"N-no," I stammer, "sorry he was so rude to you. What's his deal?"

"Um." She looks over her shoulder to survey the path Cass has just taken out. "He's kind of a dick." She leans into me. "You want to get a drink and get out of here?" Her voice is breathy and low.

"Yeah." It's all I can manage to say. Suddenly, my heart is pounding.

"Come on." She smiles and walks past me through the

main doors. I look back to see Bain and Mike watching us as we leave. Bain holds his glass up and tips his chin toward me. *Cheers? Really?* Have I won some small victory with this little trip?

I try to keep up behind her; she has a long stride, amplified by her heels. I try not to look at her glorious ass directly in front of me. *Sweet mother...get a hold of yourself.* I realize all too quickly that I will need to grip myself up, sooner rather than later.

We walk into the main area of Eden, now vacated and seeming slightly less magical. People are cleaning up and the bartenders are cleaning house.

Diesel walks behind the bar to cheery greetings and quickly makes herself a dirty martini.

"And for the gentleman?" she says to me, hands resting on the bar.

"I'll have a beer." It's all I've had all night. No sense in mixing and paying the consequence.

She pulls the draft and passes it to me along with the martini. She scoots out from behind the bar and says goodbye to the staff.

She grabs her drink and walks toward one of the exit doors. "Come on," she says when she sees me sitting on the bar stool, "we're not staying here!" She smiles, at my expense I think, and I quickly get up and follow her.

"Where are we going?" I ask.

"Up," she says with a mischievous grin.

She punches a code into a cleverly disguised panel on the wall and the exit door buzzes open. "All the doors to get through to the upstairs have key pad access. People can walk in and around the main area of Eden and backstage, but to get upstairs you have to know the access codes."

"There are codes, as in more than one?"

"Yup," she says as we climb the stairs. "There is the code to get in, a distress code, a code for if you've forgotten your code." She rolls her eyes. "So many codes. It's Bain's idea. For as much of a daredevil as he is, he's a bit of a freak about being safe."

"I suppose there are worse things in the world," I offer as we continue up.

"True," she agrees without missing a step.

The stairwell has an institutional feel about it. Wide steps of steel and concrete with clearly worn marking from years of traffic are utilitarian and oddly intriguing. Properly maintained from the original building, the steps twist upward to the highest points of the massive building. *Where are we going?* We pass a large steel door on one of the landings and continue our ascent. We are really high and I don't dare look down to see the flights of stairs below us. "Okay," she huffs, "here we are." After punching another code into an identical pad, she opens the door and steps into a fully furnished living area. It's a large, open design with the living area, kitchen, office, sitting area and bedroom sectioned off by furniture. The bed actually faces the large floor-to-ceiling windows on the exterior wall.

"So," she says quietly, "this is my place." She looks at me and raises her eyebrows slightly. "We can sit on the patio." She gestures to the windows. "It's my favorite place to relax after a night in Eden."

"That sounds great."

A comfortable patio set welcomes us. She flops down in one of the chairs and promptly kicks off her heels.

"Ahhhhh," she moans as she stretches her feet out and promptly curls her legs into her body. "I should totally switch apartments with Mike and Bain." She looks at me and laughs. "Those bastards should have to walk all the way up here!"

"Are they below you?" I ask.

She nods as she takes her first sip of her martini. "Yeah, we own the entire building. When we bought it, it was literally just a shell. Mike had some great design ideas and made it what it is today."

"Wow." I'm shocked at the talent between the Three Musketeers. They each have unique and singular talents that flow together. "So, uh, what's the deal with that guy...Cass?" I try to sound less annoyed with his actions and fail miserably. His behavior was deplorable and I'm still having a hard time accepting that he was so derogatory to her.

"Ugh," she says, rolling her eyes and setting down her drink. "He's been trying to get me to hook up with him for months now. First, he would just hit on me, then he wanted to be friends with benefits. When I told him no, he took his campaign public."

"Oh." I look at her. She appears impassive and shrugs lightly.

"He gets drunk and out of control. The bouncers have kicked him out a bunch of times but he always manages to weasel his way back in. Mike and Bain get all serious when he's around. He's never done anything more than be verbally disrespectful but I'm planning to talk to them about blacklisting him." She smiles lightly, putting me at ease. "Let's not let him ruin the night, okay?"

"Okay." Fuck. Why can't I talk around her? "So, what do you do after a night at Eden?"

She glances at me before looking out over the skyline. "This."

I instantly feel overwhelmed. Why am I here? "Do you want me to go?"

"Do you want to go?" The inquiry is direct and quick.

"Not really."

"I don't really want you to go either." Her admission is soft, breathy.

"Good. I'll stay."

She stares at me with eyes that hold me in place, arching her brows. "We're not fucking, just so you know."

I choke on my beer. "No," I sputter, "no, I, uh, no, that's not what I was thinking."

She looks at me with a light humor in her eyes. "Just checking."

"You're safe with me." I offer quietly.

"Am I?" Again, she pins me to the chair with her look. It's as if she's assessing every thought I've ever had, every moment I've ever experienced. For a moment, I think she can see my fascination with her. She looks slightly amused as I shift in my chair. Holy shit....she's got to stop staring at me!

"I think," I say while looking away and taking a pull from my beer, "you are very safe with me." I look out over the skyline but manage to see her from the corner of my eye.

She turns her head, taking in the skyline and nods. "Okay," she says.

We sit in silence for a while, taking in the sounds and sights of New York in the early morning hours. Our conversation is brief and only focuses on Eden. She is casual and light but guarded. Happy to have pulled off another successful night.

I take my leave of her begrudgingly, citing the early morning hour and the need to write. I thank her for the evening and she walks me to the door. She leans against the doorframe and looks up at me, her full lips parted slightly. When I take a step closer, she straightens, our eyes assessing the lines and valleys of the others face. She swallows and exhales before dropping her eyes to the floor. Every inch of my body screams to pull her to me. I clench my fists to stop from pushing my fingers through her hair, tilting her head back and taking what I want, which is every inch of her. The heat of her body pressed firmly against mine. To taste her lips and tongue. To feel her hands explore my body and for me to return the favor. Instead, I bid her goodnight and start my slow descent down the belly of Eden.

Chapter Nine
DIESEL

SATURDAY NIGHT IS usually reserved for recouping or heading up north to see family, but tonight we are going out. Bain's convinced me to go to a club with him, Mike, and the gang for some blow-off-some-steam time. Pulling on my sexiest nude heels, I examine the black, almost backless, dress I've poured myself into. *Not bad. You'll do okay standing next to Bain tonight.*

As if on cue, my phone pings with a text from Bain.

FYI – Elliot's meeting us at the club.

I huff with indignation. I didn't know this was part of the deal. It's bad enough Elliot's been with us every day, now we're hanging out with him socially? I struggle to ward off impure thoughts about him when he's at Eden. Now I have keep myself in check when we're out and I'm drinking. Fabulous.

Is there a reason you're telling me this now? I'm ready to walk out the door.
Perfect! I've been waiting on your pokey ass all night as it is. Let's go.

Dick....

Why is he going to be there?
Why not?

Do I really need to explain this to you?

I know he's new but do we really have to be besties? I'm sure he's capable of meeting new people.
I'm sure he's very capable at meeting new people. He met Jess just fine.

I roll my eyes, irritated at Bain's incessant need to rub salt in wounds. Yeah, like Jessica would give a guy like Elliot a second before sinking her curious claws into him. If that's friendship, I want none of it. Regardless, this sucks. I never should have crossed the boundary with him last night. What was I thinking, bringing Elliot Archer up to my apartment? The fact that I even suggested we would end up sleeping together was asinine. Now I have to re-establish a limit I never should have breached.

Just stay close to me, okay?
Of course, love. Always.

Chapter Ten

ELLIOT

IN THE UPPER level of the posh nightclub Bain texted me about, I walk into what appears to be a mini Eden. While more modern than industrial, the club is swarming with the usual suspects from Eden, making me feel only slightly comfortable. Before I can scan the crowd closely, I see Jessica making a beeline in my direction.

"Hey sexy," she croons, "I'm glad you're here." Wrapping her arms around my waist, she pulls me into the throng of bodies which undulates in rhythm with the blaring music. Her stagger is slight but present nonetheless. I'm glad I didn't pre-game this event. Jessica uses me to steady herself as we weave though the crowd until reaching the other side. Why we needed to walk directly through the eye of the storm, I have no clue, but Jessica does not appear to be a reliable navigator.

"Hey guys," she hollers above the music in a tone that could only be labeled 'drunk girl,' "look who's here!"

I immediately see the pair of them in action. Bain and Mike command conversations at separate tables, their backs almost touching. Eyeing me, Mike raises his glass and his eyebrow at Jessica's close proximity. I offer a noncommittal shrug as Mike leans back slightly, nudging Bain. Engrossed in his conversation with two stunning beauties, Bain reaches back, never breaking the conversation in an attempt to capture the offending nudger. The women erupt in laughter before he drains his drink and turns to Mike, who shoves his chin in my direction. Bain's reaction to Jessica's physical affection is less restrained than Mike's, looking full-blown irritated as he holds a hand out to me. I step out of Jessica's hold and move to Bain, who begins introducing me to the women he is clearly enchanting.

"Jessica," Bain barks over the noise, "why don't you get Elliot a drink?"

As she scampers away on ridiculously high heels, Bain takes on the task of introducing me to the entire room. The names, faces, and brief informational nuggets of information Bain tosses at me are lost the instant we move to the next group. Some work for Eden, others are just connected though a web of mutual contacts. Jessica returns with beers for Bain and myself and quickly reestablishes her space next to me. Despite the close proximity of Jessica and Bain, I scan the crowd as coolly as possible, eager to find Diesel.

As introductions continue, we weave through and eventually emerge from the perimeter of the tightly-woven group. Finally, I see her. Tucked quietly into a dark recess at the end of the bar, Diesel is engaged animatedly with several people. I recognize a few from Eden but the others are suspect. Bain sidles us up to the bar where we are immediately surrounded by several women and a few men. From our vantage point, I have a direct line of sight. She is coy at best with a guy who is using all the classic moves on her. Leaning in to whisper in her ear, making sure her drink is topped off, touching her bare arms. She responds with reserved flirtations. She flashes her gorgeous smile, offers doe-eyed glances, and occasionally puts a hand on his arm. Without even knowing this wanker, I fucking hate him.

The conversation is difficult between the noise, my focus on Diesel, and the man who has taken obvious interest in her. Thankfully you can appear to be engaged in any conversation in a crowded bar by nodding your agreement and buying the next round. As the night progresses and Jessica becomes more and more like inebriated Velcro, I watch Diesel move through the room. Just as in Eden, she is seamless in her interactions with everyone. She glides between tables, chatting and laughing with everyone she engages. Her affection toward some of the guests is clear. She hugs and offers warm kisses to the cheeks of various men and women over the course of the night. The man she was flirting with in the corner has deftly followed her throughout the evening, clearly enamored with her. He tries to buy her more drinks, which she refuses. I watch her sidestep his efforts to get her alone by pulling friends into their conversations. He pulls out all the stops and she halts him at every turn.

Eventually, she pulls from a group of several people and begins scanning the crowd. When she catches me looking at her, I swear she flinches. Her eyes skate across me, assessing me from head to toe before restarting the swift search of the group. Once she finds Bain, her smooth stride resumes and she appears only slightly relaxed.

As if he knows she's moving toward him, Bain extends his arm, welcoming her to curl into his body. They look at each other for a brief moment before she pushes up on her toes to whisper in his ear. She pulls back and steps into the circle we've formed at the bar as Bain moves to find the guy who's been tailing her all night. I watch the conversation between the two men, which, while calm, is purposeful. The guy appears to be placating Bain and while his back is to me, it's clear that Bain is providing some level of redirection. The guy nods in acceptance and turns to find someone else to help him fill the evening.

"Do you like what you see, Mr. Archer?" Her voice is a purr that emanates to my left. I turn to find her leaning back against the bar next to me. I'm not sure how long she's been there but she obviously watched me stare down Bain's actions toward her lothario.

I lean into the bar, facing her. "What do I see, Miss Diesel?"

"Diesel, Elliot." She quickly corrects me as she brings her drink up to her lips. "I told you before, there is no 'Miss.'"

I watch her swallow her drink as she looks out into the crowd. To outward appearances, it looks as if she is ignoring me. Her face is passive and not at all animated in the way I've seen her all night. From the periphery, I see Bain walk toward us and then away after she casually waves her hand. She just detoured Bain when two minutes ago she pulled him in to redirect someone else. Is he her bouncer? Her helicopter parent? It's clear to me he has both eyes on Diesel at all times.

"What do you think I see, Diesel? I see you. You look beautiful this evening." It's true and I want her to believe it. Her dress hugs her body perfectly and her heels amplify her long legs. She is stunning and eclipses all others in this crowded room.

She turns her head to me slightly. "How's Jessica?"

"Drunk." Thankfully, she got sidetracked during the evening and peeled herself from me. For all I know, she's passed out somewhere. "How's Mister Man who was trying to get you to go home with him?"

Her eyes narrow at the question. "Gone."

"Is that your doing or Bain's?" I need to know where they stand despite the fact that it is none of my business. If she is his, I'll make more of an effort to squelch this urge to get close to her.

She finishes her drink before placing the glass on the bar and facing me. "Mine, Elliot. What does it matter whose doing it was? It's done."

"I see that. I was just curious." I feel dangerously close to pissing her off.

She sighs as she pushes off the bar. "Don't be the cat that curiosity catches, Elliot. It won't work out the way you want it to."

My mouth gapes, trying to formulate a response, but before any words escape, she is gone. After pushing off the bar, she breezes by Bain and Mike, holding up her hand and wiggling her fingers in a blasé *goodbye,* before she's out the door and disappears into the night.

Chapter Eleven
DIESEL

WITH MY SUPERIOR sex kitten skills, I've lured him into my apartment. He came into the club and I wanted him instantly. A specimen of male perfection, he is gorgeous, perfectly primped and has a slight arrogance to him that makes me want to do whatever, whenever, wherever only for him. We cat and mouse each other throughout the night. We lure each other around the club, on the dance floor, at the bar, and into dark corners which are suitable only for dark deeds.

With minimal resistance, he is now gloriously naked and sprawled on my bed. I trail kisses from his ankle to his chest and back down again. He doesn't talk, and frankly, I don't want him to. Just the sharp hiss as I take him in my mouth is all I need to hear. After a brief moment of teasing play, I feel the hard grip of his hands on my upper arms as he pulls me up to meet his face.

He shifts, pinning me below him. *Yes...* He's on me, kissing me hard and urgently. We've played for a little too long. He ravages my mouth before trailing kisses down my neck to my breasts. He worships my sensitive nipples with his tongue, forcing me to arch into his body, which teases in a hover over mine. With the deft fingers of his strong, slightly rough hands, he skims my ribs before grasping my hips to hold my body still against his sensual assault. I can feel the mastery of his skill building in the core of my body. Lightening pulses of heat shake my core with every delicious tease he has to offer.

My breathy pleas for more are met with a low grumble, as if he is irritated I've pulled him from his life's work. As he comes back up my body, kissing and nipping the sensitive skin of my neck, his face comes into focus. He is no longer my fantasy man from the club. It's Elliot. It's Elliot hovering over me, pinning me to the bed. It's Elliot kissing me. Elliot who wants to fuck me and tells me this fact directly and clearly before he takes me with such powerful force, my breath is lost.

I come quickly and loudly in the confines of my shower.

Blinking into the water as it rains down on my head and body, I try to savor the bliss of my orgasm. Unfortunately, it is quickly lost on feelings of confusion and the effort to calm the tremor taking over my body.

"Holy shit." Pressing my forehead to the shower wall, I try to calm myself and fail miserably.

✧   ✧   ✧

"SO...HE WAS in your apartment and you just talked?" Holly's disappointment is blatant.

"I know the guy for two minutes. Are you kidding?" I admonish her with my tone. Holly has been my best friend for what seems like forever. I'm so grateful for the limited time we have together. She reminds me that, yes, I am a woman despite the full-blown testosterone scene I'm in every day.

"All I'm saying is it's been a long time for you. I want you to get on that horse!" She says it in a rampantly sexual undertone as she rolls her hips toward the rack of brightly colored shirts. Oh, do I tell her about my one-woman sexcapade this morning? I'm still a little shaken from the whole incident.

I look at her with pursed lips and an exaggerated eye roll. "Give it some time."

"Okay, I'll give you time, but if you think you like this guy, I'm not sure what you are waiting for."

"Holly, again, I met him two minutes ago, and he's good-looking but he's here on business." I feel the blush push forward and she is on me like a heat-seeking missile.

"Holy shit, Diesel. You are smitten. You are a smitten kitten!" Her tone is excited and loud. I'm so grateful it's the middle of the week and we are pretty much alone in the store.

"Okay," I hiss, "enough with the kitten talk. I can't do anything, anyway." After Holly looks at me with wide, imploring eyes, I explain, "Jessica asked him out already."

"That whore," she says flatly and turns to a pair of jeans. "You may not want him after she's done with him anyway." She snorts.

"Tell me about it."

"What does Bain say?"

I look at Holly from the side of my eye. "What does Bain say about what?"

"Deese, don't be coy with me. Does he know you're a smitten kitten?"

I feel the rush of warmth hit my cheeks and have to remind myself that at this point in time, I'm not in trouble.

"No, he knows nothing. He told me that he thinks Elliot is

curious about me, that he keeps looking at me, but nothing more than that." My voice is quiet.

"Well, at least he knows there is some potential interest." She looks at me and I feel like I want to explode. "I'm going to try these on; I'll be right back."

"Okay." I breathe a sigh of relief that this conversation is over. It's Wednesday, we have two days until the show, and I'm anxious. I've never been nervous before. I'm mean, there's usually some jitters but this time I'm my entire being is nothing but butterflies and nausea. I've seen Elliot during the week but we've not been alone, not since he was in my apartment. Despite the fact that we were by ourselves, we didn't talk much beyond sharing anecdotes about the evening. We enjoyed our drinks and the skyline. He left like a gentlemen and I reeled about him for the next three hours. He seemed so comfortable in my apartment and I liked him there.

He really is very attractive...damn it. What I wouldn't give to run my tongue over that jaw and down his chest. The pull of desire consumes my entire stomach. I imagine myself pulling on that messy hair then smelling him...

I have to stop this. I did stop this. I gave him the cold shoulder at the club, so hopefully he gets the hint. This will not happen here. It cannot happen. Not that anyone is helping me to not make it happen.

Bain is relentless and has been for the past three days. *He's looking at you again. He's all about you, Diesel. You should talk to him.* I can't take it, really. Am I too old for this? Feeling like a teenager staring a boy down across the lunchroom. At twenty-five when a yummy piece of man barrels into your life, do you just go for it? Do you throw everything aside and put yourself out there? He's a year younger than me, but somehow I feel years older. Like the past has aged me, and not kindly. I've never been involved with a younger guy before. But, it's only a year, so that's not that much younger. I have always appreciated the strong masculinity of an older guy, not sugar daddy old, just a little more established than me. Someone who is emotionally and mentally strong. Who can push against seemingly impenetrable barriers without flinching. *Like Elliot just blew through the doors of Eden?* Now that I think about it, I've never dated a guy that rides a motorcycle. I'd be lying to myself if I didn't think that was hot.

Really? This is the conversation I'm having with myself? Ugh. I'm so nervous about Friday. Why do I let Bain talk me into this shit?

Because that's what Bain does. He's a talker and he knows what to say to you. I roll my eyes as Holly emerges from the dressing room, catching me in deep contemplation.

"Oh, boy," she muses, "you got this bad." She smiles and puts her arm around me. "Come on. Let's find you something sexy for Friday night."

I groan in anticipation. I really do think I'm too old for this.

Eden's profile picture, Friday night:

Chapter Twelve
ELLIOT

A WEEK'S WORTH of work has created the amalgam before me. People are everywhere. Inside Eden, some are doing last minute preps, sound checks, checking scant outfits in the mirrors. Outside, I see the crowd and can hear the buzz of anticipation and excitement. I figure now is a good time to take pictures, so I walk backstage.

Down the hall, from one of the rooms, I hear Jessica's voice.

"I'm not sure why you think this is necessary?" She sounds frantic.

"Look," Mike replies with a flat tone, "it's what we do. You know this. What's your problem today?"

"Nothing." Jessica is irritated, huffy.

I can hear an interior door open and close.

"Oh, well there she is. The woman of the hour!" Jessica drawls in a sarcastic tone.

"Ugh, Jess. What have I inadvertently done now? Did I breathe your air? Step on your earth?" Diesel responds, her voice sounding dismissive and somewhat cold.

"Worse. I went out with Elliot for dinner and we couldn't even get through drinks without him asking a million questions about you!"

Oh boy. From that tone, there will be no getting a second date. Not that I necessarily wanted one. She was right about the whole 'no knickers' comment. I am momentarily distracted by how she knew British slang but I am brought back by Diesel's voice. I've not seen her since Wednesday.

She sighs audibly. "Look, Jess, I think he's just curious. This is new for him. He's trying to get his footing. There is a lot here. Give him a break. He seems like a nice enough guy. Just go easy on him."

"Really? That's what you want me to do?"

"Or not. The decision is yours. You're an adult."

I hear Jessica huff and she stomps toward the open door immediately to my left. *Shit, I've got to get out of here.* A second later, Jessica is flying out of the room and runs directly into me.

"I-I'm sorry." I have no choice but to apologize profusely, I think for more than slamming into her. "You look lovely tonight, Jessica."

She glares at me with unspoken hostility.

"Good luck tonight," I try to muster as she storms past me. *Hell, that was awful.*

Before I can escape the hall, I am pulled back to conversation in the room. Eavesdropping has never really been my thing, but Mike's tone peaks my interest.

"Diesel," he asks, curiosity lacing his words, "what was that all about?"

"What? Jessica having a spaz? That's rote; you know that's how she is."

"You've never complimented Elliot since he's been here."

Mike truly sounds shocked and amused by this change in her.

"Look, I just said he seems nice. There's no harm in observing nice."

"If he such a nice guy, why are you feeding him to her? Are you observing more than his personality, darling?" His tone is clearly teasing. I can hear the smile creep across his face.

"Enough." Her comment is sharp but she sounds like her night is already off. Maybe nervous? "Are you serious that this is the conversation we are going to have right now? Do you know we are on in a few minutes?"

He snorts before responding. "More like an hour, but I'll leave you be. I'll make sure everyone is where they need to be."

"Thank you, Mike. You know how to make me oh so happy." Her tone is amusingly sarcastic.

"Yes, I do." I can hear Mike's smile. "Best wishes, darling. You will be amazing."

"I hope so." She says it with what sounds like a sad sigh.

"I know so."

Ten minutes later, Mike finds me, and we banter about the set for the evening over a beer. I've taken up my favorite spot, the back corner, a prime position to observe everything and everyone. I can stand on one of the huge windowsills and truly be above the audience if need be.

The evening begins with Bain in the booth. The crowd comes instantly alive under his tutelage. He really is very good at what he does and clearly loves every minute of it.

As the night rolls on, various other DJs take over for Bain. It's a very democratic feel, no one person is fully responsible for spinning the whole evening. I've observed the audience for the majority of the evening. The chattering, laughing, drinking, and hook-ups are all typical evening-out behavior. I've seen pretty much everyone, Mike and Bain at various places and times, Jessica and several others who are connected with Eden. But no Diesel. *I heard her getting ready. She was putting on makeup. I heard her tell Mike they were on soon. Where is she?*

My thoughts are cut short with an increase in noise near the stage. The base has begun to pound in a rhythmic tone, the lights on the stage pulsing in time with the sound. Everyone, including me, is rapt by the event. One by one they come to the stage, the women and men of Eden moving in time with the music. Individually, they come to stand at various points along the perimeter of the stage and look out into the crowd. Everyone goes ballistic, screaming, yelling, hands thrust towards those on stage. I watch until the entire stage is lined with people. Mike and Bain stand shoulder-to-shoulder at center stage. They are both looking out into the crowd. Bain catches my eye and smiles. I raise my glass in acknowledgement. Bain laughs and points to me, then quickly focuses back to the swarm of girls at his feet.

What the hell is going on?

Over the speakers, the DJ addresses the crowd. "Anyone ready for a little bit of fun tonight?" Again, the crowd goes wild.

"Are we all ready and accounted for?" he inquires. The crowd responds, willing him to begin.

"I think our ship is short a captain? What do you think?" His words instantly change the stage lighting. All the lights on stage go dark with the exception of a space that has opened between Bain and Mike that is lit by a single over-head spotlight.

The audience, now riotous, begins to chant what at first is inaudible, then becomes a more unified and clear demand for Diesel.

As if on cue, the music shifts, slow and sultry, and she emerges. She stalks downstage and comes to stand between Mike and Bain. Dressed in nothing but heels and a belted black dress with flowing sleeves, she surveys the crowd as if she is ready to devour someone.

"Ladies and Gentlemen of Eden," she coos to the crowd via a handheld mic, "you know it is our tradition to, well, stay with tradition. As we have grown over the years, we've had more and more people come to see us. From what I'm guessing,"—she turns to Bain, running a finger down his chest and abs—"you like what you see. Isn't that right, ladies?" The women scream at a pitch I can hardly stand. She laughs, playing the crowd as she lightly smacks Bain's rear end.

"Now boys," she continues, "I think you've seen some things you like as well, yes?" Diesel struts over to Emily, a stunning blonde whom she kisses on the cheek and spins for the admiring men. The response is one that would rival a cheer from a winning touchdown by the home team.

"You see, it is our tradition to offer up a sacrifice to those who make Eden what it is." She is all sex and purrs into every word. Diesel turns her back to the audience and raises her arms in offering to everyone on stage. "My friends, choose your sacrifice."

The music turns to a hard-core rock song that bleeds with dark and dirty lyrics. The feel is hedonistic and the crowd immediately responds. Some members of the group jump into the crowd and pull various audience members to different places in the club. I watch Jessica lead a guy up into a suspended cage they've put up especially for tonight. Mike and Bain each grab willing participants and pull them up on the stage. The others cast members follow suit until everyone has positioned themselves around the club with an audience member.

Diesel remains on the stage watching the mayhem, rocking back and forth on her heels in time to the music. She only moves when everyone is in position, talking to the audience, engaging the guests who have come on stage.

She is the ringmaster to the circus of all circuses. Is this the intended effect? To get the crowd hot and bothered? It's working. She's working. Without a doubt, she is there to ramp up the crowd. Controlled. Sexy as hell. Those lips. Those legs. That voice. All pieces of a puzzle I'm not sure I will ever figure out. In this moment, she appears free, laughing and engaging the people who have come to Eden. She is happy, light. This woman on stage is not the same one who walked away from me at the other club. The woman from that night pales in comparison. The Diesel before me is more vibrant, more real than the plastic shell that tried to put me in my place on Saturday.

Diesel looks at every member of Eden's cast, now standing in front of a chosen audience member. She smiles as she receives nods and thumbs-ups, relaying that each is ready for whatever is about to begin.

Diesel addresses the crowd. "Well, it appears as if we are all set and-"

"Wait, Diesel," the DJ interrupts her, "don't you think it's proper for you to offer up a sacrifice, as well?"

The entire crowd is screaming now. It's deafening and bordering on unruly.

Diesel smiles. "Thank you, Marco, you are right. I have my guest ready. You know I like to sneak up on my prey."

Marco bows his head to her and smiles. He turns back to the music consoles, turning it up to a pounding rhythm that sets the tone for the event at hand.

Suddenly, as if consumed by the song, the dancers do nothing but focus on their guest. Circling them, tousling hair, kissing cheeks, unbuttoning shirts. Snapped from my curiosity of the onstage antics, I see Diesel take the hand of a bouncer before she descends the front stage steps. She surveys the crowd as she begins her tour of the possible guests she can bring on stage. Men and women clamor to her, begging, holding out their hands. She touches them, acknowledging the pleas, but keeps moving. I am immediately anxious and fearful as she catches my eyes. She walks toward me slowly, as if stalking me. She stops inches from my face, slowly breathing in and out. *Fuck, she smells good...*

"Put down your drink." Diesel purrs it in my ear. I drop the cup unapologetically on the floor, beer splattering across the concrete. Diesel smiles and runs her hand down the buttons of my shirt, all the while looking at the various parts of my face, eyes, and lips. In my reverie from having her so close, I don't realize she is pulling me forward by my shirt collar. I see her sway in front of me, the strut indicative of one proud of her capture. I have no choice but to follow. My heart is pounding and I am immediately sweating. I only faintly hear the crowd as they champion her on.

All too soon, I realize she is pulling me on stage under the hot, bright lights for everyone to see. She turns me to face the crowd before I am pushed into a chair. Diesel immediately begins to survey me as I've watched the other cast members do to their chosen ones. From my periphery, I have the opportunity to see the other dancers with their sacrifices. Bain already has his shirt off, tilting the chair on two legs as he undulates his body against a beautiful redhead who is clearly enjoying herself. Jessica has straddled the guy she snared, circling her hips in perfect time with the music as she whips his shirt in a circle over her head. A primal roar erupts from the opposite side of the club, sparked by Emily, who has lost her flimsy tank and is eagerly rubbing her ass into the crotch of a guy who looks ready to blow. Then it hits me.

Holy shit. It's a lap dance!

Diesel pushes her hand through my hair to muss it before she begins to unbutton my shirt. My initial instinct is to jump and run; however, I am paralyzed. By fear? By desire? This woman just pulled me up on stage and I can't move. I am dumbstruck between being on stage and Diesel and the music. The vibration of the bass resonates through my chair. It's the metronome to her movements around me. She runs her hands down my legs before shoving them apart. As she straddles one of my legs, she gently cups my chin, tilting my face to meet her eyes.

She smiles at me and makes a sensual demand in my ear. "Pull the belt." I look to her waist and with trembling hands, I pull her soft satin belt. I see her flesh peek through what was nothing more than a well-disguised robe. She rolls her head back and peels off the robe to reveal her naked body in nothing now but a black lace bra and panties. I am breathless and can feel my reaction to her everywhere.

She hovers over me, rubbing her soft skin against mine. She presses her beautiful ass into my crotch. She straddles my lap before running her hands through in my hair again, down my chest and over my legs. I'm not sure when, but I am no longer aware of the music or the people or the vibration of the bass. It's only her. Her breath on me. The brush of her bra on my bare chest. Her smell. The feel of her hair tickling my skin. The warmth of her body. I am lost in her. I want nothing but to touch her. To kiss her. To pull her hips into my lap and hold her there.

I am quickly snapped back into reality as she pulls me up off the chair. I am acutely aware that my pants are tighter than when I first sat down.

"I–I can't," I stammer. Through some grace of God, she hears me and puts her arms around my waist to cover my erection. Before I can be relieved, she hitches a leg up on my hip and leans backward. *Oh yes, this completely helps the situation.* The audience howls with excitement. I have to resist the urge to push my blazing cock into her body but I can't resist touching her. I curl both hands around her ass, holding her close to me for a moment. She rights herself and looks at me for a moment. I drop my hands from her body and wonder if touching is off limits despite the fact that she's all but molested me.

Without a word, she turns the both of us so I am no longer facing the crowd. She pulls me toward the darker shadows of the stage. I am relieved she has concealed my predicament with ease and grace.

Once we're offstage, Diesel pushes me into a small side

room.

"Stay here," she says and quickly disappears. I can hear the audience respond to Diesel returning to the stage and offering her closing well wishes for the evening. The music continues and I do my best to calm myself down. My jeans are choking my aching dick. I'm brimming with pent up frustration and desire.

What the hell just happened? She was all over me. Shit! And now what? We can't just leave each other like this. I adjust myself, which does nothing to ease the urge to pounce on her the second she returns.

Diesel comes back into the room, closer to me than appropriate given she continues to wear only the lace essentials. Both our breaths are still ragged from our mutual physical exertion.

"Are you okay? Did I hurt you?" Diesel looks genuinely concerned that in some way, I've been injured. She puts her hands on my upper arms before running them lightly across my chest. I am officially going to explode. Do I kiss her?

"Am I okay?" The benign question is a punch to the gut. She chose me for no other reason than to make a scene. "You just rubbed yourself all over me like a stripper in front of hundreds of people! How do you think I am?" I can't figure out why I'm yelling. "What was that? Some kind of sick joke!"

"N-no. It's just something we do." She sounds confused; she pulls her hands of my chest, holding them up in resignation. "I thought you'd like it for your story. You know, you can recount how you were sacrificed for Eden. We've all done it, or rather, had it done to us. Bain thought it would be a good idea—"

"This was Bain's idea?" My interruption is abrupt and she looks wounded. "Your boyfriend wants you to strip for a complete stranger? That's his idea of fun?"

"Look, it's just something we do. Like frat parties do virgin sacrifice." She's visibly put off, irritated at my outburst. "I thought you'd enjoy it. I did! And Bain's not my boyfriend."

She turns and stalks out of the room. How is it she is so calm? How did this go from me wanting to fuck the daylights out of her to me yelling and her leaving?

She enjoyed it? She had fun?

Despite having every urge to run after her, I leave Eden.

Chapter Thirteen
ELLIOT

THE FOLLOWING MORNING, I return to Eden to find it buzzing with activity without the structured pace of show prep.

"Hey," Bain calls, sidling up beside me, "where did you run off to last night? Someone like what you had to offer and you took 'em up on it?" He laughs after nudging my arm with his elbow.

"Eh, no, more like I had a bit too much fun and needed to take a break." I'm still off-kilter from last night's exploits. I'm thankful I don't see Diesel in the group. I'm not sure how she would react to me after I lost my mind. I can't decide if I should apologize for my actions or ignore the fact that she rubbed herself all over me.

"Right." Bain looks at me sheepishly, snapping me from the replay of Diesel's body smoothly draped across mine. "Look, it wasn't her idea. It was mine. She told me about the whole closet situation. I thought you'd like it, maybe find it interesting, because she's our number one here. I didn't want to make you uncomfortable."

"Really?" I scoff. "Not make me uncomfortable? Just put me on a stage and lay a half-naked woman on top of me?"

"Okay, look, I'm sorry." He puts his hands up and laughs. "But you've got to admit, she's pretty fucking awesome." Bain raises his eyebrows and nudges me again. *No shit she's awesome. I had to jack off when I got home because she's so fucking awesome.*

"That's not the point," I huff, trying to resist agreeing with him. "Besides, I thought you two were..."

"What, Diesel and I?" Bain steps back, clearly affronted. "Oh no, dude, you are totally up the wrong tree there. She's like a sister to me."

"And Mike?"

"Mike and Diesel have a working relationship. They are close but can be like oil and water at times. He's a little too laid back for her, she can be too domineering for him. Overall, they accept each other for who they are. If it weren't for this place and me, I don't think they would ever associate."

"So she's unattached?"

"Oh, yeah. She's not been with anyone in a long time. Diesel's legit. She's not like some of these other girls; she doesn't take home random guys." Bain looks at me with a questioning glance. "Why do you ask?"

"Curious."

Bain looks around to see who is close. "Remember she said that Jess was all fur coat and no knickers?"

"Yeah."

"Well, Diesel is the fur coat and the knickers, or, however you guys say it. She's the real deal." Bain says this without any real tone or inclination.

"Brilliant."

"All right, well, good luck with that, bro. Despite all that, she's a tough one." Bain looks at me with slight sympathy. "Okay look, sometimes after we do a show, we take off for a place in upstate New York. Diesel is there already. It's just a blow-off-some-steam long weekend. Next show is straight DJ and it's someone we're bringing in. We usually don't come back 'til Wednesday or Thursday to help them get situated. We are heading up in a few hours. Why don't you pack up and meet us here at one o'clock?"

"Are you sure that's okay?"

"Yeah." He shrugs. "You are sticking close to the three of us. Mike and I are going up, so that's two of the three. She's already up there. If she has any concerns about it, she can't really fault us for following her rules, right?" His grin is pure devilish delight.

I offer a shrug, agreeing with Bain's logic. "Sure, I'll see you here then."

FOUR HOURS LATER, we meet outside of Eden with bags packed in a sleek grey BMW. Apparently needing increased revenue may not have been a concern for these three in accepting my offer about the blog. They seem to be doing just fine on their own.

"So where are we going?" The curiosity surrounding this little trip has my mind racing since leaving Bain this morning.

"We are headed to Diesel's place," Bain offers. "She's had the house for a while. It just gets us out of the city and offers some reprieve. Diesel is usually there longer than the rest of us. She has some friends close by. I think she likes the change of atmosphere."

I can only consider this briefly before dozing off, exhausted from the lack of sleep and nerves that kept me up all night.

✧　✧　✧

THE CRACK OF gravel wakes me up faster than I would like. No sooner are my eyes open than the car bottoms out, jarring me from any comfort I had.

"Holy shit, Mike! Can you not completely mess up the car?"

"Well," Mike responds with a calm huff, "if you weren't be so fucking hell-bent on buying the next Batmobile, maybe your car would be more than a half inch off the ground."

"Blah, blah, you love this car."

"I'd love it more if it was able to get through this driveway. You need to take Deese with you next time. She is at least sensible enough to get a car that is functional and won't get stuck on road kill."

Deese? As is short for Diesel?

Collecting myself from the too-brief nap, I peer out the window and am shocked. "Diesel's place," as described by Bain, is an elaborate lake house that's equipped with a wraparound deck, three-car garage, floor to ceiling windows, skylights, and at least three thousand square feet of living space.

We pull into the garage and I eye Diesel's silver VW Jetta parked next to a black convertible Fiat Abrath. Bain is immediately out of the car and opening the door to the home. Pulling myself from the back seat, I am hit with the sweet scent of baking. The house smells amazing. Bain inhales and looks at Mike with primal eyes. "She's cooking!" He's gone in an instant, as if no other explanation is needed.

I look at Mike with a questioning glance.

"Diesel cooks and bakes when she's here," he offers. After pulling the bags from the trunk of the car, he begins to walk into the house. For a brief moment, he pauses next to me. "Just so you know; she is truly amazing." His information is offered to me with a level of earnestness I was not expecting. Before I can respond, he moves toward the house as if nothing was said, an apparition of an admission without a clear goal or agenda.

We hear echoes of Bain yelling with his mouth full about cinnamon buns that are still warm. Mike passes a glance over his shoulder with raised eyebrows. "Bain, on the other hand, lives for nothing but food and sex."

I stifle a laugh at this obvious admission, especially given Bain's enthusiastic performance with the redhead he pulled on stage last night. Besides, with these two sharing a place, I'm sure Mike is witness to all of Bain's sins.

As we enter, the house appears empty with the exception of the three of us, and Diesel.

"Deese? Where are you?" Bain yells through the house.

We turn as her voice emanates from upstairs. "I'm up here. You better not have touched those cinnamon buns!"

Bain laughs sheepishly and shoves the rest of the cinnamon bun into his mouth. "No one tell her. We'll find someone to blame it on." He snorts with jovial pleasure as he climbs the stairs. Mike shakes his head but follows, motioning for me to come along.

I can hear the muffled discussion between Bain and Diesel as Mike leads me through the house. As we climb the stairs, the surrounding area begs for me to take it in. Through the enormous windows, I see a lush wood held back by a sizeable pond on the property. It is serene and beautiful, the antithesis of Eden. The house itself is well maintained and decorated with simple but beautiful photography. The entire structure is open, calm, and pristine, with natural light. I don't realize it until it's too late that I've blindly followed my guide and I'm standing in what appears to be an office with three people staring at me.

"Hello," I offer to Diesel, who returns an irritated gaze.

"Hey," she replies. "I didn't know you were coming." Her tone is flat and without any indication that she is remotely pleased with this arrangement.

"Well," Bain interjects, "that was a bit of my doing." After Diesel looks at him in a please-explain-this sort of way, he goes on, "You did set the rules explicitly that Elliot was to be with one of the three of us, and here we all are. I couldn't leave him there all by himself." Bain lays his hand on one of Diesel's, softening his eyes in a mockingly sweet gesture. "You would have never forgiven me, sweetheart."

"I'm not sure I will ever forgive you." Her tight smile speaks of retribution rather than thanks.

"You will, because you love me." Bain kisses her on the cheek. "Where shall we house Mr. Elliot? Your room? Don't you have a pole in there?"

"Har har. You are so comedic, my dear Bain," Diesel replies as she turns back to her work. "He can stay in one of the spares. I think it's just us this weekend. Everyone else is usually here by now."

The entirety of her response is given without looking at Bain, Mike, or myself. Her back is turned to everyone as she resumes typing on the computer.

Bain looks at me and shrugs. "Come on. We'll let her finish her work." Before fully exiting the room, he tosses a mischievous glance back toward her. "What's for dinner, my dear?"

"You on a stick."

He laughs again and turns to me. "Told you she was a tough one," he mutters. "I'll show you to your room. We just usually chill until dinner. Feel free to walk the grounds."

"And Elliot." Diesel's voice causes me pause. It's calm but direct, the same voice she used to tell me not to fuck with Eden. I realize instantly I love the sound of my name rolling off her tongue regardless of the tone or intonation. When I turn back to look at her, she is staring directly at me.

"Yes?"

"Everything here is off the record. It's enough for you to expose what we do for a living, but our private lives will remain just that. Understood?" She is clipped and all business again.

Ah, it's official. The closet freak-out has totally fucked this up.

"Of course. You have my word." It's all I can offer.

"Thanks." She turns back to her computer. "Dinner is at seven thirty."

I follow Bain down a hall of closed doors. Every one Bain walks past, he pushes open.

"This is my room," Bain turns the doorknob and the door falls open without missing a step.

"This is Mike's room." He opens the next door and proceeds. "And you can stay in here. I've always liked this room. It's usually reserved for guests and the like. I think you'll enjoy it."

"Where is Diesel's room?" I ask the question before I can even register that it might be an inappropriate inquiry.

Bain considers the question before answering it. "She's upstairs, bro." He looks down the hallway from which we have just come. "Enjoy it here. It's really nice." He lowers his voice, leaning toward me. "And don't worry about Diesel. She'll ease up."

I nod in Bain's direction and look around the room. It is simply decorated, clearly a guest bedroom, with a bed, dresser, and closet. The view is amazing. It overlooks the lake with a clear view of the forest behind.

After unpacking, I set out for a walk around the perimeter of the lake, taking in the beauty and grandeur of this place. One is forced to compare and contrast the areas Diesel lives in. There's Eden with its combination of rustic industrialism and modern chic, and then this place, where everything natural and calm. It's two sides of a coin. Two sides of her. But, despite the change in scenery, she seems held in the city. Because of me? Because of how we left things? Skimming rocks into the lake, I look up at the house and hope Bain is right. I want her to be relaxed despite my presence.

After an hour and a half, I return to the house, take a shower, and lay down for a nap. I am jarred awake by Bain yelling from downstairs.

"Hey! Elliot! Dinner is ready!"

I get up, straighten my slept-on hair and head down the steps. The closer I get to the kitchen, the more I am overcome by the delicious smells of pork, potatoes, and biscuits. Bain is hovering over the table like a wild dog as Mike flips through his iPod for dinner music. I stand in the doorway as Diesel enters from another door carrying two bottles of wine, a red and a white. She has changed from her previous outfit into a simple green dress covered by an apron. As she removes the apron and readies herself to sit down, I can see that the dress highlights her fair skin and accents the copper highlights in her hair, falling in it's typical unruly pattern across her shoulders. I notice how small her waist actually is and how her hips are so...enticing.

I am pulled from my thoughts when Mike claps me hard on the back. "Grab a seat, man. You'll want to get something before Bain eats us out of house and home." He smiles, shaking me gently by my shoulder. He caught me staring, again.

Diesel laughs lightly. "It won't be the first time," she says. "Come on, everyone get a glass."

She pours wine into each of the four glasses then raises hers.

"To another successful event and for many more to come," she toasts and lifts the glass to her lips.

"And to a few more wanted, er, uh, unwanted lap dances," Bain interjects, causing Diesel to choke on her wine.

"Really, Bain?" she says with a laugh that hugs the border of discomfort, before catching a small drop of wine escaping from her lip with her fingertip. She gently purses her lips around her finger, savoring the deep red liquid before sweeping her eyes to me. Finger still held to her plump lips, we hold each other's stare for a moment before her cheeks flush and she breaks the connection.

"Okay," she says with a slight wobble to her voice, "let's eat!"

I look at Bain and Mike; they exchange a glance before

taking turns looking at both of us. Only Diesel snaps Bain from whatever his thoughts were, deftly tossing pork onto his plate. Again she has salvaged an awkward moment.

Thankfully, as dinner continues, the atmosphere gradually becomes more comfortable. We talk about the production and planning that goes along with each of the shows. Bain continues to quiz and question me about how I got into writing. I share my brief history as a mildly successful college blogger for the underground London music scene and my transition to the States for more opportunities. Mike and Bain are the most interactive, with Diesel interjecting here and there. By the end of the dinner, we are all warm with wine and the lighthearted nature of the evening. Mike and Bain offer to clean the table because Diesel did the cooking. I offer to help but am quickly turned down by both. Diesel thanks the guys for cleaning up and moves into the living room. I watch her from my seat as she takes in the sunset over the lake from an enormous bow window.

Bain shakes me from my reverie as he returns and looks at me with what I think is amusement. He glances into the living room. "If I were you, I'd check out the music." He smiles as if he's just given permission for a covert mission before grabbing more dishes. I nod my assent and walk into the living room with an awkward pace. I am immediately unsure of how to approach her, given our last one-on-one interaction was made up of me yelling at her while she was practically naked in front of me.

"Thank you for a wonderful dinner," I offer despite her back being turned to me. Good. Polite is good.

She looks at me over her shoulder. "I'm glad you liked it. I don't get a whole lot of opportunity to cook anymore." She smiles. "It's nice to know I've still got it."

"Um, yeah. Good to know." I feel so stilted compared to her breezy response. Shoving my hands in my pockets is the only way to manage my anxiety and the screaming desire to touch her.

"Hey." She quickly turns to me, causing me to teeter a little. "I just want to say again that I'm sorry about last night. I feel really bad about it. Most guys enjoy it...I think you are the only one who ever didn't." The entirety of her statement is made without looking at me, as if she's embarrassed or ashamed of what happened.

I cannot control the flush on my face. "Look, I'm not saying I didn't enjoy it. I couldn't stand up without everyone seeing how much I enjoyed it."

Her light laugh is accompanied by a rueful smile. "Yeah, sorry about that."

"Really," I offer, "I assure you that it's okay. I was just very surprised. Looking back on it, it was really great."

"Really?" she asks, looking up at me through her lashes. I nod in approval.

"Well, okay," she says, "I just don't want things to be strange, you know? I mean, you're here and it's just easier for everyone to be cool."

"I hear you. I'm cool." Of course, saying it and being it are two completely different things. I do my best to be relaxed as I stomp down the urge to wind my arm around her waist and pull her to me, to have her as close to me as she was last night. Our conversation, meant to be private, has pulled us into each other. I can smell a light mixture of lavender and vanilla.

"Okay, good." She stops short. We are caught in each

other, looking at eyes and lips. Diesel's breath catches as she hears Bain enter the room. She immediately steps back and I have to clench my fists in my pockets to stop from grabbing her and bringing her close to me again.

"Okay, I'm going to head up," she says as she is walking out of the room, "good night everyone. See you in the morning."

No one responds. Her escape is too quick. We can only watch her leave. Once she's gone, I take a moment to survey my shoes before looking up at Bain, who is now watching me intently.

His face twists with empathy. "I told you she was tough, dude. Come on, we're having beers on the deck."

"Right." I nod and take a final glance at the stairs where Diesel had made her great escape before following Bain outside.

Chapter Fourteen
DIESEL

FROM UPSTAIRS, I can hear their conversation through my open balcony door. They talk about the evening and the show, and they drink late into the evening. I gather as much information about Elliot as possible in the hope that my burning curiosity about him will be dismissed by some outward flaw.

Please be some kind of horrible asshole. Please say something terribly douchey so I won't like you anymore!

Despite listening intently for several hours, my hopes are dashed. I have to admit, I am intrigued. I have this stirring in my chest, which I've not felt in years. Of course, that's by my own doing. I've spent years intentionally blocking myself off, protecting myself. It's easier to be the voyeur, to watch everyone else fall in and out of relationships. Years ago I fell and that wound still stings at times. The pain has lessened, but it lingers like a ghost haunting the possibilities of what could be.

I pull myself from the balcony door and crawl into my excessively large bed. Lying here alone, I wonder what it would feel like with someone next to me again. Maybe it *has* been too long.

✧　✧　✧

"DIESEL."

"Hmmmm?"

"Diesel. Wake up!"

Bain?

I open one eye to see Bain standing at the foot of my bed, fully dressed and polished.

"What are you doing?" It's a whiney, sleep-filled response.

"Can you come downstairs?"

"Um, yeah." I look around for a clock, something to orient me from my abrupt awakening. How can he be up? I was asleep well before him. What the hell is going on? Before I can question him or get out of bed, he leaves the room.

I slowly navigate the two flights of stairs down to the kitchen. Even if he's up and running, I don't see an apparent need to rush. Pulling on my robe, I stifle a yawn as I make my way through the house in my bare feet. I enter the kitchen to see Bain standing in the kitchen with Mike, who's also dressed and sitting at the kitchen table. Elliot's head is propped on one hand, the other holding onto a cup of coffee as if it was the final lifeboat on the *Titanic*. He is also in his pajamas, or more clearly, pajama pants. I snatch a quick inventory of his toned torso complete with deliciously cut biceps before pulling my robe closer. I am immediately aware of how thin and short my nightgown is, and that I have nothing but underwear on underneath.

"What's going on?" I try to sound nonchalant as I go for coffee.

"Mike and I are heading back." Bain spits the words as if he has been rehearsing this in his head.

"What? Already? Why?" I narrowly miss smashing the coffee carafe into the counter. *Why are they leaving so soon?*

"We have *business* to take care of." Bain smiles.

I immediately raise my eyebrows.

"Business?" I repeat before resting my hand on my hip and glaring at him. "What kind of business?"

"You know, Diesel." His brow raises in a way makes me want to smack myself in the forehead. Stupid girl, they have *business* to attend to.

"Oh...well, okay." I respond. Of course he would have this conversation in front of Elliot. Clearly, they aren't going to out themselves to him. They need to ensure they are alone before any *business* takes place.

"So, we are going back. Elliot is going to stay here with you for the next few days. Make sure you bring him back when you come home." Bain speaks with a clear focus and intent. I am very aware that he's told me, not asked me, if this situation is agreeable.

I look to Elliot, who has now found the conversation more interesting than the coffee. As Bain begins to walk toward the garage, I am on his heels.

In the privacy of the garage, I lose my resolve.

"What the hell is this? You are going to leave me here with him? What if he is some kind of mass murder?"

Bain laughs. "He's not, trust me. We talked a lot last night. He's legit. I actually like him a lot. I think you should spend some time with him. Take him on your little jaunts and have some fun."

"My *little jaunts*? Have some fun? And how do you propose I do that?"

"Take him to meet Greggor. He'll get a kick out of Elliot, make him some dinner...and then I suggest you sleep with him."

"What!" The blood rushing to my face is instantaneous. My heart is pounding so hard I'm convinced it is visible through my robe.

"Look, he's single. I'm convinced he's got the hots for you. He keeps asking about you, if you are single, what you like, and those kinds of things."

"That's for his blog."

"I don't think so, Deese; it's not like that. Besides, you told him everything was off the record here. I've not seen him write a single thing down."

I look at him with a mix of betrayal and anxiety.

"He couldn't take his eyes off you last night, sweetheart. A bomb could have gone off and he would have only heard you."

I roll my eyes. Despite my desire to fight, I know this battle is futile. They have *business* to take care of.

Mike walks into the garage. "Okay," he says, "are we out?"

Bain hugs me and kisses me on the cheek. "Have fun, my darling. You deserve it."

"I agree," says Mike coolly. "Let him touch you in your special place, Deese."

I am instantly horrified at Mike's suggestion. My gaping mouth is enough to send both of them into hysterics.

"Oh, and darling," Bain calls as he is getting into the car, "Mike just put condoms in your nightstand drawer. Enjoy!" He is in the car and pulling away before I can move.

You have got to be kidding me. With fists clenched at my

sides, all I want to do is punch something. Rather, someone. *Two* someones. I inhale and open my fists.

Okay, we can do this. It's just like any other day.

Despite my pep talk, I know it is not. I hope that my face is not going to give away the warring struggle between my intense discomfort with this situation and my fascination with this man. Elliot and I, alone....in this house....alone...with condoms. Can I do that? Can I do him? Well, yes...but....

I take some more stabilizing breaths before returning to the kitchen....which, again, does not really help.

Elliot is still at the kitchen table, now looking out over the lake, admiring the morning. I have a brief moment to take in the lean muscles of his arms, shoulders, and back. Holy crap... My entire body pings with excitement, and I feel a bolt of desire singe my stomach. I am caught staring when he turns to me with expectant eyes.

"Good morning?" he offers.

I smile meekly. "Yeah, good morning."

We actively try to avoid each other's glances for a few minutes and fail miserably. Oh, yes, and here is the uncomfortable silence that is so much fun. Breathe in and out. Okay, here it goes...

"So, I'm going into town to see some friends and do some shopping. Would you like to come with me?"

"Of course. That would be great." He smiles and runs his hand through this hair then across his stubbled chin. He looks so...yummy.

"Give me an hour or so. Feel free to help yourself in the kitchen. There are eggs and stuff in the fridge." I quickly turn to get out of the kitchen, intent on finding something to cover my ass just a little bit.

"Do you like eggs?" he asks.

I pause in my tracks. I look at him and nod.

"Brilliant. You get ready and I'll make us eggs for breakfast." He's up and moving toward the refrigerator. "I need something for this hangover."

I am caught off guard. I stare at him for a moment. "You are going to make me eggs?"

"Yeah. Are you okay with that?"

I pause to consider this for a brief second. Is he serious?

"Yeah, I'm okay with that."

"Good." Elliot opens the fridge door and peers in. Shocked with the current turn of events, I am frozen in place, watching him rummage through the contents of my fridge.

Go upstairs and get ready, Diesel. This is okay...it's okay....this will be all right.

I shower and spend an excessive amount of time primping, shaving, doing my hair. My outfit is not one I would normally wear to see Greggor but I'm anxious and want to make a good impression. Holly would be proud.

I leave my room, knowing I look good in jeans, a coral top, and beaded sandals. I used the makeup that highlights my hazel eyes. Here we go. Now or never.

I walk into the kitchen to see Elliot leaning against the counter, looking at his phone. Whatever his activity, he is so engrossed he has not heard me come down the stairs.

"It smells really good." I try to sound nonchalant as he snaps out of his activity.

"Well, yeah, it is good!" he responds with a smile and gestures to the table.

Oh, God! Don't smile like that! Why do you have to have beautiful lips and teeth? Why do you still not have a shirt on? I hope these eggs are awful. Please, God, let these eggs be awful.

Elliot walks two plates of eggs, sausage, and toast to the kitchen table, which is already adorned with orange juice glasses, napkins, and utensils.

"I'm impressed," I offer. "This is a pretty good spread."

"Well, after last night's dinner, I figured you deserved a little break from the stove." He pulls my chair out for me.

I sit and pick up my fork. "Ah, that's my pleasure, though," I respond with a smile of embarrassment and gratitude. "I do love to cook. I just don't get to do it often."

"Where did you learn to cook like that? Your mum?" Elliot asks.

With a mouthful of eggs, I smile ruefully at him. "Um, no actually. You know those bottles of wine we had last night?"

Elliot nods.

"My mom taught me how to open those." I look at him with a silly slyness I know he's not seen before. It's easier to be myself here. Maybe too easy. I offer a half smile and scoop some food into my mouth. Damn, the eggs are really good. Crap!

Elliot laughs at my dig and holds my stare just a little too long. "Your dad, then? He taught you?"

I feel instantly nervous and break my stare away. "No. I never really had any steady interaction with him. I was pretty much left to my own devices once I was old enough to feed and clothe myself. I actually learned to cook from Greggor. He's the friend we're going to see today." I point to the plate with my fork. "So where did you learn to cook?"

"My dad," Elliot offers. "My mum died when I was three, so he became the ultimate in managing dual roles."

"I'm so sorry for your loss. Where is your Dad?"

"Thanks. I don't remember too much of my mum but Dad tells me good stories once in a while. He's still in London. I'll never get him out of there unless he's in a box. He loves it just a little too much."

"Yeah, it's a great place to be," I respond.

"You've been to London?" Elliot's interest is peaked.

"Yup." My mind launches me back to my time in England, and I can't help the smile on my face. "When did you get here?"

Elliot sits back. "A year and a half ago. It killed my Dad for me to leave, but there was an opportunity, and I couldn't wonder my whole life if I'd given something up if I didn't take it. So I'm here."

"For how long?" The question flies from my mouth so fast, I don't have time register its gravity. I feel my cheeks grow red.

"For as long as I want to be," he offers coolly.

We look at each other for a brief time before Elliot excuses himself, citing he needs to make himself presentable to visit people. I finish my breakfast and clean the kitchen with a fervor I've not had in a long time. As I scrub the sink, I think about how much I really hate cleaning and other random things as distraction to my errant thoughts about Elliot upstairs, naked in the shower.

OUR DRIVE INTO town is highlighted by awkward silences

and stolen glances across the car at each other. Of course, the Fiat does not allow for much distance between people, especially when one of those people is well over six feet tall.

Back at the house, he'd looked oddly confused when I walked to the Fiat and not the VW. "That's my city car," I offered, pushing my chin toward the VW. "This one is for tooling around out here on the weekends." He shrugged in acceptance and folded himself into the Fiat. I couldn't help but feel instantly self-conscious that all this man came to New York with was a motorcycle and a backpack.

While pulling into town, I break our silence. "So, Greggor has been a friend of mine for a very long time. He's like an adoptive dad to me. He's protective, and highly embarrassing, but very loving. With that said, I'm going to apologize now for anything that is about to happen."

Elliot looks at me with amused delight. "Really, it's going to be that kind of a visit?"

I laugh. "Well," I say while looking out the window, "Greggor is a trip. You never know what you are going to get. His wife, Natalie, is a gem. She's much more refined than her husband."

"What is he going to think about me?" Elliot asks.

"Oh," I laugh knowingly. "I think he and Natalie are going to love you, no worries there. You'll see. Come on."

I lead Elliot through the town from the community parking lot. The streets have a leisurely feel, with people walking, enjoying the beautiful day that has become warm and inviting. People say hello to each other, visibly joyful walking through the streets. It's such a difference from the pace of the city. I've always felt so comfortable here.

"Okay," I stop short, feeling mildly apprehensive, "we're here." I look at Quinlan's storefront; Elliot follows my gaze with a curious look. "Fair warning, he can behave like a Labrador without manners."

I can't wait for him to respond and move though the front door, making the bell on the door jingle lightly. I watch the amazement on Elliot's face as he's hit by nuances of his home on all senses. The place smells of tea and biscuits, there are goods from the UK carefully placed on shelves, and speakers waft out music from classic English artists.

From behind the counter, Natalie emerges wiping her hands on an apron. She sees me, immediately breaks from her previous thought, and rushes to embrace me with arms extended.

"Oh my, dear! We've been waiting for you!" She kisses me and pulls me into the warm and inviting hug of a mother. I wonder if Elliot has registered her English accent. Before I can offer any introduction, Natalie realizes I'm with someone. Still in Natalie's arms, I follow her gaze to see Elliot wordlessly taking in the shop.

"Oh, my," Natalie offers, looking at me with surprised amusement, "I see you've brought a friend." Before I can even form the thought to introduce Elliot to Natalie, the Labrador named Greggor emerges from the back to the store.

"Natalie! Where are you, woman?" Greggor abruptly ends his rant when he sees the three of us in the middle of his store. "My darling Diesel is here!" He lumbers out from behind the counter and hugs me with a force that blows air from my body as he picks me up off the ground. The man is contradiction in form and function. He is physically intimidating with dark eyes and hair, barrel chest, and meaty arms and hands; however, his mischievous smile and affectionate hugs that feel more like a headlock give away his playful mien. He has always been strong and loving for his family. I'm so grateful that 'family' includes me.

"Hello, Greggor. It's wonderful to see you. Greggor, Natalie, this is Elliot."

Without any opportunity to explain further, Greggor is on Elliot like a hungry dog on hamburger.

"A boyfriend! You've got a boyfriend! Finally! We have been praying to all gods out there for you! Come here, boy!" Before I can stop the train wreck from happening, Greggor embraces Elliot with a force that I'm sure could crack ribs.

Greggor releases Elliot. After a slight sense of relief that he's not crumpled to the floor, feeling compelled to protect Elliot. I move my body between them for the next divulging of information.

"Wait. Elliot is not my boyfriend. He's a writer doing some pieces on the club. We're here this weekend because we just had our show and it wouldn't be right to leave him in the city without any of us. So he's here with me."

"Huh." Greggor takes a step back, rubbing his chin with his massive paw of a hand. "Then where are Bain and Mike?" he asks with an irritated curiosity as he assesses Elliot.

"They had to go back to the city," I offer.

"So they left you with a total stranger?" Greggor's demeanor changes suddenly. He's now glaring at Elliot with a fatherly *you're-not-getting-near-my-daughter* look.

The anxiety of the moment is overwhelming. I shift from one foot to another, debating if I should scream for Elliot to run because Greggor is going to take both of us down.

"Greggor, it's not like that. He's okay. He's been around us. I promise he's cool. I thought you'd like to meet him."

"Why?" Greggor asks gruffly.

"Say hello, Elliot," I implore.

"Hello, Greggor, Natalie, pleasure to meet you." Elliot says with his clear British accent.

The thawing of Greggor's mistrust is so immediate, a snicker bubbles forward louder than intended.

"Why didn't you say you were with a Brit?" Greggor demands.

"The opportunity was kind of lost a little while ago." I offer playfully.

"Come here, boy. Let's get you some tea." Greggor claps Elliot on the back and pulls him toward the counter.

Natalie glances at me, raising her eyebrows. I laugh and roll my eyes, "I know...I know."

"He'd be delighted if you dated a Brit, you know," Natalie whispers.

"Okay, I know," I respond quietly and look across the store at the newfound friends. "He's really cute, right?"

"Right," Natalie responds.

"Natalie, he made me eggs." It's a whisper and I'm proud of myself for not screaming it.

"Well, that's something, isn't it?" Natalie offers as we watch Elliot and Greggor become immersed in tea and talks of home.

✧   ✧   ✧

WE SPEND THE afternoon at Greggor and Natalie's shop and

catch up between tending to patrons. During afternoon tea, a blonde, well-built young man walks through the front door as if it's his own personal runway. I know this bad boy just a little too well and that knowledge warms my heart.

With an English accent, he hollers, "I just smacked up some piece-of-shit Fiat in the public lot. I hope that didn't belong to anyone here!"

Elliot looks at me with curiosity as I laugh behind my teacup. Quin walks toward us and immediately hones in on Elliot.

"Who is this suitor?" he asks me.

"Quin, this is Elliot. He's a writer spending some time with us. Elliot, this is Quin. He's Greggor's son. God help the world."

I immediately realize that I did not redirect his notion of suitor but maybe I'll let it hang and see what happens.

"She loves me best, don't ever forget that fact," he says, shaking Elliot's hand. Quin offers me an overzealous hug and kisses my check, staring at Elliot the whole time. This man, heavens! "What are you two doing tonight?"

"Nothing." I look at Elliot. "I was going to make dinner, and that was it."

"Well, you must come to my show then," Quin says before turning to Elliot. "We're in a band and we're pretty amazing."

"Puff those feathers a little more, there, love." I playfully jab at Quin. He's grown so much but his mere presence makes me nostalgic for the old days of our youthful fun and lighthearted play.

"I think a show would be great," Elliot offers.

"Whoa, you're Brit! Deese, why didn't you say?" Quin has

his full attention on Elliot now.

"If you guys would be less focused on the fact that I walk in with someone rather than who the person is, I could tell you these things." My response falls on deaf ears.

"Yeah, yeah." Quin brushes me off and begins talking to Elliot in the same fashion that Greggor did.

That's my cue. I sneak behind the counter to Natalie and Greggor, looking over the books.

"Hey, we are going to head out soon. Where is Quin's show tonight? We can meet you there."

"Nonsense!" Greggor bellows. "You come to the house for dinner and we'll all go together."

I chew on my lip for a brief moment as I consider asking if Elliot can come also. Truly, I have no choice but to bring him. If I leave him, I'll do nothing but think about him.

"Be there at five," Greggor instructs. I nod and turn to walk out of the office. "And, Diesel," he calls, "bring him along, too."

I look at these marvelous people who have done nothing but love me unconditionally for years. Greggor's mouth curls into a mischievous smirk and Natalie, with her huge grin hidden behind her hand, tell me everything I need to know about their approval of Elliot. I offer a slight smile as I shake my head.

"Okay," I offer, "we'll be there then."

I say good-bye to Quin, informing him we will be over for dinner then the show. Once we are outside and alone, Elliot begins asking questions.

"How do you know them?"

"I met them when I was in Essex. I was really young, like

seventeen, and we've known each other since."

"Okay, how?"

"My last year of high school, I got into the student exchange program at my school. Natalie and Greggor were my host family. Once I graduated, I wanted to stay and they let me live with them until I was able to afford a place on my own. I worked at Natalie's brother's bar for a couple years."

Elliot nods in understanding. "They seem really great."

"Oh, yeah, they are amazing. I'm truly blessed to have them in my life." I have no choice but to be honest, anything less than that would be a lie I'm not willing to live with. "I'm sorry I didn't check with you first about the show and dinner. I figured you didn't want to be in the house alone."

"No, it's great. I'm very excited for a night out with you." He truly looks it, and I immediately feel a jump of anticipation, too. I'm going out tonight with this man! I try my best to tamp down the burst of giddiness, but it's impossible. Can I call this a date? Why am I calling an evening out with my family and a guy I barely know a date? *Good God, get a grip.*

The ride home is more comfortable than this morning, which is a much needed improvement. In fact, the tension has lifted so much that Elliot has decided to weed through my iPod with a fine toothed comb. He quizzes me on song titles and singers, highlighting our common likes, and remarks about my overall eclectic tastes.

"I never tagged you for a lover of show tunes. Or Jay-Z."

"I like a lot of different things. It depends on my mood."

"What kind of mood do you have to be in to listen to Nine Inch Nails and Dave Matthews Band?"

I snort a laugh. "You're telling me you don't listen to different things?"

"No, I listen to everything, but this is your playlist, not mine."

"Even show tunes?"

"No. No show tunes." He gasps in mock surprise and clutches his chest. "My favorite!"

The mellow music filling the car abruptly changes to *Buttons* by The Pussycat Dolls.

"Hey!" I laugh, mostly from his antics but there is hint of embarrassment. "Cool it with the critique. I bet there are some real winners on your playlist." I tap my chin in contemplation. "I'm guessing you'd go the homegrown route. One Direction? No, even better, The Spice Girls, right?"

His warm and playful laugh sends the butterflies in my stomach on a wild course. They dive bomb the depths of my belly when he reaches across the car and places a warm hand on my leg.

"Don't tell anyone my secrets, Diesel. I've kept my Spice Girl addiction private for a long time and intend to keep it that way."

I glance at his hand while trying to stay focused on the road. "Your secret is safe with me but I will use this newfound knowledge as blackmail if needed."

"I'm sure you would but there won't be any need for blackmail."

"No?"

"No."

Stopped at a red light, I find him looking intently at me. His smoldering gaze sends the butterflies careening out of control again. I look back at the light, willing it to turn green, squirming in my seat. The Dolls fade away and are replaced by *I'm On Fire* by Springsteen. The butterflies dive bomb again and explode in a fiery crash of need and trepidation.

Chapter Fifteen
ELLIOT

AFTER PULLING UP to Natalie and Greggor's house, Diesel tells me to get out of the car quietly as she sneaks us up to the door. She gives me the 'shhh' signal with her finger held closely to those beautiful lips as she pushes me into a little alcove to the left of the door. From my hiding place, I have full opportunity to ogle her in her black skirt, lace tank top, and silver sandals.

Her style outside of Eden is alluring and feminine. Oh, she's got "feminine" going on at Eden, but here, it's as if she expresses herself with her clothing. She has a glamour I've not seen before. Not pretentious or vapid. It's the genuine beauty she hides behind the industrial film of toughness at Eden. At Eden she's a rock star, here she's the hot girl next door.

"Just stand here for a second," she instructs as she rings the doorbell. She is giddy and appears lighthearted. Since we left the shop, she's been more at ease and open. It's been nice to see her smile. She was so warm with Greggor and Natalie, even Quin. I could tell they were strongly connected and care for each other very much.

I am riveted from my thoughts as Greggor pulls the door

open with a loud, "Hello, darling!" and immediately notices that she appears to be alone. "I told you to bring that man with you! Are you daft, girl?" His tone is surprisingly chastising. The quick jolt of excitement surprises me. *They want me with her.* "You know you are too stubborn for your own good!"

As soon as Greggor must have turned his back, she grabs my arm and pulls me to her side. The movement is so quick, my arm automatically curls and settles on her hip. I feel her shift, pushing her hip into my hand. When Greggor turns back to look at us, his shock is apparent.

"Too stubborn for my own good?" she asks coyly.

Greggor takes us in and shakes his head. Diesel's head rolls back with a warm and infectious laugh. She looks at me with such an inviting smile, I immediately want to kiss her. *Just one kiss on those full lips...*

She looks as if she is sharing the same thought but then breaks nervously from our place on the porch.

We walk into the house, and I instantly feel comfortable. The delicious smell of sausage and potatoes married with the purely English décor reminds me of my own home. Around the dinner table, we engage in friendly conversation about customers, Eden, family, and Quin's pending tour back home. Greggor drills me about my family and living in London. They share similar stories from their lives in the UK and settle us into a comfort that I had not anticipated.

"So Diesel, did you stun Elliot with your tales from Essex?" Greggor asks with the raised eyebrow of a meddling father.

"Um, no," she says, glancing at me. "He knows I was there, but he doesn't know the whole story." She is looking at her wine glass, playing with the thin stem.

"I would like to know the whole story but she's a little shy. How about someone fills me in."

She looks at me, clearly taken aback by my overt prying. I know that Greggor is willing to purge this story like a burst pipe. I smile at her and succumb to the restless urge to drape my arm across the back of her chair.

"Well, she was what, seventeen when she came to us," Greggor begins without any reservation. "She was really rammy but looking for something different. We had our shop in town; my brother-in-law runs it now in addition to his pub. The shop has a flat above it, and she rented it for a time after she graduated. We were so busy with the shop that we needed an extra set of hands, so she would work and help us out."

Natalie chimes in then. "Quin was a real handful. We just couldn't do for him what we wanted to and run the business. So, Diesel would help us manage Quin."

"And how long did this go on for?" I ask.

"Four years she was with me," Quin offers from the end of the table. He holds a wine glass up to her. "The best four years of my life."

Everyone laughs at Quin's unabashed affection for Diesel. "Yes Quin, it was a wonderful time," Diesel responds.

"You know I'd marry you in a heartbeat, darling," Quin offers across the table.

I snap my eyes at Quin, who's looking at Diesel with nothing but clear admiration.

"I know, Quin," she responds slowly, examining her plate with clearly flushed cheeks, "but I may always think of you as that skinny, awkward twelve-year-old boy."

Greggor laughs with gusto. "No matter how much you

push him off, he'll still come after you, darling."

"True," Quin responds. "I've grown, Diesel. I'm a man now." He lifts his eyebrow at her, egging her on.

"Oh, gross. I think it's time for you to go," she offers to him. "You know I will always adore you."

"Okay," Quin gets up from the table, "just make sure you are good and greased before you come to the show. We sound better when you're drunk."

Diesel laughs as Quin hones in on me. "Get her while you can. She'll be mine some day."

"Challenge accepted." The words roll so effortlessly off my tongue that I can't stop them. I hear Diesel suck in a breath beside me. I look to her and raise my eyebrows, imploring her to respond. She says nothing, just curls her mouth into a slight smile.

Quin says his goodbyes as dessert and tea are served. Natalie, Greggor, Diesel and I continue to talk about her time in Essex and how many places we may have crossed paths. During our conversation, I notice that she's shifted toward me, as if she is comfortable with my arm around her.

"So, when did you come back to the States?" I ask.

"Four years ago."

"Why did you decide to come home?"

Diesel pauses and looks at Greggor and Natalie as if she has no idea what to say. "Family issues, you know how that goes." She finally offers.

I look to Greggor, who appears saddened by the vague statement, his lips a thin line as he looks at Diesel. Natalie quickly stands and begins picking up dishes.

"Yes, well," Greggor says with a loud clap of his hands, "let's not let this wonderful night of my son's horrible music pass us by."

Diesel quickly helps gather dirty dishes and redirects my efforts to help. After clearing the table, she excuses herself to freshen up and change her shoes for the club. Greggor and I continue to chat until she calls to me that the bathroom is free for me to use. I excuse myself from Greggor and head up the stairs to where I think I heard her voice.

The dimly lit hallway is illuminated by a single open door. From the hallway, I see her sitting on the bed, attempting fasten the ankle strap to her high heel. Her hair falls down over her face as she fumbles with the tiny buckle, fingers fighting with the thin piece of black leather.

"Need help?"

A gasp escapes from her lips as she is snapped from the focused work. I see the blush rush across her cheeks.

"I," she tries to regain her composure as quickly as she's lost it. "I love these shoes but they are a bitch to get on."

"Here," I walk into the room and kneel at her feet. "Let me help you."

"Elliot, that's really not necessary. I can get them."

I ignore her. My hand on her body in any way is better than standing in the doorway. I've always loved heels on a woman, but these on Diesel are beyond anything I could have fantasized about. I pull her leg to rest on the side of mine, holding her ankle with one hand while fastening the leather strap with the other. I run my thumb over the delicate bone of her ankle before releasing her. Her breath is audible and hitches when I move to her other shoe. With both beautifully fastened, she stands and looks nervously around the room.

"Thanks. The bathroom is through there," she waves absently toward an open door and she teeters on the heels ever so slightly as she walks toward the door. "I'll be downstairs."

"Don't go."

She stops and looks over her shoulder at me before turning to face me. Her obvious anxiety about this situation is at war with the sexual tension clinging to the air. Her breath causes her chest to heave as she bites her bottom lip and fumbles with her hair. The pink flush of her cheeks calls to me. I can't wait anymore. This has gone on for too long. I take two strides toward her, leaving mere inches between us. She's not retreated or offered any type of resistance. I wrap my arm around her waist, closing the gap between us and kiss her lightly, testing my theory. I pull back and she exhales, her lips parting.

I need no other cue. I slant my mouth over hers, pushing all the pent-up emotion from the past several weeks and the stolen glances from today into her. She runs her hands up my arms before snaking them around my neck. With our bodies melded together, I roll my hips into her belly, pressing my desire upon her, and am rewarded with a low moan. The moment is a mess of roaming hands, frenetic kisses, and ragged breaths. It is blazingly clear that both of us are involved in this purging of restricted emotions.

The call of our names from downstairs breaks us from each other. Though our mouths are no longer touching, we still cling to each other. Our foreheads are pressed together as we attempt to collect our breath.

"We'll be there in a minute," Diesel forces out. I can hear the strain in her voice.

We look to each other, not knowing what to say. We release each other and move in opposite directions.

✧　✧　✧

THE CAR RIDE is quiet and thankfully short. The downfall of being a guy is that your desire to fuck is blazingly clear. I needed some time away to calm down, but now, with her next to me in the car, the respite was useless. I want her. Badly.

"Here we are," Greggor announces as he parks the car. The club is swarming. Women and men outside are hollering to each other through the crowd. Patrons recognize Greggor and Natalie and offer their welcome to the singer's parents. There is a reserved table for the four of us in the center of the club. Quin is already on stage, crooning. We walk through the crowd as he finishes a song and takes in the applause.

"Ah," he calls into the crowd, "I see my family has arrived! Wonderful! Everyone, I would like to you welcome my parents, and my beautiful Diesel, and her friend, Elliot." The crowd responds in kind.

"Now," Quin says, "I thought I would have built up to this, but, I think now is a good a time as any. Diesel, darling, are you a little buzzed?" The crowd laughs at his question.

"A little," she shouts to him, "why?"

"Well, I was wondering if you would come up here and do something for me?" The crowd hoots in agreement that she should go to the stage.

Greggor leans to me. "This will be good. This is why we fell in love with her."

Diesel looks at Quin with questioning and he motions for her to come up on stage. "Come on, my lovely Tess, you know you want to."

Tess? Her name is Tess?

I am flooded with warmth at the knowledge of her actual

name. Suddenly, in the dim light of the club, she looks different. The contrast between her outward appearance and being called Diesel seems outrageous. There is no way this woman should be called anything other than her beautiful name.

"Fine," she finally acquiesces. The crowd hoots as she walks toward the stage toward Quin.

"Ah, I always get her with the name," Quin says triumphantly. "For those of you who are a bit confused, my nanny's name is Tess, but we all call her Diesel. She's tough like diesel but she has the heart of her very feminine given name." Even in the darkness of the club, I know that Quin is staring directly at me.

I am amazed at how comfortable she is on stage with Quin, as if she has been there before. But she makes her living on a stage. It could be her second home.

"Today," begins Quin, "I had the wonderful opportunity to be with my dear friend, who helped raise me when I was doing a fantastic job of raising hell. I wondered if we might have one of our special moments here, to share it with everyone."

"What do you have in mind?" She is light and confident as she smiles at Quin's obvious attempt to bait her.

"Sing to me like you did when I couldn't sleep," Quin implores.

"What will you have me sing, my darling boy?"

"You are taking this very well, my Tess." Quin is clearly playing cat and mouse with her.

"You are not going to let me be until I do this, so let's do this!" She laughs and shakes her head. "Can someone get me a shot?" she calls into the crowd.

"I want you to sing *The Weight* for me. For us."

"Really? You want me to sing *The Weight*?" She is handed a shot from a server in the crowd and does not hesitate to take it. The crowd roars as she downs the drink then holds the empty glass up.

"It was truly my favorite," he says to her with a sincerity she had obviously not been expecting. He turns to the crowd. "This woman is amazing in every way. She is strong, beautiful, smart, fun, and above all else, an amazing human being. My life is better because of her."

The crowd simpers with Quin's unabashed affection for her. She turns her back briefly to the crowd and appears to wipe her eyes. "Okay, okay. I'll sing if you put a cork in it."

From the audience, I watch Diesel sing to Quin as if they were the only two people in the room. I am spinning with her name, her voice, the loving affection for the young man on stage. She is so different here. So soft and feminine. She's the jewel of this family, and she's not even a blood member of it. They clearly love her and she obviously loves them. Why is here so different from Eden?

When the song is done, the crowd is on their feet, clapping, hollering, and loving everything they just witnessed. On her way back to the table, she is handed a napkin with a phone number on it. Just as I guess this is a potential hook-up, a drink is set in front of her, sent from a man across the dark bar. Thankfully, she politely acknowledges the sender but pushes the drink to the center of the table.

She sits down and settles into my arm around the back of her chair.

I pull her closer to me. "Your name is Tess?"

She bites her lower lip and nods her head, looking at me through her lashes. After a moment of contemplation, she releases her lip, leans in and kisses me on the cheek.

"Do I get to call you Tess, too?" I ask.

She smiles fully, considering the request. "We'll see."

Chapter Sixteen
DIESEL

THE REST OF the night is a blur of drinks and singing along with Quin. Once the set is complete, he joins us for a few drinks before last call. I can easily say we've enjoyed the full scope of the evening. Dinner, the show, drinks, it's all been light and uncomplicated. Despite my goal to keep up the veneer, I can't be anything but myself with this crew. Even with Elliot here, it seems too normal. I can't say that I haven't enjoyed his company this evening. He's been kind and funny. I threw him into a possible shark tank and he swam with ease and grace. On the way out of the club, the chatter continues, lively and excited despite the late hour.

I can't recall the moment during the night when he took my hand, but I felt the silent but booming gesture under the table and had no desire to stop it. In fact, Elliot did not let go of my hand even when we exited the club. He released me as we got into the car but as soon as we were buckled, he took it again. I could only glance in his direction and met a raised brow, begging me to challenge him. I didn't. Of course, I didn't stop the kiss upstairs either, and I did kiss him after singing with Quin. I couldn't help it. It just happened. I wanted it, I wanted him, and so I took what I wanted.

Back at Natalie and Greggor's home, we have no choice but to release each other. I kiss Greggor and Natalie good night. Quin attempts to get a bedtime song out of me again but we are able to escape.

We get into my car and the nervous anxiety settles in again. I am immediately ignited by memories of Elliot throughout the night. The kiss, the looks, him holding my hand, the feel of his grip in my hair. Driving home in silence, I touch my lips and secretly hope I'll feel the pressure of his mouth on mine again.

The drive back to my place is thankfully short but utterly confusing. What do we do? How do we manage...this? We're alone. In my house. Together.

We walk into the house through the garage and my body is forced by the anxiety of the moment to surge forward and hide. Without a word to Elliot, I dive into the bathroom, slamming the door and abruptly locking it. *Big. Fat. Chicken.* I shake my hands out in an effort to stop the relentless shaking but nothing seems to help calm the tremor.

A light knock comes to the door. "Hey, are you all right?"

Breathe in. Breathe out. Do not sound like a crazy woman. "Oh, yeah," I offer as nonchalantly as possible, "just should have ducked into the bathroom before we left." That winner of a statement, followed by the most ridiculous nervous laugh, has won me mega points in the game of seduction. *You are so fucking sexy right now, Diesel. Completely spank bank worthy.*

I hear him head upstairs and bolster myself. I check myself in the mirror and fix my hair. Why am I so nervous? Because it's been three years since I've had sex with someone other than myself. Because I don't know this man. Because I like this man and he's practically living with us for the next six months. Because I might have to explain why I'm sleeping with someone when everyone assumes Bain and I are together.

But, in all reality, no one is here now. Only us. I would like to have sex with someone that does not exist only in my head or requires batteries. However, these possibilities mean nothing if Elliot is already asleep. Maybe he's a test-the-waters kind of guy. Start out slow and take incremental steps. A handhold here, a kiss there. Chaste actions that don't really mean anything in the grand scheme of things. I guess there is really only one way to find out.

If my heart could pound any harder, it will be audible to anyone within a five-foot radius. My belly curls with a mix of desire and nausea as I walk down the hall, battling with myself as I walk toward Elliot's room. The little devils in my head dare me to go to him, the saints beg for my retreat. To my delight, the devils are louder.

I pause inside the doorframe. Elliot stands silent in the room, looking at me as if he heard me coming. His hair is tousled from taking off his shirt. His belt is undone as if my movement down the hall stopped him in the middle of his task. My breath hitches as he moves toward me, and a wave of anxiety crashes over me. Taking my hands in his, he pulls me toward him, deeper into the room, and I pray he can't feel the quaking tremors resonating through my body. I'm overwhelmed by him and this precarious situation into which I've willingly put myself. Elliot is a dream and has the potential to be a living nightmare. He pulls back from me, looking in my eyes and running fingers through my hair.

"You looked unbelievable tonight. And hell, that was before you got on stage. You...you amaze me."

His words permeate the remnants of what whatever boundaries I had in place. They may be said with ulterior motives in mind but right now, they make me soar. I run my hands down his sides and lean into his chest, greedily taking in this man on all senses. The smell of him, the feel of his strong body flexing as it responds to my touch, and the sound of his breath...it all overwhelms me. I nuzzle his neck as I hook my fingers onto the top of his pants. He pulls back, kissing me lightly before pulling my blouse over my head. I am immediately self-conscious as he surveys my body. I cross my arms in front of my stomach.

He laughs, pulling my arms down and away. "I have seen you practically naked already."

I feel the heat of my blush. "Ah, yes, how could I forget?"

He shifts and reaches behind me, quietly shutting the door.

"No escape now," I say lightly as he moves back toward me.

"Did you want to go somewhere else?" He kisses me before I can respond.

"No," I offer breathlessly when he pulls his mouth from mine.

I am rewarded with a half smile before I pull at the already unbuckled belt hanging from his pants. As he toes out of his shoes, he holds me by the nape, kissing me with urgent lips. I reach behind and quickly unzip and push my skirt to the floor. I step out of it before kicking it away. I have the fleeting assumption that my heels will be staying on.

He steps out of his jeans and I take greedy inventory of him. He has a lean, muscular chest with clearly defined abs dipping into that gorgeous V. I shudder as my body seizes, desire curling around my womb, making me undeniably needy and wet. I run my hands across his chest, down his abs and trace the V with my fingers. He jumps as my fingers skate across his hipbones, I try to pull back, but he catches my wrist before any major ground is lost.

"Ticklish." He smiles sheepishly before remembering the goal of this endeavor. "Keep touching me."

I nod and continue to explore the ridges and valleys of his body. I brush my hands across his thick and attentive erection, straining the fabric of his boxer briefs. At my touch, he breathes in sharply, head rolling back with a groan, the sound whipping my arousal into a barely restrained frenzy.

His hands, which had been immobile at his sides as I explored his body, finally move. He curls his fingers around my hips before following the curve of my waist, up my sides, to my breasts. He hooks his fingers under each strap of my bra before pulling them down to expose the soft mounds. Cupping them, he feels their weight and leisurely runs his thumb across each nipple. My knees buckle under the sensations, forcing me to teeter on my heels. Despite still being sheathed by his boxers, I wrap my hand around his cock, applying the slightest pressure to his engorged flesh, and receive a rumbling growl of approval.

He leans down, running his tongue over each nipple before sucking the stiff points into his mouth. Pushing my hands though his hair, I moan and arch into his body, allowing for full access. Without realizing it, I am lost. The curl in my belly has exploded into a full-body hum of wanton desire. My breasts ache, my core clenches with the need to be filled. My clit throbs with a fervor that happens when a body is awakened after years of being dormant. It's perfect, the pressure and touch of his tongue and hands. For this moment, we can take what we want. It can all change tomorrow for all I know but this, right now, this is what I want.

He moves his hands down my hips, finally pushing down my barely-there panties. Once around my ankles, I step out of them and widen my stance, giving him full access to my needy sex. I am wet and beyond ready for this man. All the looks, the innocent touches, the build-up to this has been relentless and I can't wait anymore. His fingers glide over my clit and my entire body convulses. I wrap my arm around his neck, holding him to me, kissing his jaw and nibbling at the stubble from the day.

"You are so wet," he murmurs into my ear.

"That's what you do to me." It's the truth and I don't know what else to say.

He smiles. "Clearly you see what you do to me." I huff a breathy laugh and finally dip my hand down the front of his boxers. I take his length in my hand, hard and unyielding, and begin the slow pull from base to smooth tip. It's been so long since I've had the ability to enjoy the aesthetic beauty of the male form. Any sculptor would be lucky to have Mr. Archer as a model.

"You're gorgeous," I murmur, as I trace the veins of his arousal with light touches. He's bigger that I expected, long and thick. "And impressive."

He pulls his head back slightly and looks at me. "I'm already impressive? I've done nothing more than kiss or touch you? I would love to show you how impressive I can be. Can I do that, Tess? Can I show you how good this can be?"

The entirety of his question has been made without missing a kiss or a stroke of my wet folds. This is not the best scenario for making a sound decision.

"Yeah," I breathe out. I continue to examine him and suddenly feel the overwhelming desire to have him in my mouth. I push down his boxers, which he quickly steps out of, and begin the slow kneel in front of him, irritated with myself for making his hand leave any part of my body. I cup his testicles and run my hands over his hard cock. With his veins and nerves standing at attention, his thighs quiver with anticipation. I trail kisses along his length, breathing in his masculine scent. He jerks and groans loudly as I take him in my mouth. He curls his fingers into my hair and exhales as I worship him with my tongue.

"Tess," he says, "God, you feel so good, baby." My name rattles around my brain for a moment before I feel my heightened arousal push forward. No one has said my name in a moment of passion for years, my years of self-imposed celibacy. As I suck him, paying special attention to all the deliciously sensitive parts of a man, I am pleased to hear the satisfied hiss escape from his lips. Maybe I'm not a lost cause in this game.

"Baby, you're going to make me come." Elliot's gruff voice sends lighting though my body. Desire radiates from my core and excites every nerve ending of my body. I want to make him come in this moment but I'm also beyond needy and want this man pounding into me. I begrudgingly let his cock slip past my lips and look up at him.

He smiles at me. "You are so sexy." He offers me his hand to help me to my feet. He kisses me fervently as he pushes me toward the bed. I fall backwards, sitting with a slight bounce on the bed. He deftly unhooks my bra and tosses it on the floor. After kissing each breast, he alternates licks and kisses down my belly until he reaches the apex of my thighs. He kisses my mound with such completeness, not an inch of my bare skin untouched by his lips. I can't stifle the moan as I arch closer toward him. Oral sex is one of my favorites, always has been. I love the intimacy of it and the sheer focus of pleasure in one sensitive location. He pushes my thighs apart, his warm hands melting any resistance I might have had. I open to him, wide and welcoming. His hands run the length of my legs, stopping at my heels, still firmly in place.

"These are going to stay on. I've wanted nothing but you in these since we left for the club. I've wanted nothing since." His stare drills me, pinning me in place. I've never kept anything on during sex before. I've never been told to keep anything on during sex before. However, at this point, Elliot could tie me into a pretzel and I'd be a-okay.

"Okay." I manage to push out before he settles between by legs and pushes my folds apart with his thumbs. I buck under him and moan through my teeth. I bite on my lip as his tongue traces the length of my needy folds.

"Let me hear you, baby. I want to hear you."

Permission. It's permission to be open in this moment. To moan and whimper as he devours me. I arch into him as he completely obliterates me and am immediately rewarded by two fingers pushing into my quaking core. His mouth on my clit and his fingers nudging my sweet spot are too much. Total sensory overload. It's been too long for me and my ability to restrain my orgasm is completely depleted.

"Elliot," I push out, barely recognizing my voice.

"Tess?"

I moan as he grinds out my name. "I'm close." It's a plea

of desperation in this amazing moment.

"I know, baby, I can feel it. I can't wait to get inside you."

The thought of him being inside my body sends a new wave of arousal though my core. Elliot continues his delicious torture, fucking me with his fingers while dancing his tongue mercilessly on my clit. The sensation is overwhelming, something so foreign from self-directed orgasms. While they were good, they didn't feel like this. Like my body is going to explode, shatter uncontrollably under this man's touch. Elliot's efforts increase with the telltale flutter of my sex, sending me over the edge. My cries only spur him on, provoking more attention to my tender skin and extending the pleasure that has ripped me open. Jerking and moaning under him when the sensation of his tongue becomes too much, he pulls back and away from me before walking across the room.

I am bereft for a moment at his wordless exit; however, I am distracted by the delicious perfection that is his bare ass. Before I can comment, he turns back toward me, cock bobbing under the pressure of engorgement, and hands me a condom. I need no explanation. I quickly sit up and tear it open, sheathing my destruction with skilled hands. I lean back as he hovers over me, settling between my legs. He pushes the head of his cock against my entrance, testing the resistance he might encounter. He braces himself on one elbow, his other hand running down my neck to my breast. As he plucks at my nipple, I moan and wiggle under him, willing him to enter me.

"Tess?" My legs open wider to him at the sound of my name.

"Elliot?" I say, sounding a little too eager.

"I've been waiting for this since dinner at Rosie's." He seals his mouth over mine before I can respond. He pushes into me slowly and I feel the burn of him stretching my unused body. I groan into his mouth under the pressure of his girth.

"You are so tight, Tess. Holy shit..." Elliot sounds like a man drowning. I lift my hips to him, heels digging into the sheets. His pelvis nudges my clit with each stroke, lighting me up all over again. I can do nothing. I am lost. I'm letting go. My body and mind are his in this moment.

"Baby, I'm not going to last..." He sucks on my breast before rearing up to thumb my clit. This man is officially deadly.

"Ahh, Elliot!" I cry as the blinding sensation shatters across my body again. He's right behind me. I can feel him thicken, stretching me even further as he begins pounding into me. His friction extends the wicked pleasure saturating my entire body.

"Oh, God...Tess!" He growls out between strong and powerful strokes.

He collapses on me for a brief moment before shifting his weight to his elbows. He smiles and kisses me gently before slowly withdrawing from my body. I wince. It's been a long time, too long, and I will be sore.

He rids himself of the condom and lies down next to me. Instinctively, I curl into him, saying nothing. He responds by taking my hand in his before kissing me. It's calm and quiet and for the first time in a very long time, I feel good. A man who has known me for three weeks has broken me down with charm, hotness, and now, amazing sex. What do you feel in these moments besides delicious exhaustion? This man came into my life and crept into my mind. Now I fear, he's creeping into my heart.

Elliot rolls into me, gently kissing my lips. "Will you stay here with me tonight?"

I am too overwhelmed to develop any reasonable excuse to leave.

"Yes, Elliot. I'll stay."

✧   ✧   ✧

THE NEXT MORNING, I slip out of Elliot's arms to shower and ready myself while he continues to sleep. Downstairs, I make coffee before putting out an array of English teas for his choosing. Greggor would kill me if I didn't have tea in the house. If I only had coffee, he'd call me a heathen and remind me of my evil ways for the rest of our time on earth.

I take my coffee on the porch that overlooks the backyard. The serenity is what I enjoy the most. Watching the herons on the lake, breathing in the air, and feeling the warmth of the sun on my skin. It is total bliss and the salve to old wounds.

After about twenty minutes of savoring my surroundings, I am pulled from my Zen by the sound of the sliding glass door. In shorts and a t-shirt, freshly washed, Elliot walks out with a cup of tea.

"May I join you?"

"Of course." I smile. So polite, even here with no one around.

"I thought you may have up and left me," he says with a sheepish grin as he rumples his hair.

"Nah, I couldn't leave you here. Bain would kill both of

us. Me for leaving you in the house alone and you for whatever you did to make me leave. I'm smarter than that, Elliot."

Elliot laughs in response. "So what's on the agenda today?"

"I don't know," I look out into the yard, "want to go for a walk?"

"Yeah." Elliot looks at me with nothing but kindness.

"Good." We finish our drinks and go in to lace up sneakers then head out the door to the beautiful day.

We walk through the woods and talk, filling in the blanks between the facts we already know about each other. Elliot, who has done the majority of the talking, turns to me, looking pensive.

"So, tell me how you met Bain?"

I hesitate for a moment. I knew this discussion would come up eventually. How to explain it fully was something I had yet to figure out.

"Um," I stall, "the truth?"

"Well, yeah, the truth. Is there something to not be truthful about?"

"Not necessarily. It's just, I don't really talk too much about it."

"So give me the facts. He's an alien life form you've raised from an egg. You two dated and now you're not. He's actually your Siamese twin."

I laugh. "While all your theories are very interesting, none could be farther from the truth."

Elliot looks relieved. I can only guess it's because I've confirmed again that Bain and I are not and have not ever been together. I would hope after last night he still didn't think I was actually in a relationship with someone else.

"You know I lived in Essex for a while. When I was settled and working for Natalie's brother, this guy came into the bar. His name was Jamie and we struck up a conversation or two. He was backpacking through, so I knew he wouldn't be there long. But he kept coming into the bar and asking me to dinner."

"And you took him up on his offer?"

"Eventually. He was relentless." I feel the nostalgia of those days creep into my smile. Everything was so good back then. "We did that on his last night before heading off to Ireland. He was gone for two weeks and showed up back in the restaurant."

"Ah. He couldn't stay away."

"Yeah, that's what he said anyway." I smile at the memory of Jamie standing in the middle of Barney's staring at me with heated, passionate eyes. "We started dating and were together for a couple years. He was from the U.S. also, so we had that in common. The family issue that brought me back to the states was actually his family issue, but we'd been together so long at that point, I couldn't stay there and have him be here. There was no time frame for coming back."

"And where is he now?"

"Um, he died." I can't look at Elliot after I say it. Suddenly the grassy hill we've stopped to rest on has become unbelievably engrossing.

"I'm so sorry. What happened?"

"He signed up for the Peace Corps before we came back to the States." As I pull at the grass, I can see Elliot shift beside me. "He was volunteering at a school for girls helping with music education in Iraq. The school was attacked and he was killed with several other teachers and students." I can't look at him, even though I can see him staring at me in my periphery. Despite my acceptance of the situation, it's still a burn on my heart that smolders. I still talk to him on occasion, for however crazy that may be. He was my best friend. I miss him and the realization that he is truly gone still tightens my throat and pushes tears forward.

"I'm so sorry." Elliot seems lost on what to say in his own shock. I know he would have never expected that type of a response. I'm sure it would have been easier taken if Jamie had cheated, or even beat me, something other than dying while trying to educate and protect little girls.

"Thanks," I offer as I glance at him. "It's been a couple of years so the sting is not as bad anymore. I was a mess when it happened. It was so surreal. We actually saw it on the news first before anyone was able to get a message to us."

I survey the hill where we have stopped. "I have faith he got what he wanted before he left. He had Eden, me, his family was safe. It was his choice to do what he did, I supported him in that."

"So, Eden was his?"

"Yes, Eden was Jamie's idea. He started with DJ gigs around London and it grew from there. He developed a bit of a reputation. We didn't do any of the performance stuff until we got here. When we came back, he started setting up gigs as soon as he could and it grew from there."

"So, how did you come to get it? Eden?" Elliot asks, playing with the grass.

I'm determined not to look at him now "We...were married before he left." I pause before daring to glance at him.

"He wanted to make sure Eden was protected and that I would be taken care of if something happened to him." He looks shocked, or horrified. Gah! This is always so...sticky.

"That's kind of good and also a little morbid," Elliot says finally.

"I agree," I respond with a slight laugh. "In fact, I said that to him but Jamie was firm. He didn't trust Bain to take care of things." I meet Elliot's confused look with a weary smile. "If you think Bain is a handful now, you should have seen him five years ago. I thank God every day he's still alive."

"Wait. How exactly is Bain involved?"

"Jamie and Bain are, well, were, brothers. That's why I can assure you there is nothing between us." I smile and push into him with my shoulder. "I practically helped raise Bain. He's more like my child than anything else."

The relief on Elliot's face is apparent. Amidst this outpouring of information about marriage and death, he is happy I've confirmed that Bain and I are not connected romantically.

"So, are you the CEO of Eden?"

I laugh at the thought of what my role actually is. "Yeah, I am. Bain is written into it also and he really has taken over many of the creative tasks. But on paper, I manage the trust and the everyday workings."

"There's a trust?"

"Yup. They were trust fund babies. Jamie rebelled against the family business; thus, he was a dirty backpacker. Bain relished the luxury. The drugs, cars, sleeping with whomever he wanted. When Jamie died, the family kind of fell apart.

Bain struggled a lot with the loss. The family didn't know Jamie and I got married so there was a huge legal battle."

"Oh, my god."

"Yeah," I agree, sighing with the memory of deposition after deposition, "it was awful. But we were legally married and he had actually willed everything to me. I didn't know that he had gone to the trouble of making a will but in the end, it really protected me. I think that's all he ever wanted."

"So his family knew nothing? Wasn't invited to the wedding?"

"There wasn't a wedding. We were married. It was a Justice of the Peace deal, we said 'I do' and signed a paper in front of some judge who I thought would crumble to dust in front of us." I smile with the memory of the day. "We went out to dinner afterwards and that was it."

"Doesn't really have that fairytale feel to it."

"Oh no, nothing like that. We didn't even wear anything special. No one knew, except Bain. He was there. When Jamie died and the family came after me, he really manned up. He knew what Jamie and I were and he respected us."

I stand up, brushing the grass off before offering a hand to Elliot.

"I'm sorry your wedding day wasn't what you deserved," he says before pushing to his feet, his hand curling around mine.

I can't help the internal swoon at his genuineness. "Thank you." I turn to take in the afternoon sun warming the hillside. "But I'm holding out for marriage number two. Everyone always says those are the good ones anyway!" I laugh at my own dark humor.

"Yeah, I guess so." Elliot laughs.

"Come on." I pull on his hand. "Enough of this deep shit for today."

He nods before we walk back the winding path toward the house in quiet respite.

Chapter Seventeen
ELLIOT

I WAKE TO an empty bed. The house seems quiet but I know she's around here somewhere. I review the afternoon and evening in my head. She was married, widowed, and willed a club. She has a brother-in-law with whom she collaborates, and this extended family from her time in Essex.

She's amazing.

After coming back from our walk, there was a message from Greggor with a non-negotiable dinner invite. During the call to accept dinner, Tess was strong-armed into having an extended visit with the family. Even with them last night, she was so free and open, as if the stress and worries of needing to be in control of Eden leave her when she's here. The only issue was spending the night in separate beds at Natalie and Greggor's house. I was looking forward to a replay of two nights ago.

I roll over to look at the clock. Holy crap. It's twelve-thirty in the afternoon. Without another thought, I pull myself up, quickly shower, and head downstairs.

Natalie stands the kitchen, and greets me with unconditional warmth. "Good morning, Elliot," she offers kindly. "Can I get you some tea?"

"That would be great, thanks," I reply, despite being distracted by mild chaos outside.

"Ah, yes." Natalie follows my gaze. "The boys have come over and they are up to their usual antics. You would think since they are all adults this would eventually get old, but they do it all the time."

"What's that?" I ask as Natalie put tea in front of me.

"Oh, I don't know," she breathes out, "act like no time has gone by."

From inside the house, I see the tropical oasis that is Natalie and Greggor's backyard, equipped with a large pool, bar, and built-in grill. Tess squeals as she emerges from the lush green landscaping and runs around the outside of the pool with cautious steps, Quin is hot on her heels. Davis, the drummer of Quin's band, wraps her up like a linebacker and blocks her forward progress. She screams with unrestrained hysteria. Davis passes her to Quin, who bellows that he has captured the rogue sea hag and must sacrifice her to the ocean gods.

She tries to get away, pinching him and trying to pull down his swim trunks, but he has her firmly in his grasp. Davis grabs her legs, holding her captive as Quin tucks his hand under her armpit. He grips the inside of her thigh and effectively bench-presses her over his head.

The hysteria has transferred into actual fear and bubbling anxious cries of "put me down" and "don't drop me" before Quin launches her into the pool. She comes up for air as Quin and Davis cannonball into the pool after her.

Greggor claps wildly from under the canopy of the porch as the drama of squelching the sea hag has come to a dramatic close. It's a regular family free-for-all. I am happy that

Tess has these connections.

"You know, Elliot," Natalie says, shaking me from my reverie, "she's a very special woman."

"I've been getting that impression," I reply, sipping my tea.

Tess walks into the house with dripping hair and a towel around her waist. "Hey sleepyhead! We didn't wake you, did we?"

"No," I laugh, "amazingly you didn't."

"Ah, good." She smiles at me. "Want to swim with us? The pool is really nice."

"Yeah, that would be great."

"Ok," she says coolly while running her hand through her hair. While her arm is bent, I notice a tattoo on her left ribcage. I grab her arm and lean into her, eyeing the delicate, black script.

Genesis 2:24

"What's that?" I ask, running my finger down her side. I realize when she gasps that touching her like this may be too intimate, despite our past evening together. I also realize that despite our time together, this is the first time I've seen these words. But we *were* in a darkened room...and I *was* a little preoccupied with a few other things.

She falters and looks to Natalie. "It's a tattoo."

"I can see that," I reply, bending to look closer. "What's the passage?" It must have hurt like hell on her ribs.

She looks slightly embarrassed, maybe even pained. "It reads, 'for this reason a man will leave his father and mother and be united to his wife, and they will become one in flesh.'"

She pulls her arm down, effectively covering the verse. I realize from everything she's divulged over the past twenty-four hours, I don't need to inquire about the inspiration for the verse.

"It's beautiful," I say, and truthfully all I can muster.

"Thanks." She blushes and looks at her feet before looking into my eyes with a softness that I think is only reserved for this place. After a moment, she breaks from me. "Go put on something to swim in, okay?"

"Okay. I'm going right now."

She walks out of the kitchen and I turn to look at Natalie, who has witnessed the entire exchange. She raises her eyebrows at me and winks.

"Enjoy yourself with her, Elliot," she says knowingly.

LATER THAT EVENING, after dinner and drinks and a rousing game of Apples to Apples, I retire to bed. Tess has opted to stay up and watch a movie with Quin, so I begrudgingly take ownership of the empty bed.

The days here have been eye-opening and oddly unsettling. The evolving change in her is amazing. She's free, maybe? I don't see the focused stare, the need to manage, the bonds to Bain. She's not mentioned him since he left. I don't think she's had any communication with him at all. I thought that he would have checked in on her since she was here with me alone.

Swimming away the afternoon and wonderful wine during dinner has caused such exhaustion. I melt into sleep.

"HEY....ELLIOT." A hushed voice and a warm hand pushes me into consciousness. "Elliot. Wake up."

"Tess?" I offer with a sleep-filled voice. "What are you doing? Is everything okay?"

"Yeah." She sounds like she's smiling. "Everything is great."

"What is going on? What time is it?"

"It's two-thirty. Do you want to see something cool?"

"Are you serious?" I'm mildly irritated. What could be so cool that I have been roused from sleep?

"Come with me," she says in a husky voice that is laced with anticipation. "If it's not worth it, you can come back to bed, I promise." She takes my hand and pulls me gently. I have no willpower to resist her.

As my eyes adjust, I see she is only wearing a T-shirt and panties. "You don't have to get dressed. It's warm out."

"Wait," I pull her back toward me, "we're going outside? You have no pants on."

She giggles at my apparent lack of understanding. "It's okay," she whispers, "no one else is outside. Everyone is asleep. It's fine. I do this all the time. Come on."

I realize too late that she's walking me down the stairs. Quin is snoring loudly on the couch as we sneak by him and through the sliding glass door.

Once outside, the chirping crickets are the only sound aside from the humming central air unit.

"Okay," she says in her normal voice, "are you ready?"

"Um....sure. What's going on?"

She takes my hand as she bites her lower lip to mask her smile. Beneath the nighttime sky, she is illuminated by the stars and what I can only guess is a full moon. It's bright out here. "Let's go."

She leads me down the lawn, past the pool and patio, toward the edge of the property, which is lined with enormous pine trees. She walks us down the line until the trees curve into a bend away from the house.

She stops on a dime and turns to me quickly. "You have to close your eyes."

I am instantly nervous. "Why?" This is weird and I'm not sure what the deal is.

"Come on, Elliot," she begs, now holding my hand with both of hers in a physical plea, "just trust me. It's only for a minute."

I sigh. Her excitement for this is palpable. "If you run me into something, I'm going to be pissed."

"I can assure you the only thing you could run into is me...or a bear."

"Tess! Are you kidding?" I yell. "This is nuts!" She is instantly in hysterics and I'm completely embarrassed at my discomfort. She stifles her laughter and takes a stabilizing breath in. Her look turns intense.

"Close your eyes, Elliot." She runs her hand down my forehead and over my eyes, forcing them closed. "This will be well worth it." Her lips brush mine as she speaks. I shake in the sensual wake of her action. As she takes my free hand and begins to lead me forward, I have no choice but to follow.

We only take about ten steps before she stops me. She drops both my hands and leaves them hanging at my sides for a moment before she places one hand on my chest and the other around the back of my neck. She pulls me to her and kisses me with a passion that must have been hidden away for years. I wrap my arms around her waist, pulling her to me. I part my lips to take her tongue, her breathy moans, and anything she has to offer me in this moment. She pulls back and offers me a chaste kiss to calm our fervent actions.

"Open your eyes, Elliot."

I blink as my eyes adjust in the dim night and look at her. She is beautiful, eyes dancing with mischievous delight and arousal. I run my hands over her hair and cup her chin, tilting her face toward mine. "You are amazing."

"Thanks," she offers, clearly pleased. "Look past me."

What? She must be able to read my apparent confusion and rolls her eyes as she playfully nods her head backwards. I follow her gesture and I'm immediately awed, silenced and humbled by the sight before me.

"Whoa." It's the only thing I'm able to push forward.

"I know," she says with nothing but love in her voice.

In the distant night sky, the Northern Lights dance with rhythmic grace. All glowing and bright, it's like the waves of the ocean reflected in the night sky. Thick ribbons of light entice the world to see it its unabashed glory and beauty.

I look at Tess, who is clearly enraptured by the lights. She is all blissful smiles and awe as she stares at this natural beauty.

"This is amazing," I say.

"I'm glad you like it." The satisfaction in her voice is apparent. "I come out here whenever I'm here to see it. This is the season to see it the best. I figured you've never had the opportunity to see the Borealis, so I had to share it with you."

"You come out here all the time?"

"Yup," she shrugs, "I love it too much to not. It's strange that I can always stay up or wake up at just the right time to see it. It's such a natural beauty that I feel the need to experience it whenever I can."

She's right, it is an amazing experience. I've never seen anything so pure in my life. It's a wonder of the world. I am humbled that she felt the need to share this with me.

She turns to me and grabs my hand again, leading me further into the open, tree-lined area, further under the Borealis. She stops me and steps up on an elevated platform in the middle of the grass.

"Come here," she asks to me as she slowly sinks to her knees, sitting back on her heels. Though she's only three feet off the ground, she looks at me with a passionate plea. Her face, illuminated by the night sky, is earnest as she asks me to be next to her. Only once I step up on the platform do I realize it's the size of a full bed with a plush cushion on top.

She catches me assessing the platform. "Greggor made it for me several years ago." She offers. "He would find me out here sleeping on the ground whenever I stayed the night, so he built me an outdoor bed to keep me off the ground."

"You would fall asleep out here?" I'm shocked. Was she joking about the bear? As someone who was never outdoorsy, the thought of sleeping completely exposed to the elements is a little unnerving with two people, let alone one.

"Oh, yeah. I would stay out here all night and he'd wake me up in the morning. There is nothing out here that would eat you. I've done it for years now and no one has taken a bite out of me yet."

"Well, that's good. What do you do out here?"

"I watch. I think." She pauses. "I used to cry." She looks wistfully up at the night sky. "But now, for the most part, I just marvel at it."

"Do you come out here alone?"

She's hesitates for a moment, as if she's unsure of what to say. "Always."

Her honesty breaks me in two. She brought me out here to experience this with her. The need to touch her compels me to move toward her. She's still on her knees. I wrap one arm around her waist, cupping her rear end and pulling her body flush with mine. My free hand grips her hair, holding her lips against mine. Her hands are hot on my exposed chest then move to my back as I take her deeper into our kiss. Our tongues caress each other. Taking the time to feel and explore the soft contours of our mouths.

She breaks from our kiss by pushing off my chest. She pulls her shirt over her head. She is glorious in the dim light of the dancing Borealis, smiling at me before her fingers skim the rough stubble lining my jaw. Her hands dance across my collarbone, down my arms, muscles jerking under the light touches.

"Lay down," she says in a low, husky voice.

Leaning back onto the plush fabric, Tess continues to kneel beside me as she explores my body. She makes contact with the places she didn't touch before. Her lips kiss my collarbones, ribs, and hip bones. Her fingernails lightly scrape my inner thighs, causing my entire body to tense. She giggles, pleased with her complete manipulation of my body. I know she can see my erection straining the fabric of my boxers, yet she works her hands down my legs, her soft hands caressing the lines of my calves and feet.

She moves, pushing my legs wide with her knees as she settles between them, her mouth laying pillowy kisses on my hips and low belly as she pulls down my boxers. The sensation of the night air on my white-hot skin and her hair brushing my chest as she outlines the contours of my stomach with her tongue is stimulus overload. When her tongue slowly slides up the length of my cock and her mouth consumes me, I buck, gripping the mattress.

"Oh...God....Tess..."

It's all I can muster. Her tongue on me is sin personified. Never has a mouth felt so good, and I am dangerously close to losing all abilities to make this night last. Her fingers teasing my balls have her lapping pre-come at a torturously slow, mind-blowing pace.

"Baby," I growl, "you gotta stop."

She gives my cock a kiss goodbye before sitting back on her heels and staring at me with wanton eyes.

I grip her waist once more and pull her flush against me, desperate to taste her flesh. She moans as I take each breast into my mouth in turn. Balancing on her elbows, she runs her fingers though my hair, splaying her legs to straddle me. She rolls her hips against me, her warm cleft riding the length of my cock. She tilts my head and kisses me hard. Pulling back, she nibbles my lip, jaw, and neck as her hands skate across my chest. My hands mimic hers, exploring the contours of each other in the reflection of the nighttime sky.

Her whimpers and sighs nearly undo me. The passionate exercise this trip has been is beyond anything I would have expected. The vixen that stripped for me three days ago is now a siren who has me tripping over myself at her call. I must have her.

Curling my hips to nudge her clit makes her writhe and release a cry into the night air.

"I need you."

"Yes." The single word bathes me in longing. She leans

over, grabbing the T-shirt she removed, and pulls a condom out of the pocket. Rising up on her knees, she strokes me, as if I needed additional encouragement.

She rolls on the condom and offers a throaty groan as she takes me inside her body, accepting everything I have to offer. She is tight, slick, and so unbelievably warm. She steadies herself on my chest, setting for a moment in perfect silence, feeling my pulsing flesh stretch her. As she begins to rock, my hands run over her stomach, breasts, and finally settle on her hips, guiding us as we move. With her head thrown back, she offers her fervent moans to the night sky. Her skin reflects the light of Mother Nature, dancing magically behind us as we move as one in this perfect moment.

Chapter Eighteen
DIESEL

WE HAVE TO talk about this.

About what happened and what's going to happen from here. Once we get back to Eden we are not going to have the liberties we had over the weekend. That's the reality.

It's just not going to work.

Driving back home, I feel tense. I think Elliot feels the same. He's not spoken much since we left Natalie and Greggor's. Granted, our re-entry into the house was a little less than private. We fell asleep after romping in nature as nature intended. We woke up naked, with the morning sun warming our bodies. Sneaking back into the house with clearly fucked hair, Elliot in his boxers, me in his T-shirt and my panties was instantly thwarted by Greggor bellowing, "Well, what do we have here?" from the breakfast nook. The walk of shame is bad enough without being actually being caught by your would-be father.

Regardless of all of that, this can't continue. It's gone on too long as it is. This is never going to work, anyway. He lives in Boston and he's only here for five more months. I seriously can't consider starting a relationship with this man. It's bad enough that he's good-looking, sexy, kind, and perfect boyfriend material, and would give anything for his hands on my body again. *Ugh.* Yeah, this is not going to work.

What about Bain? This little tryst has bad news written all over it for Bain and me. I know Bain said what he did, but he's not thinking about the future. Bain never considers what could be.

"You are thinking awfully hard over there." Elliot offers it quietly from the passenger seat.

I inhale. It's now or never....

"We have to talk about what happened this weekend." Despite trying to be as steady as possible, I feel the waver inside me.

"What do you want to talk about?"

"What we did this weekend...it can't happen at Eden." I hate the words the instant they've erupted from my mouth.

I can see him thinking, brow furrowed over his stunning blue eyes.

"What do you mean, this can't happen? What's happening?" He's turned to look at me and I feel instantly trapped.

"Well, the...stuff we've done in the last few days. All that's has to stop." Fuck! This is awful.

"I don't understand." He sounds insulted. "Are you embarrassed about what we've done?"

"No, Elliot that's not—"

"You didn't look embarrassed last night or even this morning when we were bang to rights."

"Elliot, it's not the same at Eden. I have different...um...responsibilities."

"What? I don't understand, Tess." His voice is quiet, distant.

"I'm not Tess at Eden, Elliot. I'm Diesel. I hate for this to sound totally bitchy but I have a reputation that needs to be maintained. We show up like we've been for the past two days and everything I've established is gone."

"So everything this weekend...the conversations, the playfulness, the sex...it's over. No more?"

"I think it has to be, Elliot." Good God! Hot pokers in my eyes would be better than this conversation. It's official. I hate myself.

"You didn't have a good time this weekend?" He sounds upset as he looks down at his hands. Oh, yes. I am officially a total bitch. But I have no choice. I try to remind myself why honesty has always been my best policy.

"No. That's not it at all. I had an amazing time. It's just different here." In this moment, I wish I could tell him everything and recant all the bullshit I've just filled this car with. Why is this so difficult?

Elliot sits in quiet contemplation, watching the highway roll by. "Can we compromise?" I can hear the smirk in his tone.

This man is unreal. "What? How do you want to compromise?" I cannot wait to hear this.

"We maintain our roles and, as you say, responsibilities." He air quotes "responsibilities," causing me to scoff out loud. "And when we have the opportunity to be alone, we can have the freedoms of the weekend."

"You want us to sneak around?" I glance at him as we're flying down the highway. I must be a loon for even engaging this conversation.

"I want what we had this weekend, during the week. If you are uncomfortable with us outside of the safety of a weekend, then we do what we need to keep you comfortable." He is matter-of-fact, as if he negotiates these kinds of deals on a daily basis.

We'll act as we normally do and sneak around behind everyone's back? Well, despite the fact that it's something I never would have considered doing before this moment, it does sound appealing. Even if this is short-lived and never going to move beyond whatever this is right now. I guess I should enjoy the ride. It has been a long time since I've had any type of romantic relationship, and this weekend was quite nice.

I look over at him and he is staring at me, intensely. "I'm not ready for this to be done just yet." He says it with a clear ferocity I can't mistake for anything other than the truth.

Oh shit! There it is. The electric current that shoots through my body causing my sex to clench and my brain to short circuit. "I think I agree with you on that point." I can't help the smirk.

"Okay," I offer after a moment of silence. "We keep our activities private and look at if nothing has happened. We'll do our best to be, um, discreet between your place and mine."

"You are going to risk me in your place? With Mike and Bain near?" He is laughing at me as if I couldn't get past those two with a cloak of invisibility.

"You'd be amazed what passes under their noses without so much as a sniff." Elliot may have been watching our every move but I know my guys like the back of my hand. They have their own situations to manage and could care less what I'm doing half the time. The benefit of being good at what you do is that the majority of people trust you to do what's best and ease the watchful eye on your behavior.

"So you won't tell Bain?" Elliot asks.

He cares about Bain finding out but not Mike?

"No, I don't think that would be such a good idea." I hesitate after I say it, wanting to say more but knowing that I can't. This is not the first relationship that I've had to be devious in.

"Okay," he sighs, "if that's how you want it." He pauses and looks at me. "I can't call you 'Tess' at all?"

My body tingles with the sound of my true name on his tongue. "When we're alone, I'd love to hear nothing but that. But when we're in front of others, it's Diesel." I can't help the sad tone of my voice.

"So, I have until we get to Eden to call you by your name?"

"I guess so."

"Well, in that case." He puts his hand on my thigh and squeezes my leg. I flex in response and silently hope to feel him slide up toward my sex. My heart begins to pound and I do my best to focus on the looming tunnel before us. "Tess?" He says smoothly.

"Yes, Elliot?" My response is breathy and soft.

"I had a wonderful time this weekend and I look forward to the next." His voice is all mischief, sex, and British civility. I want him already and we are at least a week away from true freedom.

I glance at him, longing to kiss him before we drive into the tunnel. As we plunge into the darkness of the Lincoln, I know this is the passageway that will swallow us from our bliss and deposit us squarely in a world we have conspired to deceive.

Chapter Nineteen
DIESEL

THIS IS CRAZY. You are officially certifiable.

Driving to Elliot's suite in the middle of the night might be rash, but after today I need to see him. When I saw him with Jessica, her hands lazily wrapped around his neck, the burn of rejection and fury was worsened by the complete inability to do anything about it. I saw them, he saw me seeing them, and I know he watched me turn on my heel and stomp away as if I wanted to crush the ground. I've spent the majority of today trying to get the vision of them out of my brain.

Anyone but her! If you've got to screw around with anyone else besides me, please don't let it be her!

For the past week, we've been uncomfortably awkward. I want to be near him but I'm scared. He tries to pull me to him and I flinch. Since returning, I have this nagging fear that something is off, that he is not what he seems to be. That this is not what it seems. That he's not truly interested and that makes me nuts. Granted, he did try to ease my mind after seeing him with Jessica, but pulling me into a dark corner to explain the situation did nothing to help ease my mind. I was stuck between not knowing whether to drop to my knees and show him exactly why that whore has nothing on me or engage in the drama of a hissy fit. I took the wrong path. I fully launched the grenade.

I demanded to know if he enjoyed tasting all the flavors Eden has to offer. He was calm and controlled when he told me that jealousy is an ugly beast. I responded by asking how ugly his beast would be if Bain was draped over me like a possessive lover. I didn't wait to hear his response; he sucked a breath in and stared at me as if I'd committed all the deadly sins in one day, and that was enough. The carnage of the argument would have continued, gotten louder and noticeable, so I left. He didn't try to stop me. Bain saw the look on my face before I left the club and knew it was not worth the inquiry. Smart man.

This back and forth is awful. I can't risk him calling me Tess but that's all I want to hear. I can't have him in my apartment every night but that's all I want. I want to kiss him. I want him to touch me. I don't want Jessica's whorey hands all over him! Jealous? Yes, he nailed that one. I like him, a lot. Too much, I fear, for the limited amount of time we've been doing this...whatever the hell *this* is.

So, now my jealousy has turned into guilt and I am walking up to his suite, brimming with nervous anxiety. I need to apologize and try to fix the mess I've made. I could wait until he comes back to Eden but then we'd have prying eyes. Regardless, I couldn't let any more time pass without resolving this. I knock lightly on the door, hoping he'll be alone.

He opens the door and his shock is apparent. "Hello." He opens the door a little wider to let me in.

I take a step toward him, watching for a flinch. *Please let us be okay.*

I have to touch him and I need him to touch me. I lift my hands to his face, pushing to my toes to press my lips to his. I feel his arms curl around my waist, pulling my body flush with his. His tongue pushes me further into the kiss. As I open my mouth, he growls in satisfaction. The sound reverberates in my entire body. Keeping me close, he kicks the door shut and locks the bolt with a fumbling hand. I lean back from him and immediately see his irritation.

I take hold of his shoulders and stare into his stunning blue eyes. "I'm so sorry about today. It's just going to take some time to get used to this."

His breath matches mine, ragged and needy as he looks over my face. "She was on me. I told her that we were better off as friends. She has a hard time accepting what she doesn't want to hear." He runs his hand down my hair, my back, settling on my backside with a firm palm holding me in place. "We'll do this, baby." He kisses me quickly and hard, impressing his intent. "I've told you I'm not ready to be done with this, or you, yet."

I shiver and hope he means it. I can't get over how much I want this man. I want him enough to leave my apartment and show up at his door at eleven o'clock at night.

With one hand still firmly planted on my ass, Elliot snakes the other under my hair to hold the nape of my neck. He kisses me again and grinds his hips into me. No mistaking that Mr. Archer is more than pleased with my late night arrival.

Somehow, we've moved past the first room of his suite and he's pushing me toward the bed. He lets me go only long enough to turn off *SportsCenter* and rip his shirt off. He stands in front of me, naked chest rising and falling from the exertion of moving us into his bedroom. Elliot lets me stare for a brief moment at the taut lines of his abdomen. *Just follow the V...* He snaps me from my ogling by impatiently pulling at my shirt and I assist with wiggling out of my jeans. Thank God I wore flip-flops. He eases me back lightly and I sit on the bed. He smiles slyly. "I've wanted you here for a long time. I like the look of you here, especially in this number." My pool of desire explodes into a lake as he eyes the bronze shimmer of my lace bra and panties. *How does he do this to me?*

Elliot runs his finger down my face and neck, and lingers in the dip of my collarbone before drawing a line between my breasts. I lean back on my elbows, allowing him to continue down my belly.

With my heart pounding wildly, I know that my body has betrayed all efforts to keep distant. My breath, my heart, the flush of my pale cheeks, and the flutter of my core are all dead giveaways that I want every part of him.

He steps between my legs, gently pushing my knees apart to take him in. Automatically I sit up, hands rising to his hips. I run my fingers just under the waistband of his jeans and kiss lightly across his tight belly. He breathes in and I am electrified. I look up at him as I pull at the buttons securing him. He's so close to me, my chin skims the flesh of his tight abdomen. His naughty smirk matches the wild look in his eyes. His hands are already tangled in my hair. With a pucker of my lips and a slight smile, I turn my attention back to his steely and wanting erection, now firmly in my grip. He shifts his weight as I gently kiss him. He hisses in satisfaction as I take the length of him in my mouth.

"Holy shhh...ah, yeah, baby." His grip on my hair is gentle but firm as he tries not to push into my mouth. He's holding back and I know I can unravel him right now if I want.

"Diesel, baby, you gotta stop...I'm too close already." He lets me go and I slowly release him before settling back on the bed. By the look of him, chest heaving, erection heavy with want, and a look that can only mean this night is going to go on for a while, I assume I am forgiven for today's mishap. But despite my body humming wildly for this man, I feel a frisson of disappointment that I can't name.

"What's wrong, baby?" he murmurs as he begins the slow crawl up my body, kissing my thighs. "We're here. We don't have to censor anything...I like it when I can hear you." He edges closer to my sex and as he wraps his strong and able hands around either side of my panties. Then he says it...

"Deese...I'm so—"

"Stop." It's more forceful than what I wanted but I'm so jacked up on this man, I would probably scream out a grocery list. He immediately releases his grip on my panties and he pushes off the bed and me.

I'm momentarily shocked at his unquestioning retreat at the first sign that something is wrong. Despite his obvious care about my well-being, he looks completely perplexed. I suck in a breath. Not moving from my position in the bed, I realize this needs to be fixed now.

"Say my name," I pant.

"I did, baby. I called you Deese but if that's reserved for Ba—"

"No," I hold up my hand and close my eyes. *Please don't say his name!* I open my eyes and take him in, still looking lost and terribly confused. I am, too. Never before has 'Diesel' ever bothered me...until Elliot said it.

"My name." I stare at him. "I need you to say my name." It's a breathy plea followed by seconds of nothing but the sound of our collective breaths. "Please, Elliot."

Then I see the light bulb ignite.

"Tess..." He says it slow and whispered, as if testing the word in his mouth.

My head lolls backward, taking in the verbal ecstasy that is Elliot saying my name. I moan and look at him. "Yes..."

"Tess, baby," he moves to the bed again, reclaiming the path he began up my thigh, "I love to say your name, you know that, right?" His fingers claim the edges of my panties and he pulls them off me slowly as he kisses my hips and stomach.

I run my hands through this hair as he assaults my skin with licks and bites and kisses. "I love it when you say my name, Elliot."

He pushes my legs apart with strong and controlled hands, hovering inches from my sex. Still propped on my elbow, I can see how close he is to the very core of me. The feel of his breath and the sight of his lips, both so close, ratchet my desire like nothing I've felt before. *God, please put your mouth on me...*

He plants a soft kiss on my mound, enough to show me his intention but less than what is needed to ease the painful ache. "I have a proposition to our arrangement," he says.

Are you serious? You want to talk now? "Okay," I push out, "tell me your proposition."

"I only call you Tess. No going back and forth depending on where we are." He kisses me again, forcing a needy moan from my throat. "To me, you are only and always Tess."

I can't think of all the reasons why this would be a horrible idea with him hovering so close to me. Truth be told, at this point, I would give this man nuclear weapons if he wanted. He's watching me from between my thighs, waiting for my answer.

I nod in agreement. His eyes widen, lips curling with satisfaction from winning this battle. "I never wanted to call you anything other than Tess since we left Natalie and Greggor's. It kills me to call you Diesel. That's not your name. You are Tess. My Tess."

My Tess hangs in my head as he drops his mouth on me, drowning me in sensation. His tongue dances over me, pushing me closer to the pinnacle of desire. He moans and I feel the vibration though my entire body already on edge with lust, and need. My back bows, hips bucking under his sensual assault on my body. Any leverage I had is ripped away when Elliot shifts, caging my hips with his hands and pinning me to the bed. I'm trapped, forced to feel the warm heat his mouth bathe my clit in undivided attention. Writhing under the intensity does nothing to ease the ache. The want. The need. It's too much. I came here feeling like dog shit and now I'm willing splayed and happily restrained by him. I'm *his. My Tess*. Dog shit has never shined up so fast.

The pressure behind my clit builds, causing pleas for release to fall from my mouth. The begging spurs him on, holding me tighter, nibbling and sucking harder until the inevitable shatter crashes over me and I am pulling at his hair, crying out his name. He rides the wave, not letting up until my body is convulsing with aftershocks set off by multiple kisses and quick swipes of his tongue to my sensitive mound and inner thighs.

"I'm sorry, Tess," he offers between kisses, "but I can't wait any more. This week has been killing me." He kisses up my body, lingering at my breasts. "I need to be inside you." He licks and sucks on each nipple in time, pushing me back into the fray of needy lust once more. I fall back on the bed as he crawls up my body. He's all hands and mouth and weight of his body on mine and I love it.

"Tess," he jerks his chin to the bedside table, "in there." I open the drawer to find a box of condoms. I pick up the box and raise my eyebrows at him. "I told you I've wanted you here for a while." He shrugs and smiles at me, "I wasn't going to miss an opportunity if one came up. Thankfully, one did."

"You're lucky this isn't open yet," I huff, ripping the package open and freeing one of the soldiers lined up to protect the masses.

"You are the only reason any would be missing." He is direct and sounds affronted. When I don't respond right away, he takes my chin in his hand and makes me look him in the eye. "Only you, Tess. Only you."

I pause, momentarily waylaid by his decree. "Okay."

"Say it," he says.

"Say what?"

"Only you."

I breathe in and my entire body shakes with desire that goes beyond the physical. I like this man. A lot. Too much. He's addictive, this game we've concocted is exciting, and when he's gone, it's going to hurt like hell. If I let myself believe that this could last, I will be in for one huge heartache. But for now, he says it's only me. In this moment, I want nothing more than to trust everything he says to me.

"Say it." His voice is more forceful than I ever expected.

"Only me." It's only a breathy whisper, but it's said.

"Yes, baby." He kisses my neck as he praises me and lifts off me a little further to assist me in getting the condom on his length.

He wastes no time prepping me any further. He kisses me hard as he pushes into my body. I lift one leg to his hip, encouraging him deeper into my body. His pace is hard and relentless and I know immediately I'm not the only one who has been struggling for sanity over the past few days.

"Tess," he growls in to my ear. His voice travels down my body and pulses around him.

"Elliot," I whimper.

"Say it," he commands, and I know I'm about to break under him. His body, his smell, and his demands both physical and emotional have me wound beyond tight. If I say it, I'll come undone. "Say it, Tess. Feel it." His words leave no room for questioning.

I have no choice. No control. I look up at him, expectantly waiting for me.

"Only me." I barely get the words out and I explode around him. His name erupts from my throat in a strangled cry. I dig my nails into his back as he pounds into me. He follows me moments later, shouting my name before collapsing on me.

I cling to him, sweaty and out of breath. He rolls off me slowly and removes the condom, tossing it in the trash. Turning back, Elliot rolls on his side and wraps a protective arm around my stomach. I feel so warm and blissful that I can't do anything but snuggle into his large body. All too quickly, I realize that I don't want to be anywhere else but in Elliot's arms.

✧ ✧ ✧

ADAM LEVINE BELTING out the chorus of *Moves Like Jagger* rouses us from our nap.

Who the hell is calling me in the middle of the night?

I look at my phone in horror and then to Elliot, who looks unbelievably delicious propped on one elbow as he rubs sleep from his eyes.

"What's wrong, baby?" he says in a beautiful, sleepy English accent.

"It's Bain." I stare at the phone.

"And?"

"Elliot, it's eight-thirty in the morning." I look at him and the shock registers on his face. We slept the entire night and would have continued if my phone didn't ring.

Adam stops his serenade and moments later, there is a text.

Where are you?

Shit! He would have gone for a run already and I'm always downstairs by eight. What do I do? How am I going to get back into Eden in the same clothes I left in? Elliot sees the panic on my face and looks at me with concern.

"What's the big deal? You spent the night out."

"Yeah, with you. I don't think it will bode well if I tell Bain I was shacking up with you all night because we are secretly running around. I'm not the type of girl to spend nights out, Elliot. He's going to be suspicious."

He nods in understanding. I get the sense he's not ready for us to be public yet either, and that thought warms me. "What are you going to tell him?"

"Um..." I bite my lip and the genius comes upon me as I punch out a text message, to Holly this time.

Can you cover for me?

Please be up! Please be up!

Of course! Where are you and what or who did you do? :D

Holly is my best friend for this very reason. She would bail me out of jail, help me hide a body, and cover for me during my moments of impulsivity.

With E…in his suite. We fell asleep. Bain wants to know where I am.

Well, tell Bain that you are with me. I called you late. You came over. We had too much to drink and you slept over

Thank you! You are the best.

You know it, girl! I'm excited you had a sleepover, smitten kitten!

Yeah, yeah….lunch soon?

You got it! Love you!

Love you, too! Lunch is on me!

I breathe a sigh of relief and text Bain. He appears to believe me, and Elliot and I begin to prep for my departure. I struggle against the guilty twinge that lying to everyone is bad. I've been comfortable lying to protect Bain for years. If everyone knew about Elliot and I, the work we've done to make life right again could be ruined. Bringing in Holly to cover for us is even worse. However, as I watch Elliot brush his teeth with rumpled hair in loose pajama pants, I firmly believe the sin of lying is worth the penance.

Chapter Twenty
ELLIOT

OUR SKILLS IN being covert have done nothing but improve over the past three weeks. Despite our openness with Natalie and Greggor, I think we've successfully pulled the wool over everyone's eyes at Eden, including Mike and Bain. Despite the questioning looks, they have not said anything about our relationship. As far as I can tell, we look like business partners – a blogger and a club owner.

Inside our world, that's a whole different story. Her ability to fly dangerously under the radar floors me. We've explored and enjoyed each other frequently despite being under the restriction of looking normal. Which means....clandestine operations. It's become my favorite game. How much can we get away with in plain sight? Stealing kisses. Roaming hands. She even pulled me into the closet we were crammed into after the unannounced lap dance and showed me what she wanted to do to me that night.

We text regularly. Talk when we can. She's become very good at sneaking me in and out of her apartment when she's not coming to the suite.

The weekends at the lake house have been freeing. We don't hide. Thankfully, no one has come up to the house recently so we have full freedom to be ourselves. Natalie and Greggor have never asked any questions, they just accept which is comforting.

This evening at Eden has ended in typical fashion; a happy and satisfied crowd is pouring out into the early morning hours. Tess is doing the rounds with everyone. From my position at the back of the club, I watch as Cass, that fucker, sidles behind her again. I watch him hunt her down week after week, only to be dismissed. His pursuit pisses me off more and more every time *Paws off, asshole!* She is effective in pushing him off, which always ends in his rejection. Despite the fact that it does not bother her that he curses in her face at every refusal, it infuriates me to the point of wanting to be violent. Tonight's refusal earns her the title of "frigid cunt" before Cass wraps an intoxicated arm around Jessica and they stumble out into the main area. Why Bain doesn't intervene, I'll never know, but if Tess is comfortable with managing him, I'll let her get to it.

We grab our drinks at the bar and head up to her apartment to "review the evening." I realize now that we've never actually reviewed anything after a show except each other, but it's our tradition. Upstairs, we enjoy the view and afford ourselves a few intimate moments before Bain plowing through the door like a bull unceremoniously interrupts us.

"Dieeeeesel!" His slur is so apparent he wouldn't have to stumble into the kitchen, but he does. "Diesel! I want pretzels!"

Tess and I look at each other, her arm still around my neck, my hands gripping her waist. He nearly walked directly into us, but obviously didn't see us. Collectively deciding to not push our luck, we drop our hands. Tess crosses her arms; I turn my back to both of them, desperately needing to adjust my cock.

"Bain, darling," she asks calmly, "what's going on?"

"Diesel," he huffs, "you 'member when we usta watch porn together?"

She laughs out loud when I snap my head to look at her. She offers a sheepish shrug. Her eyes are dancing with nothing but sinful delight. Bain, bag of pretzels in hand, staggers over to the sofa and settles in.

"Yes, Bain," she sighs, "I remember when we used to watch porn together."

Bain shoves a fist full of pretzels in his mouth. "Feefel! Fom vatch forn wif me!" He slams his hand down on the couch, calling her to sit next to him. He grabs the remote and turns on pay channels, determined to find a soft-core porn delight for them to enjoy.

Her hands have moved to her hair in amused exasperation. She looks at me and shrugs.

"The sooner we get him out of here, the better," she whispers.

I nod in agreement.

"Besides," she adds quietly, "maybe we could get some inspiration." She raises her eyebrows with nothing but wickedness lurking in her eyes. The previous adjustment to my pants has officially been deemed ineffective. How the fuck am I going to manage this one?

"Deeeese!" Bain bellows. "Pooorn. Wif meee. Nooow!" How did this man get pissed up so quickly? He seemed fine downstairs.

She moves to the couch next to Bain. I follow and am

forced to sit on the opposite side. He is a physical barrier between us. Even if I wanted to tease her during this little episode, I'd have to circumvent the grown man between us.

We watch the very typical porn movie for all of ten minutes before Bain's phone rings. He picks it up without turning down the volume on the television. I'm sure whoever is on the line can hear all the "fuck me harder's" and "oh's" and "ah's" this couple is belting out.

"What?" Bain yells into the phone. "I'm with Diesel." He pauses, mesmerized by the television screen for a moment, before the caller snaps his reverie. "No, that's not her!" He looks at me and mouths 'gross' before he rolls his eyes. She laughs loudly at his actions, the drunk trying to conceal when in reality, he's nothing but transparent. "Yeah, I'm down. Cool. I'm bringing Elliot." He hangs up the phone.

I'm bringing Elliot where? Tess and I look at each other with quizzical looks and then back to Bain.

"Okay." Bain brushes his hands down his pants, showering the carpet with pretzel crumbs. "We're going to go now."

"Who is going where?" Tess asks.

"Elliot and I are going to play poker downstairs." It's said as if she is stupid for even considering that this was not an option. I'm immediately questioning if Bain even knows I was here before he got here. Does he think I came here with him? How drunk is he?

"Let's go, dude. You're not staying here with her!" Bain laughs loudly with his head thrown back. "Bye, Deese!" And with that, he's gone.

I look at her as she laughs quietly. "Well, there goes our night."

"I'm really pissed that there goes our night." I can't help but laugh, too. "How long do you think it will take for him to forget I was supposed to play poker?"

"I'm not –"

"ELLIOT! Let's go!" Bain's voice ricochets around the stairwell.

"Okay." I bow my head. "I'll concede this one. This is not happening again, just so you know." I lean over where she's still sitting on the couch.

"I look forward to this not happening again." She smiles and gestures to the porn, still loudly playing on the television. "But since you're leaving, I'll just enjoy the show." She looks around me and focuses on the large-breasted woman on the television taking it from behind by a repairman-mailman-boss-type guy.

"You're evil."

"I'm human."

"I want to watch this with you again."

You will." She drops her eyes to my crotch. "Are you going to hold out until next time?"

"Don't tempt me."

"Wouldn't dare." She tilts her head up to kiss me. It takes an eternity to consciously decide to break it off before we really are caught in the act.

"I'll see you tomorrow." The words are gravel in my throat.

"Tomorrow, Elliot," is the promise that escapes from her lips.

Chapter Twenty-One
DIESEL

Ping Pong!

What the hell? What time is it? Seven forty-five? *Oh my God. Who the hell is texting me? And why is it so damn loud!* It pings again and I slap the side table, fighting the tangles in the sheets. *Ahhh, shut up!* I grab my phone with exhausted fingers and pull it to my face to look at the text, of course, from Bain.

We are going for a run…wanna come?

Is he serious? Elliot didn't leave with him until three-thirty this morning.

Pass

I drop the phone on the bed and nestle back into the soft comfort of too many down pillows.

PING PONG!

Holy shit! I grab the phone and flip the switch to silent.

Slacker. We'll be back in 30 minutes

Great. Back to sleep…

Really! Now I can't fall back to sleep. Damn Bain and his adult ADHD, or whatever the hell his problem is. Bastard.

I roll out of bed and pull on my robe over my cami and panties. It's rare that I'm here the morning after a show but thankfully, it's quiet. Since Bain, Mike, and I have the run of the place, a little bit of silence will help me work on some of the billing for the upcoming shows.

I fumble with the coffee maker before walking to my desk. Once I'm settled, I promptly realize I've left all documents in the downstairs office. *Yet again another reason why we need an elevator!*

I quickly shuffle down the steps and across the vacant room that six hours ago was filled with pumping music and thousands of bodies. I walk behind the main stage and into the office area past the sea of white couches and tables. In the office, I grab the paperwork and head to the kitchen. I grab my leftovers from the night out Elliot and I had the other night. The restaurant fell directly in line with our secret date, a little Thai place with dim lighting, low music, and a plush booth in the back corner that hid our rendezvous perfectly. I warm at the thought despite pulling the chilly container from the fridge. I think Pad Thai for breakfast sounds perfect.

I step back from the open fridge and encounter some-thing—rather, someone—behind me. As I attempt to turn, a strong and overpowering hand immobilizes me by the nape, pushing my face down. I am paralyzed with fear. *Who the hell is here? Elliot? Did he stay the night?* I am on full alarm waiting for whomever this is to make a move. I took self-defense class. I can take this fucker if need be. I feel a hand run up my arm to my right shoulder before it pushes aside my hair. The hand hooks into the collar of my robe and gently pulls down, revealing my skin. The hand tilts my head and soft, seductive kisses caress my neck, moving down toward my shoulder. *Elliot...*

I relax for a moment, enjoying his quiet affection until I take a deep breath and smell the stench of stale cigarettes and booze. My eyes fly open, panic seeping in. Who the hell is in the club? I jerk, trying to get away from him but he bands a steely arm around my waist, holding me tightly against him. I try to push against him with my hips trying to knock him off balance as I claw at his arms.

"Get off me!"

He snorts before I feel his lips press against my shoulder, a moment later I feel his slimly tongue trace my collarbone. I shudder, my stomach pitching from the grotesqueness of this situation. Bolstering myself, I try to stomp on his foot. My bare feet meet his leather boots, their effort laughable. He grips me tighter, forcing air from my stomach, before his teeth clamp down painfully on my shoulder. I scream and attempt to throw an elbow into whoever is behind me. The hand at my neck forces me to look downward as I am pushed against the counter with my forehead pressed into the countertop. My attacker's hips are pinned directly behind my rear end. I am completely immobilized.

"Diesel, you are a fucking cunt bitch."

It is a serious and dark place from which Cass is speaking.

"Why do you come parading down here like this? You think you can just flaunt yourself here, like no one cares?" He runs his hand up the back of my thigh and over my rear end. His hand pushes my robe up to my back as his hips roll again my rear end, grinding his erection into me. Nausea floods me.

Do I answer him? I try to twist my neck and push up from

the counter but it's useless. His grip on me is so hard. I have to brace myself against the countertop or he'll completely flatten me into it. It's useless. Self-defense or not, don't think I could try to defend myself if I tried.

"Answer me, bitch!" He shakes me and quickly rips his hand from my neck to my hair, pulling it hard and twisting my head so I'm looking at him face-to-face. With his hips still pinning me against the counter, I am being held in some freakish yoga pose with my back twisting upward.

He looks crazed, like he's not slept all night. His nose is red. He smells like bourbon.

"I don't know what you mean, Cass," is all I can manage to squeak.

His rage is palpable and before I know it, he slams my head on the counter. The sound is disgusting and the pain spreads like lightning through my skull. My knees buckle and the humming requiem of lost consciousness rings in my ears. *Do not pass out! Do not pass out!* I do my best to focus on breathing in and out, in and out, in and out. *My hands...*

I can feel the strain on my shoulders as he pulls my hands behind my back and secures them with something hard. I am officially bound and still a little dizzy from the ricochet off the counter top. Panic bubbles up inside of me as he pulls me upright and turns me to face him. I can feel blood ooze down my forehead.

We're nose-to-nose now and despite the haze, I can see he looks intense and more than a little insane. "Now, Diesel, here's what's going to happen. You are going to take me to your place and you are going to let me fuck you. I've waited too long for you and I'm frankly tired of this fucking cock tease game you're playing." He growls out the words before he sniffs and rubs his nose. He looks mildly distracted for an instant before walking over to one of the high tables. I sway under the pain pulsing through my skull but attempt to move, flee. My legs feel rubbery, heavy and slow as I try to push forward.

"You're not thinking about leaving the party, are you?" He glares at me and quickly snorts three lines of cocaine. *Holy shit!*

He's instantly in front of me, sniffing, rubbing his nose, and running his tongue over his teeth. Out of nowhere, he rears back, punching me in the face. Blinding pain causes a white flash through my skull, my eye threatening to eject itself from the back of my skull. I fall to the ground, unable to catch myself with my hands bound, screaming out in pain.

"Shut up, bitch!" he hisses, slapping my face. He grabs my hair and hauls me to my feet. "Let's go." He drags me by my hair through the main dance area to the stairwell with the key pad. How long can I stall him here? If he didn't have such a tight hold on my hair, I would fall to the ground in a heap. My head is pounding; I can't even hold my right eye open anymore. The lights are too bright. The hum of blood rushing in my ears is deafening.

"Tell me the code. It better not be the one that sets the alarm off or you'll wish you were dead." I know his threat is real. He's out of my league now, and I can't defend myself.

"Zero six one." I pause. "Four eight five." I look up at his hateful glare.

"Say it again," he commands.

"Zero six one, four eight five." He punches the number in

the key pad and the door clicks open. "You're lucky, whore. Let's go."

The ascent up the stairs is exhausting. He yanks me up with his hand still firmly grasping my hair. From my half-bent posture, I can see droplets of my blood decorate the worn steps. I can't keep up with him. My head is numb and I can't balance myself with the hands tied. When I stumble over the stairs, he jerks me by my head as if I'm an untrained dog on a leash.

The door to my apartment is still ajar from my quick departure. Cass kicks the door open and looks in.

"You don't have any guests, I assume. Where is your fucking Brit boyfriend?" He says Brit as if it was a foul word.

"I don't know what you're talking about. I don't know where anyone is." My voice is ragged, out of breath from the rapid climb up the steps and physical assaults.

He walks us into the apartment and throws me head first onto the floor. My face scrapes the carpet and my shoulder digs into the floor. A shooting pain engulfs my eye again. Before I can register the rug burn or the pain, he's hovering over me. "What do you mean you don't know what I'm talking about? You're going to lie to me? *Now?* I see you with him, Diesel!"

Before I can gather any thoughts, he flips me onto my back. My chest is angled upward and head tilted back by my pinned arms. He is between my legs, his hands behind my knees, pushing them apart and out. "I'm going to fuck you so hard..." His voice is menacing and chilling as he looks over my body, stopping to stare at the apex of my thighs.

Get away. Get away. How are you going to get away? I quickly twist my hip and free my right leg from his hand, driving my heel directly into his chest. As he falls backwards, I try to scramble to a sitting position. I'm too slow and before I can get my bearings, he's leveled me with a slap and returning backhand. The pain is unlike any I've felt before. It's as if his hands are concrete and I am a bruised peach. I can taste the blood in my mouth. I try to scream and liquid pours out...blood, vomit...I'm not sure...I'm beginning to lose hold on myself.

In an instant, his hand is around my throat. I try again to yell and all is lost on the rasping breath leaving my lungs. He runs the other hand down my body, between my breasts then down my stomach. He hooks his fingers into my underwear and rips them down my legs in jerking pulls. An evil grin creeps across his face before he leans down between my legs. I can't see his face anymore, only his body, but can feel his breath on my inner thigh as he inhales and exhales and then suddenly bites me on the highest point on my inner thigh. The pain is blinding. Again, a futile attempt to cry out yields nothing more than gasping breath.

"You are a fucking cunt and you are gonna pay...."

With his free hand, I can tell he is fumbling with his pants but my vision narrows, getting darker, less focused under the pressure on my throat.

I don't want to die.

I don't want to feel this much pain.

Just stop this pain.

Numbness takes over my limbs as the pressure on my neck lifts and I fall into blackness, into a weightless nothing.

Chapter Twenty-Two
ELLIOT

"YO, ELLIOT! YOU up?"

I am jarred awake by Bain's chipper voice. He's standing over me, smiling as if he's the only cat in town who's caught all the canaries. I must have fallen asleep on his couch, in his apartment.

"I am now," I say as I rub my eyes. "What's up?"

"Mike and I usually hit up a run in the morning. You game?" He asks.

"Yeah, sure. I'm game." I'm certainly not going to fall asleep now and the idea of a run to burn off all of last night sounds like a very good idea.

As I change into shorts and a t-shirt provided by Mike, I replay the night. After Bain's impromptu entrance into Diesel's apartment, he dragged me down here to play poker with Mike. I think that lasted all of three minutes before he was distracted by food and passed out. I found the couch and now I'm going running. *Does this guy sleep?* Back in the main part of the apartment, Bain and Mike chat lightly about which route to take.

"Diesel isn't coming with us, so we can just head out," Mike offers. I am shocked that Diesel would run with Mike and Bain, but the majority of what she does shocks me, so why can't running be on her list, also.

We head down the stairs and out into the bright Saturday morning. It truly is a glorious day. The temperature is cool with a slight dampness to the air. Birds are singing and there is no one on the roads or sidewalks. It's a calm and beautiful morning in the city.

My innocuous thoughts are halted by Bain's phone going off. Without breaking stride, he pulls it from his pocket and looks at the screen. "What the hell is this? An eight hundred number this early in the morning?" He looks at Mike, who shrugs as he ignores the call.

A minute later, Mike's phone rings. "What the hell is going on?" He looks at his phone. "Hey, Bain, what's that number that was just on your phone?"

"Eight hundred, five two six something, why?"

"This is the same number." He says as accepts the call. "Hello?"

We can hear the clear voice of another human being on the end of the phone. "Yes, that's right. That's our location. What do you mean the silent alarm was activated? Yes, there is a woman in the building. When was it activated? Yes, send police and fire. We are not there but we are on our way back now. Thank you."

"What the fuck is going on?" Bain asks as Mike turns and starts to run back toward Eden. We look at each other and follow him.

"That was the alarm company," Mike yells over his shoulder to us. "They said the silent alarm was activated about five minutes ago and were calling to make sure it wasn't a false alarm. They tried to call Diesel and she didn't answer. They tried to call you and you didn't pick up, so they called me. We have to get back. Now!"

What the hell is going on? A silent alarm. Tess did say something to that effect when we went up to her apartment the first time. *There is the code to get in, a distress code, a code for if you've forgotten your code.*

The pace of the run is no longer casual. It's a full-on, dead-heat sprint. The anxiety about what we are getting into and worse, what could be happening to Tess, pushes me to run faster.

At three blocks away, we begin to hear the sirens for police and fire. Thankfully, it's early and there is no delay in the traffic. *Please God, let her be all right.*

We get to Eden at the same moment the police show up. Mike and Bain identify themselves and we enter the building with three officers. They quickly sweep the downstairs and report no one is there. The security door to the stairwell is ajar and I am slammed with an overwhelming sense of doom.

"She's upstairs. The door's open." I can hear the waver in my voice. "She's all the way at the top," I offer as they rush the stairs with weapons drawn.

Like lamb to slaughter, Mike, Bain, and I follow up the stairs to who-knows-what. Her apartment door is gaping wide open and we can hear scuffling but no noise. Suddenly, clear as day, we hear it.

"You are a fucking cunt and you are going to pay."

The police creep up the remaining stairs before bursting through the door screaming all manner of commands, "Freeze!" "Hands up!" "Step away from her!" Shouts, curses, and the sounds of physical altercations emanate from her apartment.

Bain looks at Mike with horror. "That's Cass."

No! In an instant, I am through the apartment door, Bain and Mike shouting behind me. I have to know if she is all right. I scan the room, anxiety building when I don't see or hear her. Then, the tinge of the carpet catches my eye. A swirl of pink leads to her body on the floor, crumpled and covered in blood. The sight of her unhinges any restraint I had.

"YOU MOTHERFUCKER! I'LL FUCKING KILL YOU!" My advance toward him is halted, Mike tacking me from behind, barely able to hold me back from attacking Cass despite two police officers pinning him to the floor. I rail and buck, trying to get out of Mike's hold. Bain moves between the police cuffing Cass and me.

"Elliot, they have him. Let them deal with him. We need to help Diesel."

"He's right," Mike agrees, grunting against my efforts to get free.

Seeing the police jerk Cass with a little more muscle than necessary satisfies me only slightly. The urge to pound his face into a bloody pulp still racing through my body makes it difficult to calm down. I stop resisting Mike when I have enough clarity to look at Bain, who is visibly distraught and distracted from where we all need to be because I'm bordering on feral.

The three of us rush to Tess, who is being attended by a female officer. The rug around her, once white, is now fully decorated with macabre swipes of pink and various pools of red. She is a crumpled figure, her robe hanging open around her half-naked body.

"Stay with us, honey, help is coming soon," the officer says to Diesel as she strokes her hair. I wait to hear her response but there is none. Walking toward her, I can see the full scale of Cass's assault. What I thought was horrible at first glance now becomes gruesome.

Her hair is black and sodden from an apparent head injury. Her face is covered with blood and I'm sure both her eyes are black. Her lips are swollen and cracked. Her shoulder is rug burned and there's a dark red indentation in a perfect crescent shape above her collarbone. Smears of blood paint the insides of her thighs. I've seen MMA fighters look better. Her neck has a perfect imprint of his hand on it, slowing turning purple at the edges. Her breath is ragged and uneven. *He choked her?* He beat the living shit out of her. I see her underwear is torn and discarded next to her. The realization of what happened here falls on me like a freight train. He tried to rape her. Fuck.

Fantasies of killing Cass flash through my mind at a lightning pace, each more painful and sadistic than the last. I'm sure some of my Southie friends in Boston would be more than happy to help me teach this shit stain a lesson.

Bain steps forward first. The officer immediately stops him by putting her hand up. "Sir, we have to treat this area like a crime scene, including her. I can't let you touch her." She is calm but firm.

Bain buckles under her direction and drops to his knees. "Diesel?"

Her only response is ragged, uneven breaths. If it wasn't for her breathing, I would swear she was dead. Bain explodes in uncontrolled sobs, holding his arms out to her, knowing he can't touch her. He rocks and howls her name. Mike stands beside him, looking at her, hand over his mouth, frozen.

Bile rises in my throat as I look at her body. Even Cass being hauled off by the police doesn't help. *He beat the shit out of her and wanted to rape her. He beat the shit out of her and wanted to rape her. Did he rape her? He was here? Was he waiting? We were gone. I was gone.*

I choke back the urge to vomit and move as close to her as the officer will allow, laying on the floor next to her.

"Diesel," I hate not calling her by her name, but I need to keep my head, for her. "Diesel, we're here. You're safe now. They have him, love." I inch closer, hoping she can hear me. "I won't let him near you again."

The three of us are pushed aside, made to watch as the ambulance crew descends upon her. They assess her injuries, quickly starting an IV line and waving a smelling salt packet and wave it under her nose. She opens one eye briefly but rolls back into unconsciousness. An EMS member rubs his knuckles roughly on her sternum, causing her entire body to convulse. I fight the urge to roar at him after watching her body flail. The EMS team briefly discusses their plan of action before putting a neck brace on her. They talk to her like she's a wounded kitten as they cover her with a sheet. She looks so broken and I have to grit back tears. Mike and Bain are immobilized at her feet, holding onto each other.

The medical crew transfers her to the gurney, taking all potential evidence with them in paper bags, including her underwear. Bain follows them out of the building since he elected to go to the hospital in the ambulance with her. Mike shouts out plans to meet him there after calling Natalie and

Greggor. He quickly asks me to stay until the police have cleared the apartment.

With the EMS crew gone, the police bring in the crime scene investigator to snap pictures of the apartment and stairwell. I watch him move through Tess's private space, documenting every inch of furniture and flooring that Cass infected. Mostly, he takes pictures of the white and pink carpet with a large red sphere where Tess's head lay minutes prior.

Chapter Twenty-Three
ELLIOT

"SHE IS STABLE but still dealing with a wicked headache from the concussion," Bain says with the edginess that has defined his tone for the past hours. "I don't know when she'll come home."

We climb the steps to her apartment before Bain opens the door. The smell of dried blood lingers in the air. He swiftly moves to the patio door and opens it, standing with his head outside for a moment before walking back to me.

I don't know what to say to him. He looks like he's been raked over the coals. His hair is a mess. His beard is growing out. Not that I'm any better. I've not slept for the past twenty-four hours. The thought of her nearly dying in front of me is haunting. I need to see her conscious. I need to hear her voice.

In the few hours after she was taken to the hospital, the SANE nurse found there was no actual penetration but Cass has been charged with attempted rape and numerous assault charges. He's also charged with possession of a controlled substance and public intoxication. He'll be incarcerated for a long while. The police catching him was best. They witnessed everything firsthand. Her injuries were so severe, they had no choice but to throw the book at him.

Tess suffered two black eyes and a concussion. Her wrists are bruised from the zip ties. The bite mark on her shoulder will heal on its own, but the damage to her thigh required stitches. From what they tell me, her voice is raspy from being choked.

"I don't know what to tell you, dude." Bain puts a hand on my shoulder. "Are you able to take a little break from the blog until we get this sorted out?"

"I guess," I offer half-heartedly. "She was going to look over everything before I posted it. I can work on what I have until she's well enough to read it. Or I could read it to her."

Bain looks at me, seeming confused. "Yeah, that could be a good idea." He pauses and I realize I'm holding my breath, waiting for his response. "Let me talk to her and see what she says, okay?"

"Sounds good to me."

"All right," he says, "let's get this out of here."

Together, we start to roll up the stained carpet from Tess's apartment and carry it to the dumpster.

TWO DAYS AFTER the attack, I pull up outside Natalie and Greggor's after a good hour of searching for the house. I cut the engine and hear the deafening quiet of the neighborhood after being overcome by the growl of the bike.

Lingering vibrations from the bike's power meld with the anxiety of actually seeing her. I haven't been able to lay eyes on her since she was carried away. Mike and Bain held vigil at the hospital, so I couldn't sneak in to see her. I planned to text her but thankfully, a text from Holly resulted in her phone pinging in Bain's pocket. For now, it's better for them not to know what we've been doing. It's bad enough I lost my mind when I saw what Cass had done to her. Thankfully, neither one of them has asked for an explanation for my explosion.

Once she was discharged and whisked to Natalie and Greggor's care, I knew I had to come here despite not being sure where their house was. Tess always drove us and I focused on her more than the route. They don't know I'm coming. Bain and Mike think I'm on my way back to Boston. I didn't want to risk her refusing to see me, so I figured out how to get here. Despite my GPS royally fucking up the trip, I've finally arrived.

Before I'm fully up the walkway, the door is wrenched open and Natalie flings herself toward me, enveloping me in a strong hug.

"We're so happy you're here." She pulls back, tears building in her eyes. "Bain told us what happened when you saw her." A jolt of anger shoots through me, the image of her damaged body is the last memory I have of her. Even knowing he's locked up, the desire to beat the shit out of him has not lessened.

"Dear?" Natalie's voice snaps me from the fantasy of getting to Cass first instead of the police.

"Can I see her?" The desperation to see her is clearly communicated in the rasp of my voice.

Natalie directs me to Tess's room. Every part of me screams to barge in, to pull her into my arms, to tell her it's going to be all right. But, I don't know what to expect. She may not want me. I don't know what this event has done to her. What *he's* done to her. The aftereffects of the trauma could cause her to avoid any male interaction. Natalie is here, not Greggor.

"Can you come with me? I don't want to scare her."

Natalie presses her lips into a thin line, obviously saddened by the possibility that I might be right. I have this terrible image of Tess waking up to me standing in the room and traumatizing her even further. Natalie nods and leads me upstairs into the dimly lit room.

I inch into the room after Natalie, standing on the opposite side of the bed. I can hear the low, steady breath of her sleep. The calming scent of her lavender and vanilla soap hangs in the air. Unfortunately, the aroma does nothing to ease the churn of my gut once I see her. Her eyes are still puffy and the bruising has seeped down onto her cheekbones. The broken skin around her lips looks dark as if it's healing but painful.

Natalie sits on the bed next to Tess, lightly rubbing her arm to rouse her. Tess shifts stiffly under the covers as she wakes. "Darling," she coos, "Elliot is here."

She moves too quickly, shifting to her side and curling into a ball with her back to me, forcing her body to convulse from the pain. Her strangled grunt sounds parched, painful. "No."

"Tess," I choke on her name. She jerks again, causing me to wince as she tries to hide in the mass of blankets. "Please, baby." The strangled tone of my voice gives me away. Being this close and having her refuse me is more painful than I would have expected.

I watch her sides rise and fall as Natalie strokes her hair, talking to her in hushed tones.

Slowly, she unfurls, rolling onto her back and shifting her face toward me. Her chin quivers before she pulls her arm from under the covers and holds her hand out to me.

Natalie quickly removes herself from the room, closing the door with a soft click as I sit next to her. Our fingers entwine before I pull her hands to my mouth, desperate to feel her warmth and softness.

She swallows hard, her eyes looking everywhere but at me. "Elliot," her voice strained, "I look horrible."

I huff, "I don't care. I just need to see you conscious." I run my fingers across the deep red bruise around her wrist. "I shouldn't have left you." The words catch in my throat, forcing a shuttering breath. "This arrangement, the secrecy, is complete insanity."

She blinks, looking at me with pursed lips. Her eyes slide shut for a brief moment before taking a breath. "He knew."

"Excuse me?"

"Cass. He knew about us." She swallows hard, her eyes closing from the pain of the movement. Her voice falters, cutting in an out as it succumbs to the damage he did. "He must have seen you in my apartment."

Sick dread fills me. "He was watching you? Even on nights there wasn't a show?" The realization of what could have been hits me. Blood pounds in my ears as my heart hammers against my chest. I resist the urge to stalk around the room howling obscenities at his sick pursuit of her. My jaw clenches as I pinch my nose, blowing out a breath in an attempt respond calmly when every inch of me wants to explode. "This could have been so much worse."

"I can't think about that right now." She reaches for my

hands, tangling her fingers with mine. "Elliot," her voice turns low, watery with tears. "I was so scared."

I want to pull her to me, hold her close and vow to never leave her unprotected again. I want to press my lips to every inch of damaged skin. Tell her no matter how black or blue or red her skin is, it's beautiful and it's mine. Demands that we come clean and tell everyone we're together fly through my head. If we were out, then any asshole that feels the urge to pursue her would have to go through me first.

I feel her hands caress my forearms, soothing the ticking muscles betraying my anger. I blow out a deep breath and shake my head. Chastising myself for my primal thoughts, I rub the back of my neck trying to ease the tension. She needs me to support her, not overwhelm her with testosterone-laden dominance. *Be a gentleman.* "I don't see how you wouldn't have been scared." I don't want to ask, but I have to know. "Can you tell me what happened?"

She pushes herself up to sit up in bed and tells me what she can remember of Cass's assault. She allows me to look at her shoulder, inspect her face, neck and wrists but the blanket stays firmly over her lap, silently refusing to look at the bite mark on her inner thigh. I know it's the worst of the injuries, requiring numerous stitches and causing her pain with any movement.

Tess looks exhausted after only a short time and stifles a yawn.

"I should let you rest, baby. I'm sure this is the most activity you've had since you've been home."

She nods as she picks at the comforter. "Don't leave."

"I'll be right downstairs. I'll see if I can stay in one of the spares. If not, I'll be back first thing in the morning."

"No."

"You don't want me to come back?"

"No. I don't want you to go." The flecks of gold in her eyes shimmer under the threat of tears. "Can you stay with me?"

"Of course." I stand up, kick off my boots and climb into bed next to her. She sinks down, body tucked under my arm, her head on my chest. I dip my head, inhaling her beautiful scent. "I'm not going anywhere." *Ever.*

IT'S BEEN A week since the incident. Mike and Bain are doing their best to put on good faces for the group but I can tell they are off track. They both look haggard, as if they are not sleeping. Every other word out of Bain's mouth is *fuck* or *shit* or *fucking shit.* Mike is more quiet than usual, trying to take on Tess's behind-the-scenes tasks. He is stressed and irritable. In her absence, everyone is aware that her presence and focus were steering this ship on all accounts. I'm doing my best to stay out of everyone's way. I just watch and wait.

Two days ago, Mike announced that she would be gone for an "indefinite amount of time" to figure out how to manage what happened. Thankfully, I've been able to have some brief communication while she's with Natalie and Greggor. She's continued to be tired but I've been able to have a few short phone calls. Still, it's not enough to soothe me in any way. I last heard from her three days ago.

I've been staying with Mike and Bain for the past couple days. After few days of miserably trying to cope with what happened, we drank ourselves into oblivion and tried not talk about what we all saw. Unfortunately, we ended up purging our souls to each other under many beers and shots of tequila. Tears and punched walls and expressions of wishing we'd never gone for a run engulfed us for well over an hour. I've been here ever since.

Unlike Tess's apartment, Mike and Bain's place has a solid construction with their bedrooms adjoined by a joint bathroom. On the opposite side of the main living area, there is a spare bedroom and a full bathroom that I've taken over. It's a good arrangement, more homey than the hotel and I'm able to contribute to food even though they turn me down at every opportunity.

Still sitting at the bar in the club, attempting to write my next spot and watching a half-hearted run through, I don't notice Mike walking up until he's immediately next to me.

"Yeah," he says into the phone, "he's right here." He's looking at me and I can't quite read his expression. "Okay, I'll talk to you later. Here he is." Mike hands the phone to me and raises his eyebrows. "She wants to talk to you."

I do my best to keep calm. "Okay, thanks." Mike nods and takes a few steps back, trying to assess the situation. Thankfully, he lifts his watchful eye and goes back to the stage.

"Hello?" I ask into the phone, tentatively turning my back to the stage. I would get up and move to a private place entirely but I don't want to seem obvious.

"Hi." Her voice is raspy and sounds as if she has laryngitis or throat cancer. She sounds horrible.

"How are you?"

"I've been better but I'm on the mend." Her voice cuts in and out.

"Geez, Tess," I say quietly, "you sound really awful." The sound of her voice is a punch to my gut. He hurt her so badly.

Her laugh is hoarse, which causes a brief stir in me. "I know I sound really bad but it doesn't hurt as bad as it sounds, if that's any consolation."

"I guess that's all right, then."

"I just wanted to say hi." She offers. "I'm hoping I'll be back soon."

"This place is rudderless without you."

"I wish it wasn't that way. Bain knows what he's doing; he's just really unsure of himself." How is it that from wherever she is, in whatever condition she's in, she can still be strong and complimentary? I want her here, badly.

"Yeah, he's in a bit of a rough way. He's all piss and vinegar."

"Oh, I'm well aware he gets like that sometimes. Just watch him if he starts with the tequila, he gets really saucy when that starts flowing."

"That warning is too late. We had our dance with Jose Cuervo the other night. I think I'm still a little buzzed."

"Oh," she pauses. "All of you?"

Well, I might as well talk to her now that I have her. "Yeah, it was not pretty. I think we are all still coping with what we saw. We were all struggling and we were drinking." It's out of my mouth before I can curb it.

"I'm so sorry, Elliot." Her voice sounds more distant.

"Don't apologize to me; it's Cass that needs to be apologizing. I've had all manner of horrible thoughts about what I could do to him."

"Yeah, me too. I really hope someone has made him their bitch already." She sighs. "I'm really glad you came to see me," she pauses, "even though I closely resemble one of those goldfish with the googly eyes."

"I'm glad I came to see you, too. Fish eyeballs and all." The light chuckle fades quickly and we hang on the line for a minute in silence.

"Is it weird that I miss you?" Her tone crackles under the words.

"I don't think so. This call is the best thing that's happened to me since I left you." It's true and I'm not in the market to tell her anything that's not honest after what's happened.

I hear a throat clearing behind me. Mike has returned, looking at me expectantly. I wonder if he's heard my admission to her.

"Oh, hey Mike," I say, not completely into the phone, "we're just wrapping up." I need to find some way to keep our ruse between us. "So, you can give me your email address and I'll send you the copy?"

"Sure," she encourages the ruse, and I'm positive she's smiling, "I'd like you to send me the copy." Her tone is as playful as it can be.

"Right, let me get something to take down your info. Okay, shoot." I quickly type her email address and confirm Greggor's phone number since Bain still has her cell, for texting of course.

"All right, I'll give you back to Mike now," I offer to her while looking at Mike, who's now drilling me with an inquisitive glare.

"I'll look forward to hearing from you soon, Elliot." She says. "Good cover," she whispers in a conspiring way, still sounding like a smoke stack.

"Bye!" The salutation is a little too enthusiastic and defiantly awkward.

"Bye, Elliot." She snickers and I hand the phone back to Mike.

He immediately begins talking to her and walks away. Relief floods me. She sounds better, not good, but I know she's on the mend. Even better, I have unrestricted access to her. Now I just need to tighten this story up and send her an email.

Chapter Twenty-Four
DIESEL

THERAPY IS EXHAUSTING, especially if you don't remember everything that happened to you. I remember parts of it, but others are lost. I remember Cass bouncing me off the counter and tying my hands. I remember being dragged up the stairs but once he hit me, I'm a blur. I can't remember anything after he had his hand on my neck. The therapist tells me that he pulled my underwear off and police caught him undoing his belt. Thank God for Bain's alarm system and the NYPD.

I briefly remember the hospital and the sexual assault nurse specialist. I think they gave me medication, which didn't help my ability to stay conscious. I remember Bain looking at me and choking on tears as if I was his dog run over in the street. He told me about all three of them being in the room, witnessing the police take down Cass and me on the floor.

I didn't really react when Bain told me Elliot was in the room. I think I feel the same about all of them seeing me completely beaten to shit. It's horrible. I think Bain was worried about Elliot seeing me naked. Well, too late for that one, Bain my boy! From my conversation with Bain, I don't think he suspects anything about Elliot and I, for which I am inherently grateful.

The hospital offered me different options to help deal with what happened. I elected for this intense, short-term therapy to process the assault. I think my own efforts to work through what I remember and the fact that I don't want to dwell on this is helping me. I find some comfort in the fact that he didn't actually rape me. For whatever reason, I can handle the beating laid on me. If he would have raped me...I can't even fathom it. I will always have visible wounds but they will remind me that I survived the battle. The scars are etchings on my skin that will forever mar the landscape of my body. I can live with physical damage. Being raped? I don't know how I would feel. Could I ever feel clean again? Trust a man again? Would I be the same? But, then I think, how would I know if I can't remember it if he *did* violate me? This whole thing is confusing.

In Greggor and Natalie's house, I feel at home but they treat me like a sick baby bunny. I need to do something. I need to have some worth. But then, I want to stay put and do nothing but read. Then I want to see Elliot and then I get concerned that I shouldn't be thinking about the guy I'm secretly sleeping with when I was just assaulted. *What the hell!*

Ugh. I'm a train wreck. I go from normal to thinking about all manner of craziness...from worrying about Eden to thinking about what will happen when Cass gets out of jail. I'll be protected by a restraining order and all the security guys at the club will know who he is, but he'll still be out. It's unnerving to think Cass will eventually be released and he could the same thing to someone else.

Stay focused on what you want to accomplish. That's what Gretta, my therapist, keeps chanting. She's nice enough. A little too hippie for me, but she's open to hearing that I can't be all peace, love and roses with her.

What do I want to accomplish? I want to go home. Yes, that's what I want. I want my life back on track. I'm not doing any good here. I need to see if I can handle the stress of it all. I feel like this is a dress rehearsal. I'm here but this is not my life. My life is at Eden. My life is my home. My home is my apartment where I was brutally beaten and almost raped...

I drop my head into my hands and try to calm the heaving in my chest.

Thankfully, Greggor's phone, which I have commandeered as my own, pings with an email, pulling me from the vortex of unhelpful thoughts.

To: Tess
Subject: The copy

Hello Miss Goldfish,

Attached is the copy of the latest draft for the blog. I talked to Bain and he wants me to put in about what happened with you since it was on the news. He thinks it's a good opportunity to get our side of the story out there. Let me know if you want me to change anything.

It was nice to hear your voice yesterday, even though you sound like some old lady who frequents a smoky bingo parlor.

When do you think you'll come back?

Take care,
The Gorton's Fisherman

I laugh at his cheesy attempts to e-flirt and realize I've smiled for the first time since yesterday. I miss him more than I thought I would.

To: Elliot
Subject: re: The copy

Dear Mr. Fisherman,

Thank you for the copy. I think I would have to agree with Bain on this one. I'll look it over and send you my feedback.

I will have you know that in a brief period of time I have become quite skilled at the seemingly random game of bingo and have amassed a purse full of blotters and quirky good luck charms. I've also purchased three cats and have begun eating dinner at 4pm.

I'm not sure exactly when I will come back. Please don't tell me they are burning the place down without me!
Talk to you soon – Goldie

There, a little bit of humor and I feel better already. I contemplate picking myself up off the bed when my phone pings again. On the draw, McGraw.

To: Tess
Subject: Cat woman

Please get rid of the cats, I'm deathly allergic.

I'll support your bingo habit only if you are winning and not wooing old men with your charms. I know the lure of an Early Bird Special is strong but you should stay focused on your bingo and not those geezers.

No one is burning the place down. I'm just missing you. There, I've said it and typed it.

Be well and I'll see you soon.
E

What? He misses me? I mean, I know I told him I miss him but he didn't really respond. He was at the club, maybe he couldn't. Can he really be sweet in person and over email! What to do?

To: Elliot
Subject: Ex-cat woman

E –

The cats are gone. It's bad enough with one of us having swollen eyes.

I can't say that I'll stop wooing old men. They are moths to my flame. I will not sucker any of them into the Early Bird Special...again!

I'm missing you too. Be patient. I'll be there soon.

T

Is this real? Am I really doing this? Am I flirting? I can't remember the last time I consciously did this with someone. Is this something I should be doing right now? I really must ask Gretta if this is okay. Why wouldn't it be okay? The phone pings again.

To: Tess
Subject: Your flame

I am very familiar with the subject of this email. I am with the old men on this one.

I'll take you to whatever Early Bird Special you want.

I'll also be here when you return.

E

Okay, I think that's a full-on swoon I feel. I've not talked to Gretta about him in such detail but now I think I might have to.

It's been so long since I've let anyone in. I mean *really* let anyone in. Not since Jamie, and we see where that got me. Widowed, tied to my brother-in-law and a dance club I had no idea what to do with. But he's not Jamie and this is allowed...right? I am allowed to flirt and have a relationship.

Yes, I am. But shit, I'm really bad at all that cat and mouse stuff. Honesty and humor...I'm good at that.

> *To: Elliot*
> *Subject: Mr. Moth*
>
> *I am quite happy to hear you are with the old men.*
> *Don't tease me with an EBS date if you don't intend to follow through!*
> *I'm anxious for my return as well.*
> *Good night and take care,*
> *Tess*

I roust myself from the bed and while brushing my teeth create a mental list of things to go through with Gretta.

1. Dating
2. Elliot
3. Dating Elliot

After I finish getting ready, I check my phone, happy to see Elliot's response.

> *To: Tess*
> *Subject: Your Date*
>
> *Miss Tess,*
> *I'll pick you up at 3:30 for our EBS date.*
> *On a side note, of all the old men after you, I'm the one with the best hips...*
> *Is that even appropriate given the reason you're so far away?*
> *Good night,*
> *Elliot*

I laugh out loud. *You cheeky bastard!*

To: Elliot
Subject: Your hips

Despite the reason I'm so far away, you make me laugh...hard.
Thanks...I really needed that.

Talk to you soon...
Yours, Tess

✧　✧　✧

THE NEXT DAY, I flop on Gretta's couch and dump the beans about Elliot. It's good to get it off my chest, to purge all the secrecy. I do feel guilty that we've conspired together as we have. Why do we need to keep it a secret? I know why but I can't delve into all that with Gretta. Not now.

"So," I say, "I think I want to have sex with Elliot again. Is that wrong?"

"Why would you think it's wrong?" she asks. Her voice is soothing and calm. She's warm tea with honey personified.

"I don't know." I think for a moment. "Because of what happened?"

"Well, the thing to remember is not all traumas are the same and not all people react the same way."

"Okay..." I look at her to urge her on. Thankfully, she takes my cue.

"You may not have the same reaction to physical sex as someone who was fully raped. You were physically assaulted and threatened with rape. You may feel some aftereffects, so prepare yourself. They may happen if, for instance someone were to come up against you suddenly or put their hand in your hair."

I take moment to process her words. "But the fact that I want to have sex is okay? Even normal?"

"I think you are a resilient woman who is able to process through the logical pieces of the assault. The aftereffects may take you time to process but I think you'll be able to manage."

After a moment of reflection, I look at Gretta. "I'm really scared to date."

She smiles at me, "I'd be really concerned about you if you weren't. Dating is difficult and it requires a level of vulnerability that some people are not comfortable with."

I nod my head and stare at the carpet for a moment. "I think I want to be done with therapy. I want to go back home."

She looks at me for a moment. "Let's skip our next session and see how you do. We'll meet on Monday and see how you feel. If you think you are good, then we'll end. Sound good?"

"Yeah, that sounds do-able." I'm happy to have a definitive plan in place. She walks me to the door and ushers me out. I walk to the car thinking that maybe I am not such a lost cause, after all.

COMING BACK HOME has not been the relaxing transition I hoped it would be, mainly because of Bain. Upon my return, he instituted a 'must-have-all-eyes-on-Diesel' protocol. I can understand his concerns, but his guilt is woefully misplaced. His protective hover volleys between annoying to tear-jerkingly endearing. Thankfully, after three days, he has eased up and I am able to function independently. He's planned for Eden to have guest DJ's come in for the next couple of shows, which makes life a little less stressful for everyone.

Elliot has been able to extend his residence with us, also due to the delay. He has been fervently writing about how Eden came into existence, tracing Jamie back to his Essex days and highlighting how it came into my hands. It's a handsome piece and I am very pleased with the outcome.

Since I've been back, Elliot has been staying in the apartment with me full time. It's nice to have him here and we seem to be doing well together. It's easy. We've worked out a schedule for when Elliot comes and goes to not raise any suspicions. It seems to be working and that's all I care about right now.

Despite our ever-evolving skills at being covert, we go to the lake house so we can just be us. Armed with some confidence to try something new, I leave the office and climb the stairs to my bedroom, where a stunningly handsome British man is sleeping with bare back begging me to straddle it and tease him awake with my tongue. *Stay focused!*

"Hey, wake up," I jostle Elliot unceremoniously.

"Huh?" He squints at me. "What? Why are we up so early?"

"It's nine-thirty and I'd like us to go for a run." My enthusiasm piques his interest.

"You'd like to run? With me?" He's propped on one elbow, looking at me with eyebrows raised.

"Yes, I have a bit of a wager for you." I wink and sashay out of the room.

I hear him clamor out of bed. He's downstairs in full running gear in five minutes. I hand him his iPod. His expectant look begs me to divulge this little bet I've concocted.

"Okay, here are the rules of the wager. We both run the same course but in opposite directions. This way, our courses are the same length and intersect each other at various points. Whoever gets back home first, wins. What do you say?"

"What do we win?" Elliot is eager to hear the prize. His eyes scan up and down my body.

I laugh at his lack of couth. "Well." I pause for effect and in the sexiest voice I can muster, "winner takes all."

Elliot's eyes dance with delight. "Sign me up!"

"Good. But there is one rule that must be followed."

"What's that?"

"I've made a special playlist for you. I've already uploaded it to your iPod. You must listen to it while you run."

"You made a playlist for me? For running?"

I nod in wicked delight.

He sighs and grabs his ear buds. "Let's go. I've got a race to win."

I can't control my laugh. *Please let this work!* I've never been good at being overly sexy, but I've been inspired since the incident with Cass. I'm not willing to give up any more time worrying about what is right or wrong. I feel strongly for this man and I know our time is limited. I refuse to allow any more minutes to be wasted. He has been infinitely patient, taking small steps so as not to overwhelm me, especially with intimacy. But I've had enough of paced niceties. It's time to get back to Elliot and Diesel, pre-Cass-trastrophe.

"My iPod has the same playlist, so we'll be listening to the same music on the run."

Elliot looks at me with curiosity. "Why?"

I can't hide my smirk. "I just think it's a good idea to know where each other is at, that's all."

"Well, let's go," he says, but quickly turns back to me. "What kind of music is this? Is this your crappy pop garbage?"

I roll my eyes and fake deep contemplation. A breathy laugh escapes from his mouth and I bounce in giddy anticipation. "Just trust me. Okay?"

"I trust you." It's more of a confession than a statement.

"Ready?"

"As ready as I will ever be. I'm hitting play." He unceremoniously hits play on the "Run" playlist. I quickly hit mine as well to keep us as synced as possible.

He stands immobilized for a moment, listening to Christina Aguilera belt out *Ain't No Other Man.* He looks at me with a confused look, eyebrows elevated. I wink and quickly turn to begin my run. I've always been a good sprinter, not so good with long distances. I run harder than normal to ensure I'll get home before him. Before I turn the first corner, I turn to look back. He's taken off down the street.

Yes! I flawlessly execute a leaping fist pump.

Christina transitions into an old Divinyls song, *I Touch Myself* and I laugh out loud. *So cheesy, but oh-so-perfect!*

I run across the train tracks and into town. Elliot and I should be crossing paths any minute now. I can see him coming as *I Touch Myself* morphs into *I'm a Slave 4 U.* We cross paths, Elliot looking at me with a level of slight irritation. I wink and blow him a kiss. He rolls his eyes in frustration and pushes forward.

Thank you, Britney! I want to scream out loud but I have to stay focused. He's a better runner than me and I have to get back to the house first.

We are in the last leg of the race and the club mix of Katy Perry's *Peacock* is pumping into my ears. I love these girls! So fun!

I don't see him coming down the main street so I cut into the backyard and take the stairs to make sure I'm in the house when he comes in.

I hear him pounding up the front steps. I reach the kitchen a second before he does. With ragged breath, he bursts through the kitchen door, glaring at me.

His harsh breath matches mine. He's glistening with sweat and pauses for a moment to lean forward and put his hands on his knees.

"It's cruel to make a man run like that." He pushes it out between breaths. "I almost had to stop, like, three times!"

He's so sexy! I am so proud of my efforts; I laugh loudly. This worked! I wanted him hot and bothered, and here he is.

"You think that's funny?" He takes two steps toward me with eyebrows raised, which causes an eruption of laughter to escape my lips. "We'll see what's funny." He rushes me, picking me up over his shoulder and smacking my rear end.

I squeal with delight and repay the action. He swats me again and carries me up the stairs. "I know I lost that race, but I'm taking this as a win because you used sex to hamper me."

"I think you are just fine." I can't stop the hysteria. "I listened to the same music you did and I'm just fine!" He's carrying me down the hall to our room. *Oh, this is awesome.*

"Really?" he says as he drops me on the bed. "Take it off."
He gestures to my clothes loosely with his hand as he pulls his
shirt off. "All of it!"

I am all too happy to comply.

Chapter Twenty-Five
ELLIOT

Where are you?

I CAN HEAR the irritation seeping through her text.

I curse at Bain under my breath. Damn him asking questions about the blog and holding me up. I'm late to meet Tess.

I talk into my text messaging system.

On my way to you.

For the first time, I'm driving up to Tess's lake house alone. It's a little private rendezvous since she's opted to not be at the show tomorrow night. Bain and Mike have other plans, so no one will be coming here after the show. Since she didn't have anything to do during the show, she left.

I have to drive back to Boston to "take care of things at the office," so I left today, as well. However, I left well behind schedule. Two hours behind schedule, to be exact.

I turn the corner onto her driveway and begin the slow progression up the gravel. The sun is setting and I am starving. I'm also anxious to see her. Our arrangement of keeping things under wraps has been difficult at best, especially in the weeks since she's been back after Cass attacked her. I still have this driving need to constantly watch over her, care for her, protect her, even though I know she's safe. Spending every night together since she's been back hasn't lessened my need to be near her. I'll do whatever she needs to feel safe and normal again. But in my eyes, she's coped with everything beautifully. Only a few skittish moments here and there but nothing that would have me encouraging her to go back into therapy.

The moments where she unwillingly succumbed to the stress of it all nearly snapped me in two. I could see her fighting with herself until she worked it out. Her crying has got to be the single worst thing in the world. The few nightmares she did have left her shaking, angry that Cass still had power over her. Despite her telling me that all I need to do is "be here", I have a lingering feeling of helplessness and a growing desire to rip Cass's balls from his body.

We've made significant efforts to be slow, paced. I need her to know I care for her and that we will work through the murky shit. She surprised me with the naughty sex run but we hit a snag a few days later. The first time I tried to kiss her beautiful mound, she froze. My lips touching the scar on her inner thigh caused her knees to jerk together despite my body being in the way. It's been a process, but she's made it clear she wants to be back to normal.

Since then, she's been focused and has continued to wow me with attempts to re-establish herself sexually. She's not tied me up yet and I hope she doesn't need to go there but if she does, I'll give it a try. The wickedly twisted part of me hopes she'll let me do the same someday. Truthfully, I'll do anything to help her heal. Until then, I'm her willing subject, eager to embark on whatever experimentation she needs to feel better. My girl is too amazing to be held back by the insane actions of a derelict.

Climbing the driveway, I take in the looming house before me. While admiring the architecture illuminated by the setting sun, my eye is caught by a sheer fabric moving in the summer breeze.

What is this?

She's standing on the balcony, staring down at me in nothing but a black bra, panties, and garters that hold up the sheerest stockings. A sheer robe hangs loosely around her, creating a smoky backdrop that highlights her fair skin. Her long hair is artfully draped around her shoulders as she leans forward on the balcony railing, peering down at me with sinful, heated eyes. Her only physical movement is the slow rocking of her foot back on the three-inch heel before slowing tapping it on the deck's floor.

There she stands, a waiting sentinel in lingerie, until I scramble off my bike. As soon as I do, she turns on her heel, waiting long enough for me catch a glimpse of her ass, and walks smoothly into the house.

I take the steps to the main floor two at a time before busting through the kitchen door. She waits in the middle of the room, hands on her hips, head cocked to one side, staring at me. It takes me a minute to register that the house smells amazing and the table is set for two, candles, wine, the whole nine.

She drops her gaze and looks at her red painted nails with an impassive look. "You're late." It's a flat statement. I can't tell if she's mad, put off, or being playful.

"I know. I am so sorry. Bain wouldn't shut up." I move to

touch her and she takes a defensive step backwards. *Oh, fuck, do not be mad. Not when you are looking like this!* "I didn't know you were planning anything, um, special, for this evening."

She smiles at me; I can see the inner sex kitten wildly at play in those eyes. "Well, I guess that's true," she offers with a husky voice. "I've been trying to keep busy while I've been waiting."

I openly stare, my gaze caressing every inch of her. I have to swallow past the dryness in my mouth before responding, "Dinner smells wonderful, Tess. You look amazing."

"Thank you. We'll eat soon." She glances at the table before looking back at me. "But first, there are some other chores we need to take care of."

"Really?" My stomach leaps with excitement. Sex before dinner? Best appetizer ever!

"Yes, Elliot. We must complete our chores before we sit down."

"What chore would you like me to complete, love?"

"Well, I think it's obvious, don't you?"

"Yes," I agree and again take a step toward her, though she again steps back and puts her hand on my chest. The heat of her palm sears into my chest and stokes an already raging fire.

"No no, darling," she admonishes, "not yet. You see, I waited; now you'll wait a bit. I don't like tardiness, Elliot. I'm a stickler for being on time." She breathes out and takes off the sheer robe, laying it on the counter. Now she's in nothing but bra, panties, garter, stocking, and those fucking heels that click deliciously on the floor. "You need to do your chores first." She begins to pull warming dishes from the oven and walks them to the table.

"And, what chores are those?" I would mow the fucking lawn in record time if that's what she needed me to do.

"Well," she playfully ponders, "I think you need to do some laundry."

"Laundry?" I ask.

"Laundry." She says with a smile.

"Do I smell?"

"No, baby." She continues to move back and forth between the oven and the table, dressing it with plates of roasted lamb, mashed potatoes, and vegetables. She opens each vessel in front of me, letting me be assaulted by the delicious scents. I can't see anything but her, I can't smell anything other than that food, and now she wants me to do laundry! *What the hell?*

"Elliot," she turns to me, perfect ass perched on the edge of the fully dressed table, "do your laundry." It's a command. Clear and direct.

"I don't understand, Tess. I didn't bring any laundry to do." I hold my hands up. She's fried my brain in the five minutes I've been here. *Solve this for me, baby, I can't think like this.*

She smiles, "Elliot, I did my laundry today, and all I have left to wear is this." She moves her hand down her body, showing herself off as if she's a prize on a game show.

"What?"

"Elliot." Her tone is directive and immediately registers in my cock. "Put your laundry in the wash."

She wants me to put these clothes in the wash? Now? I shrug. "Where's the laundry room?"

"It's that door right there," she gestures to a closed door just outside of the kitchen.

I move toward the door.

"Don't you dare," she snaps, stopping me in my tracks. "Take it off right here."

She wants me to strip in front of her while she watches? *She's* in control of this? If so, it's fucking hot.

I begin to fumble with the buttons on my shirt. She stands five feet in front of me, rocking on her heels and running hungry eyes all over me. Her stare makes me more nervous, more excited, and renders me all thumbs. Never has getting naked been so troublesome.

"The longer you take, the longer it takes for us to eat dinner, the longer it takes to get to dessert." Her smirk is wicked and all in control.

I toe off my shoes and rip off my jeans, my cock grateful for the release. I look at her, clearly pleased at the undoing she's created in her kitchen. This is a power play and I love it. If she needs to be in control, then have at it. Hopefully this is one more step toward her healing.

"Can I keep my boxers on?" I ask.

"For now." She moves toward me, looking me up and down. When she's inches from my face, I breathe her in. "Are you hungry?"

I scoff at the notion. "Am I hungry? For what? Food? You? I think you know the answer to that."

"Good." The corners of her mouth curl in wicked delight. "Let's eat, then." Again, she turns on her heel and undulates from me to the table. I think she pushes her hips out more than she should, knowing how the curve of her backside makes me crazy. For as much as I want her to have this moment, I don't know how long I can play this game. That beautiful ass has to be mine.

Chapter Twenty-Six
DIESEL

I WALK AWAY from him, pleased he's buying the whole "pissed vixen" bit. I hear him behind me, following the path I've taken to the dining room table that I've laid with dinner, candles and wine.

Before I can turn to order him to sit, he runs his hands around my waist and pulls me against him. My eyes roll to the heavens as he pushes his attentive erection into my rear end. He gathers my hair to one side and begins torturously slow kisses up my neck. I shiver when he presses his lips to the scar Cass left. He feels it and tightens his grip around my waist, leaving no space between us.

"It's me, Tess. This is us." His quiet affirmation centers me, reminding me that this, that he, is safe. I lay my head back, melting into his chest. Even though I'm in these heels, he has the size advantage; he deliciously traps me. It's a feeling I've been craving all day. I could escape if I wanted to, but right now, I need to play.

"Dinner is getting cold, Elliot." The words are meant to be distant, dismissive even, but my voice betrays me. He knows my weakness—and it's him.

"Put your hands on the table and lean forward for me." I

fall forward, head dipped down, waiting for his next move, touch, command. He shifts his feet so one leg is between mine. I want to push back into him, grind my ass into him, urge him to be quick, but he moves before I can grapple for dominance in this little tryst. He grips my hips before running his hands down my thighs and calves while dropping to his knees behind me. I can see him take in my stance from below. He playfully runs his fingers over my ankle as he brushes his lips across the back of my knees. I close my eyes and grip the tablecloth lightly. I bite my lip to hold back a moan as his kisses move north. *So much for being all in control of this one...* Elliot Archer is the little bottle that says 'drink me' and I'm the fool that gulps it down.

"Are you still angry about the tardy thing, sweet Tess?" His question fans warm breath across my sex. My entire body buckles under the sensation. I need him and he knows it. I can't finds the words to tell him I want him. Thankfully, my body informs him...explicitly.

"Tess?" He runs a finger under the edge of my panties and lightly teases my folds. "Tell me. Are you still angry?"

The precisely laid dining ensemble shifts as I grip the tablecloth while he pushes his finger inside me. The moan I've done my best to restrain escapes as he kisses me through my damp lace panties.

He stops, withdrawing all touch from me. I open my eyes the instant his hands leave my body. From between my legs, he hovers close to my body, looking up at me impassively. My body, thrumming with desire and longing and want, screams for his skin to be against mine again and all I can do is breathe and stare at him and bite my tongue.

He is waiting for my answer, patiently. More patiently than I would have.

"No." I push the word from the back of my throat.

"Are you hungry?"

What? I look at the meal I've prepared. The food can be warmed. The wine is fine in its decanter. I blow out the candles with a long, slow breath.

I look at him, still poised to strike from beneath me. He looks like a mechanic checking out the undercarriage of a car, eyes boring into the apex of my thighs as if he knows precisely what he's going to do to me. My stomach clenches with anticipation, sending waves of awareness through my core and hardening my nipples under the thin fabric of my bra.

"No, I'm not hungry." The strain in my voice is apparent. He knows what he's done.

He smiles at me. "Good." He lightly grips the insides of my thighs, effectively pushing me wider. "Keep your hands where they are."

I can't respond because there are no words. How does this man do this, say a single statement and turn me into a mess of want and desire? I started this, so how is he finishing it? How does this happen? How do I let this happen?

Because I love it. I love his command. I love the secret life we are leading. I love his polite reservation in public and his strong will behind closed doors. I love the feel of his skin on mine, the sound of my name rolling off his tongue. I miss him when he's not with me. I am jealous when other women hit on him. I am his. Whatever he wants, however he wants it...I would give it to him.

He pulls his head away, stopping the gentle kisses he's

trailing up my thighs. "Tess, you stay here with me. No daydreaming." Before I can respond, he pulls my panties to one side and runs his tongue over my clit.

The plates, food, and candles jerk under the force of me pulling on the tablecloth. I splay my hands out to try and push the fabric away, smooth it out, but his mouth is hypnotic. I groan his name as he pushes more fingers into my sex, my trembling legs supported by his shoulder pressing into my thigh.

I look down at him. He examines me before each kiss, kisses me before each touch, and touches me as if I'm the only woman who exists. In this moment, I think I love this man.

"Elliot," I rasp, "please...."

"Please?" He says between sweet kisses. "Please, what, Tess? Do you need to be pleased? Am I not pleasing you?"

"I can't stand here much longer." It's true. My legs are weak and my arms are shaking from holding myself up.

He considers this plea for a moment and stands up behind me. He snakes his arms around my waist and he curls over my body. His hips press into me and I feel his steely urgency, pushing my desire higher.

"Why can't you stand here much longer?" He questions it into my ear, as if he is dumb to the entirety of this situation.

What does he want me to say? *Oh, fuck it...let's just be honest.* "Because I want you, Elliot. Now."

"I want you too, Tess." He says it as he moves one hand up to my breasts, releasing each from the sheer fabric barely holding them in place. The other moves slowly down my belly. I whimper, pushing my ass into him, gripping the tablecloth.

He turns pulls me around to face him and for a moment, we just look at each other in collective silence. Then he is on me. Hungry and passionate, he grips my hair and dives into my mouth. He releases my hair but not my mouth and grips the backs of my thighs, pulling my legs around his waist. He walks us into the living room and sets me on the ledge of the bow window, overlooking the lake.

He efficiently divests me of my panties, shredding the fabric with two quick tugs. Now it's just me, and garter, the stockings, the heels and my breasts displayed over the fabric of my bra, which is somehow still attached.

He takes a moment and looks at me perched on the window, wrapped around him. He holds my face in a caring grip before assaulting my mouth with his.

Pulling away and moving down my body, he murmurs affectionate words. "You're beautiful, love. I've thought of nothing but you all day. The feel of your skin on my lips is heaven." He adores my breasts in a way that has me all but screaming in pleasure. He could be the man to make me orgasm by sucking on my nipples alone, I'm sure of it.

I grip his hair and pull him up to me. "Elliot, I need you." I rock my hips toward him. Kissing me deeply, he affords me the quickest moment to push down his boxers and pull him toward me.

Our combined gasp as he enters me has me teetering on the edge. The pleasure is blinding and I have no choice but to think this is perfection. This moment, though it didn't go as planned, is pretty damn awesome.

He takes his time, stroking me slowly with his length as I release a keening cry for more of everything he has to offer.

His hands touch every inch of me. His words praise me. His body overwhelms mine.

I love this moment. I love this place. Moreover, without realizing it, I've fallen utterly in love with this man.

Chapter Twenty-Seven
DIESEL

I AM LOVINGLY nudged awake by the warm summer sun caressing my body through the window of my apartment. In my bed, bright light beams down on us, illuminating the bronzed back and shoulders of the beautiful man next to me. I roll from my back to my side, pressing up against Elliot, my lips worshiping the exposed skin. With his eyes still closed, his breath changes from sleepy to awake and blissfully relaxed.

"Mmmm, baby..."

He shifts toward me and cradles me at the waist, pulling himself flush against me. I prop myself up to kiss his neck and jaw. *I could keep him here forever.* I run my hand across his chest, over his shoulder and down his belly. *I must get my hands on –*

The predatory rumble that erupts from his chest accompanied by the rough grip on my ass causes me to squeal as he pulls me on top of him.

"Good morning, Mr. Archer." I accompany the greeting by a not-so-innocent wiggle of my hips.

"It is, isn't it?" He tucks a random curl behind my ear before caressing my neck and pulling me toward his lips.

"You have amazing ways of waking a man up day after day, love."

"What the fuck is this?"

His voice makes me freeze. Elliot and I are nose to nose, looking at each other's surprised face before I begin the slow turn away from him – toward Bain.

He stands there, arms tightly crossed against his muscled chest, two feet from the side of the bed.

He is glaring at us. *Pissed* does not begin to describe the look on his face.

So much for covert. I pull the sheet up around my body, truly the only barrier between Bain and myself, and do my best to block as much of Elliot as I can. If need be, I can push him off the far side of the bed if Bain lunges for him.

I have to do my best to stay calm but I am annoyed that he is even in here. "What does it look like, Bain?"

"How long has this been going on?" Despite his cold tone, his arms betray the anger coursing through him as the muscles flex and his chest rises and falls on jagged breaths. I can see the veins in his neck start to pop. *Oh, boy. This has the potential for serious consequences.*

"A little while," I offer, "since you told me to 'have a little fun' while you and Mike took care of *business*." The words are laced with a tinge of sarcasm. Does it matter how long?

"I told you to fuck him, Diesel, I didn't tell you start dating him!"

"What?" Elliot's tone is a twist of confusion and irritation. "You told her to sleep with me? How fucked up is that?" He's pointed directly at Bain.

Serious...serious...consequences.

"Look," Bain says, "I thought you two would have fun together, no doubt about that. But this? You stayed with us while she was away, dude. You didn't say anything!"

"What was I going to say?" he shoots back. "Tess and I-"

"Tess! You fucking call her Tess?" He looks at me as if I have sprouted a third head. "You let him call you Tess? You don't let anyone do that!"

That's it. The spark to the firecracker. I'm no longer worried about Bain going after Elliot because I'm going after Bain.

"Now you listen here." I zero in on Bain as if he's the only thing in the room, "Right now, I'm having a good time. That's what you told me to do. I like his company. He never asked me if it was okay to call me Tess; he just does, and to be honest, I like it. We'll do this,"—I gesture to us and the bed with my free hand—, "as much and for as long as we want. We've kept, and will continue to keep, this discreet. You understand the importance of being discreet, don't you Bain?" I narrow my eyes to help focus my point.

He is dumbstruck. *Take that!* He drops his gaze to his feet and shuffles uncomfortably. "Okay," he says after a moment, "you want this. I get that. I accept that."

"Thank you."

He lifts his eyes to me yet immediately shifts to Elliot. "But you." He points to the center of Elliot's face. "You hurt her, you do anything out of line, I will completely fuck you up. Understood?"

"Bain!" I yell.

He glares at me with an unnamed emotion, forcing me to stare him down.

"I understand," Elliot says quietly behind me, "it's not in my plans, but I get where you are coming from."

Bain blinks as if he's shocked...or mollified? *What the hell is that look? He's silent? What the hell is going on?*

"Good." He turns to walk out of the apartment with his fists in his pockets. "I'm telling Mike, just so you know," he says quietly over his shoulder.

I exhale the anxiety of past few minutes. "I had no doubt you would, darling," I sigh. "I had no doubt you would."

✧   ✧   ✧

"DO YOU REALLY have to go?" I ask. It's actually more of a whine. I look up at him as he slops his clothing into a suitcase.

"Yes." He looks at me passively. "I'll be back in two weeks." He kisses me swiftly on the cheek and walks to the closet in his suite.

I am amazed at myself. Five months ago, I was ready to throw this man to the dogs, and now I'm sad he's leaving. Despite multiple friends coming to visit him over the past few months, he planned a trip to see his family back home before coming to Eden. His flight leaves in a few hours.

"You know," he says, walking back to where I pout on the bed, "you can come with me. My flat is more than big enough and you can visit your old haunts."

I smile shyly. *I don't think you would get me back here if I went.* "I would, but we have the show this weekend and Bain wants me there."

"Ah, yes, then we part ways, Tess." His saying my name has become such a joy. It's something intimate between us, even though being open to Mike and Bain has made things a little easier. We're still cautious around the other members of Eden but I'm much more at ease. Life has been good.

He kisses me, holding me close to him and suddenly I am emotional. Tears break free as I run my hands around his waist and up his back. He breaks from my lips and kisses both cheeks. He feels my tears and looks at me.

"Hey, hey, hey... What is this?" He wipes my cheeks gently with his thumbs. "I'm coming back soon." He smiles, which forces my smile. Part of me is highly embarrassed. *Could you be more of a baby? Why are you being so strange about this?*

He pulls me toward him again and kisses my forehead before tucking my head under his chin. I breathe in the smell of his soap, committing it to memory until the next time we see each other. He holds me so long I secretly hope he never lets go. I hear him sigh before he steps back, holding me by both upper arms.

"I'll text you when I'm in the airport, before I take off and when I land."

I nod. I don't think I can speak now without the tears bubbling forward again.

"I have to go now or I'll never leave you." He smiles shyly and kisses me again. I watch him grab his bag and follow him to the cab waiting at the curb before I come back to Earth after his proclamation. *Never leave me? That might be nice...*

I stand on the street and watch the cookie cutter cab until it is completely out of sight.

You can do two weeks. You did twenty-five years without him... You'll survive two weeks.

✧　✧　✧

EDEN IS INTENSE tonight. I'm enjoying being myself, dancing, and drinking. I need to blow off some serious steam. Friends have come in from out of town and seem to have brought their respective cities with them. We are at max capacity and Bain is blowing the roof off.

I'm buzzed, more so than usual, and in the company of Ben, a mutual friend of Bain and Mike. Ben and I became fast friends, and since then have served as each other's wingman and chief cock-blocker when not otherwise involved. We truly believe we were separated at birth. Ben and Bain had an on and off thing for years but they've settled their ways and now have a great relationship. His arrival in town has made Bain nostalgic and he has re-worked some of our favorite songs into his mix tonight. We are dancing, howling gratitude for "the best song ever!" and busting out signature moves all while downing tequila shots like the night will never end. I will pay vehemently for this tomorrow. But in the moment, this is great.

I miss Elliot but we talked today. He's seeing his dad, hanging out with family and friends and has been able to work on the blog when he has some down time. I'm glad he's having a great time but I'm excited for his return home. Only four more days.

Bain spins a mix that causes the cluster of us to scream and turn the dance floor into a tornado of gyrating bodies. Ben hands me another shot of tequila. We clink glasses and down yet another nail in our drunken coffins.

Chapter Twenty-Eight
DIESEL

THIS MUST BE what death feels like.

The sun has decided to hang itself directly outside my window. Either that or I'm being interrogated for some heinous crime.

Ugh.

My head is killing me. My legs, feet, and back all ache. My stomach feels like it could drop or heave at a moment's notice. *Super sexy. Are these signs that I had a good time last night?*

I hoist myself out of bed and my head spins. *Oh, I don't think I'm going very far today....*

I'm naked except for my underwear. My clothing is strewn across my room as if I systematically disassembled myself walking through the room. *Classy. This kind of a scene is supposed to happen when some hot guy is ripping off your clothes, not when you are a drunk mess and can't right yourself.*

I pull on my robe and walk to the kitchen. Coffee. Since I've not heard from Mike and Bain, I assume they are still sleeping. I hope they feel as bad as I do.

I stumble into the kitchen and tentatively smell the coffee before I scoop it into the machine. *Stomach, can you handle this?* I am pleased when the 'good' craving overruns the 'foul' feeling. I make a huge pot; the guys will probably want some, as well.

As I pour the water into the coffee machine, I hear my phone ping. I finish off the water and flick the machine on. I walk over to look at the screen. *Oh! A text from Elliot! He's up early.* I look at the clock. It's five hours difference from us to London. The text came through at four in the morning our time, so that's nine in the morning his time. I swipe the screen to unlock my phone and look at the message. It's a forwarded picture with the title "Re: When you're away, Diesel will play."

What the hell is this?

I look at the screen, my brain still a little slow from last night. It's my room. Moreover, my naked body in my bed. I'm completely exposed with the exception of my naughty bits which are loosely covered by the sheet. If I didn't know I had my underwear on, I would swear I was completely naked.

In the picture, Ben is in bed with me, loosely draped over my body. We look like a scene from Othello. Ben's mahogany arm is thrown across my alabaster chest in blissful slumber. The image is both beautiful and horrific.

No!

The message from Elliot is short and to the point.

Seriously?

"Holy shit!" I blurt.

Who took this picture? This is completely fucked up! Who the fuck took this picture? My heart is pounding and I'm pacing around the room. What do I do?

I text him back.

It's not what it looks like, I promise! How did you get this picture? Who sent it to you?

His response is immediate:

Does it matter where it came from?

Of course it matters where it came from! I am up to my eyeballs in shit, he's so pissed.

Yes it matters! Who sent it to you? I promise you, this is not what it looks like. I'll explain everything.

His response seems to take an eternity.

Not that it matters, but it came from a blocked number. Diesel, I'm appalled by this. It looks like what it is. I can't accept this.

He called me Diesel!

You won't let me explain? We didn't sleep together! Can we please talk?

Another eternity passes.

I don't think I can talk to you right now.

I blink at his text and suddenly, I'm overwhelmed. The feeling that this...whatever this was...this bliss, this comfort, is done and over...it really feels like too much to handle. It was short-lived and now it's finished. I can feel the tethers to him being cut. He is floating away like a released hot air balloon. My chest aches, tears well, and my throat closes. This is done. He's gone already. I drop the phone on the floor and cover my mouth to catch the choking sobs erupting from my body.

Now I know what death feels like.

✧ ✧ ✧

AFTER WHAT FEELS like hours, I pick myself up off the kitchen floor and grab my phone. Covered in the residue from my tears, I stomp to Bain's room. I pound on the door and open it before he has the opportunity to respond.

"Where is Ben?" I demand.

"What the fuck?" Bain yells, jerking from his sleep.

"Where is Ben!" It's a full-blown scream. I feel as if I've lost control of all faculties at this juncture. I'm sure I look wild with bed hair and tear-stained face from my emotional outpourings. Now I'm angry and ready to fight. My heart pounds and my breath is ragged.

Bain looks at me as if I'm crazy. His eyes leave me only to look at Mike, who has stumbled into the room through their adjoining bathroom.

"What the hell is going on?" Mike questions, wiping sleep from his eyes. At least he appears more together and less hung over than Bain and me.

"I need to know where Ben is." I try to level my breath. I am truly afraid I'll lose my mind in this moment.

"He left really early this morning." Mike shrugs. "He came in to say good-bye to me around seven-thirty. Why?"

I give my phone to Mike. He reviews the forwarded photo and my texts with Elliot.

"What?" He looks at me with puzzlement and shock. He hands the phone to Bain, now upright in bed and conscious.

"He can't be serious." Bain looks at me with a wry smile. "He thinks you slept with Ben? Does he know you at all? Deese, you are not a one trick pony. And especially not with Ben!" He erupts into a light laugh at the end. "Your boobs look really good though."

"Are you fucking kidding me? You think this is funny?" I explode. "Some asshole sends a text to Elliot and now he doesn't want to talk to me and you think it's funny!" I am seething. I can't remember a time I was ever this angry or felt this out of control of myself. I uncomfortably notice that this level of anger is out of character for me.

"Look," Bain offers, "just explain the situation to Elliot." He looks up at Mike who nods in approval. "I think he'll be cool with it once he gets all the info and it will be all good."

The possibility of purging the truth slows down the volcanic churn of my stomach. My breath is more even and I begin feel a little more stable.

"What if he won't hear it?"

"What's not to hear?" Mike counters. "Once it's said, he'll have no choice but to acknowledge it, right? We can get Ben to vouch for you also."

"Yeah, incidentally, how did you get that naked?" Bain asks.

"I have no idea," I huff. "I just might not have cared. I didn't think he came to bed with me. I thought he was with you two."

"He was," Bain snorts while looking at Mike sheepishly, "but then Jessica came up and he bolted. I thought he was gone for the night. He must have just come in to see you."

"Jessica was here? When?" I ask.

"Last night. I don't know. It was so late. You were already upstairs."

"Where is she now?" I'm totally confused.

"I think she went home with one of the guys she met last night. God only knows where she is now." Bain shrugs. "She was trying very hard to get Ben's attention all night. I think he really pissed her off when he announced he was going to see you."

"What do you mean?"

"Deese," Bain scoffs, "you hooked Elliot, and despite being one of the most popular girls in Eden, she will always be runner-up next to you. She followed Ben out of here like a puppy after a treat. I'm sure she wanted some action with him. You don't remember her or Ben being in your apartment?"

I shake my head. The thought of them in my space without my knowledge sends shards of ice slicing though my veins. I know Ben would never do anything to intentionally hurt me, he doesn't know about Elliot.

But Jessica does.

"Do you think she took the picture and sent it to him?"

"I wouldn't put it past her. She can be nasty when she wants to be." Bain looks back at my phone, his mouth set in a tight line. "That bitch better not have done this."

I feel myself start to boil again, incensed at the possibility that we pulled Jessica from a shitty strip club to give her a chance to have a decent life, and this is what has come of it. So much for trying doing the right thing. "I need to find her."

"We will." Mike's voice is calm, focused. "We'll talk to Ben, too. For all we know, she got him to pose with you under the idea that you would think it was funny. Just tell Elliot about Bain and Ben, and our thoughts that Jessica is trying to sabotage you. I think he'll understand. Elliot is a reasonable guy."

I take some comfort in Mike's words. He seems so confident in this moment. Can I really tell Elliot everything? Only a few people know the whole story about Mike, and Bain, and I. Well, if Mike's giving me carte blanche to tell it, I have no choice.

"Okay," is all I have the strength to muster before I stumble numbly back to my room.

Chapter Twenty-Nine
DIESEL

FOUR DAYS LATER and I still feel hung over. I'm exhausted and nauseated and feel so run down that I can't keep a solid thought in my head. I need to talk to Elliot. This stress is killing me.

He came back to Boston last night. I've had minimal text conversations with him. He still won't talk to me or engage in any conversation. I just need to see him. Once I see him, I'll be okay.

I survey the surroundings outside of his office building. I would not have come here but I need to tell him what's going on and he's been so standoffish. Every refusal to see me has been a deeper cut in the wound. Waiting has become physically painful. When he has texted me, it's been like pulling teeth. A slow death would be easier. I just need to tell him, then he'll know about Bain, Mike, and Ben. I hope we can eventually laugh this train wreck away. This is a huge misunderstanding can be fixed, overcome. Everything can go back to the way it was. I hope. I don't think I've ever felt this sick, I'd take the flu over this shit any day.

I walk on shaky legs into the building, praying to all the gods above to give me strength in this moment.

In the main office, I approach a tight-faced receptionist. "Hello, my name is Tess. May I please see Elliot Archer?"

"Do you have an appointment?" she snaps.

Yikes! "I don't, it's more of a lunch date." I try to offer as kindly as possible. *Does Elliot really have appointments?*

"Please take a seat." She rolls her eyes toward the black leather couches.

I can hear her on the phone talking to someone who I assume is Elliot. "Miss, you can go back." She seems to have thawed ever so slightly.

"Thanks." Entering the office, I'm suddenly overwhelmed with butterflies. I haven't seen Elliot in three weeks. I've missed him terribly and the fear that I've lost him completely is overwhelming. I can only hope that explaining everything will help him see what has been going on.

He's in his cubicle, back to the doorway, typing furiously. I stand in the hallway, conscious of people staring at me and whispering about me. I wonder if they recognize me from pictures published in Elliot's blog. I dip my head to try to hide the blush provoked by their stares.

"Hi." It's all I have the power to offer. My feelings for him surge forward, clamping around my chest like a vice as he turns to me. He looks distant, angry, and pained. I have to fight every urge to launch myself at him and pin him against the desk as I ravage his mouth with mine despite the fact that he is so visibly agitated.

"Hello." His response is formal, quipped, and thrown over his shoulder as he turns back to his computer screen.

Oh, this is bad. My initial desire deflates like a popped balloon.

"Can we grab some lunch? So we can talk?" I say quietly.

He snorts and turns to look at me. "You want to talk?" He's bristling with irritation. "You want to talk to me? About what?" His tone is increasingly loud.

"I want to explain what happened with Ben."

"Ben!" he yells. "His name is Ben? How lovely, maybe you can introduce me to all the random guys you fuck while your boyfriend is out of town!" He tone is deafening in the silence of the office.

I breathe in, taking the full brunt of his words. *Random guys you fuck* and *your boyfriend* rattle in my head like a sadistic pinball machine.

He stands up and runs a hand over his face. "You have no idea the hell I've been in. You can't just come in here and explain it all away. I thought we meant something to each other and the minute I leave town you are in bed with someone else. You don't even have the decency to tell me first you want to see other people. You completely flip over Jessica just touching me, and that was before anything got serious. But this shit is what you do the instant I'm gone. This whole situation disgusts me!" He's leaning into me, neck muscles straining under his rage. "I know what I saw and you know what you did."

I'm losing ground fast. "Elliot, please, I can tell you everything. We just need to be more private."

He's pacing the small cubicle. "You really expected me to believe that you and Bain were nothing? And you think I'm going to just talk this out. You've got another thing coming."

I'm vaguely aware that my head is shaking back and forth. "Elliot, please. Talk to me. I know you're angry but this has a convoluted but clear outcome. Just come with me." I do my best to keep the words quiet with the hope he will understand the sincerity in them.

"No. We're done, Diesel. You were a mistake. This whole thing was a mistake. You and that convoluted freak show you have are completely fucked up." He is blazing, completely outside of anything I would have ever thought would emanate from him. "Don't text me. Don't email me. Get out."

He would have done better to punch me in the face. "Elliot, please." Tears bubble up through the emotional wreckage he has just created.

"Get. The. Fuck. Out!"

I close my eyes as I absorb the impact of the words. The shock waves from the detonated bomb wrack my body with deafening force. I nod silently and stare at the floor. I can no longer bear to look at him. I turn to walk out of the office, acutely aware of dozens of eyes on me. I can't control my tears as they stream down my face. I can't look back. I was right. This is done. I was a fool to think I could do this.

As I walk, I feel pieces of the wreckage he created fall from my soul onto the floor. The emptiness leaves a cavernous hole that consumes my entire chest and creeps into my limbs. I move forward to the elevator and press the button. I wait for it to take me away as my pain runs down my face in raging rivulets.

Chapter Thirty

DIESEL

IT'S BEEN THREE weeks of insidious awfulness. I feel nauseous all the time. I have no energy. Leaving the apartment has become an ultimate hassle because it means I have to get dressed, face other human beings, and the August heat.

I've not heard from him. No text. No call. He's had no contact with Mike or Bain. He's not showed up to any of the shows. But then again, neither have I. I've been here, struggling to get out of bed. I think I'm clinically depressed. And I've become addicted to reruns. *Friends*, *Will and Grace*, and the *Golden Girls* all have better lives than me right now.

How did this happen? How did I go from being okay after he obliterated me in public to completely falling apart? I was good. For what, a week, I was really holding my own. But then it crept up on me like a fog. It came over me and hasn't let go since. I can't think straight. Bain yelled at me three times because I forgot menial things. I'm angry in return. He's had his heart stomped on before. He could be a bit more sensitive.

From my bed, I can hear the bolt on the door release after someone swiftly punches in the access code. *Please don't be Bain! Please don't be Mike!* I can't stand another pep talk. I feel like shit. *Let me go until I feel well enough to go live my miserable existence with a purchased skid row feline who will most likely piss on my carpets.*

"Get out of this fucking bed. Now." Holly's tone would rival that of a drill instructor.

I roll over and glare at her. She looks like Wonder Woman in her red tank top and skinny jeans. Here to save me. Fists on her hips, she looks like she would be willing to beat me if I don't comply.

"Holly. I—"

"Do you really think I want to hear what you are about to say?" She holds her hands up. "You look like hell. I'm glad I'm not in that bed with you. Neither one of us would come out alive based on the scum on those sheets. You look like you haven't showered in days. Get up now!"

Oh, boy. She's blazingly mad. At me?

"Fine," I sit up. "I'm up." I look at her with a what-will-you-have-me-do-now gaze.

She jerks a thumb to the bathroom. "In you go. Shave while you're in there, too. You may have lived in Europe but we don't live in France. We de-fur here in the great U. S. of A."

I roll my eyes and wander to the bathroom. I strip down my pajamas and turn the water on, cranking the temperature hotter than I would normally stand. I need to wash away all the grime that has attached to me over the past few weeks. Holly is right. This is bad. I've never felt or been like this before. I push my face under the water, willing it to seep in and wash away the cloud that has invaded my body and soul.

When I have shaved, scrubbed, and soaked every inch, I

towel off and take a moment to look at myself. I am thin. Okay, I've never actually been "thin" but I definitely don't have the athletic stature I did a month ago. I'm pale. I can see the outline of my ribs and my hip bones protrude slightly. I look sick. *You are a hottie.* I sigh before wrapping the towel around me and walking back into the main area of the apartment.

My bed is stripped of the bedding and there is fresh clothing on the mattress.

"Holly?"

"Yes?" She calls from the laundry room.

"Are you dressing me now?" The sarcasm is my tone is evident but I am grateful for her efforts.

"Well," she says, walking out of the laundry room, wiping her hands as if she has just roped a cow, "since you have lost all capabilities to manage yourself, I figure you need some assistance." She looks at me with her head cocked to one side, hands on her hips. "You know those sheets were disgusting."

I nod. "Yeah, they matched me pretty well." My voice is low and sadder than I expected. I can't look at her.

She sucks on her teeth and walks over to me, putting an arm around my shoulder, pressing her head into mine. "Boys make us feel like shit sometimes."

"I feel like I made me feel like shit." I can feel the tears in my throat. "Why is this so awful?"

She pulls back and looks at me, hands wrapped around my arms. "I don't know, Deese." She shakes her head. "It hurts when we open up to someone, and everything falls apart."

The tears begin and I can't stop them. "This is my fault."

"No," she says, pulling me into her as she pets my wet hair, "this is not your fault."

"Then what's the problem with this situation?" My voice is loud with tears and frustration. "It was my actions that got me in this place, wasn't it?

"He didn't listen to you. That's not your fault." She looks at me kindly. The drill instructor is gone. "Besides," she says with a tight smile, "who would want to be with someone if they didn't respect you enough to work though the difficult stuff, right?"

I sniff and swallow under her statement. She's right. Under no circumstances would I put up with this from a man before Elliot came into my life. I work from a foundation of mutual respect and understanding in relationships. If there is a problem, you work it out, not matter how difficult the conversation. I nod my head and wipe the tears from my eyes.

Holly looks at me lovingly and points to the clothing in the bed. "Get dressed. We are going to go out for a bit, okay?"

I nod my head and reach for the underwear she has pulled out for me, grateful they are reliable cotton underwear and nothing that was purchased from Victoria's.

✧　✧　✧

WE WALK IDLY around Central Park with ice cream cones and talk about the Great Takedown that occurred three weeks ago.

"He just screamed at you? In front of everyone?" Her disbelief is so evident, it makes my shame feel justified.

"Yup. In front of his entire office." I pause, debating if I want to say it out loud. "He told me I was a mistake." My words are quiet and hushed. It's the first time I've verbalized exactly what he said to me.

"Fucking dick!" Holly's loud response makes me flush due to our proximity to one of the kids play areas. "What did Bain say? I bet he flipped."

"He doesn't know. No one knows except you," I offer quietly. I can't stop looking at the large rock we are sitting on.

"Why didn't you tell him?"

"I'm not sure. I didn't want him to go after Elliot..." I pause and Holly immediately knows there is more I want to say.

"And?" she prompts.

I look at her from the corner of my eye before refocusing on the rock. "I didn't want him to agree." There it is. I don't want Bain to say *I-told-you-so*. I went out on a limb, slipped and I got my ass handed to me as I hit every branch on the way down to the concrete ground.

Holly is silent for a moment. "I think he'd kick his ass," she finally offers. "He loves you too much to rub salt in your wound."

"I don't want to risk either possibility. The thought of Bain going after him breaks my heart on two accounts. I don't want Bain out of control and I don't want Bain to lose it on Elliot. I also can't risk hearing feedback that rips me to shreds and renders me unable to manage myself for weeks on end. You have to work and I can't expect you to manage my showering and wardrobe full time."

She laughs. "You could hire me to be your personal groomer. Ah, the next celebrity need! A personal groomer to wash and shave your pampered ass." She gestures as if she is selling some crap product on QVC and I have to laugh at her antics.

"As your personal groomer, I do have limits. The week you have your period, I'm totally taking off! I love you, but not that much."

She pushes my shoulder in jest though I feel like I've been hit by a wrecking ball.

My period. It's been, what, three weeks since the last time I saw Elliot? I've not had my period since...when was the last time? At Greggor and Natalie's after I was attacked? How long ago was that? A month and a half? Two months? How did I go two months and not notice these things?

I look at Holly who sees what I can only imagine is horror on my face.

"Diesel?"

"Holly, we have to go."

✧   ✧   ✧

I THOUGHT THE longest twenty minutes of my life was spent getting to Duane Reede, pacing in front of the home pregnancy tests as Holly picked the most idiot-proof model available, then waiting in line to pay for the damn thing. Unfortunately, those twenty minutes were light-years compared to the three minutes it's taken for the little blinking hourglass on the readable screen to register my pee.

I play the game where I close my eyes and will it to read negative but the past fifty times I've opened my eyes, that hourglass is idly blinking away. *Stupid hourglass.*

I pace the bathroom until finally the stick has surrendered my fate.

Holy shit.

I sit on the edge of the tub and pull my hands through my hair. Is this real? Could this be? This can't be real. This is a joke. It's a joke. It has to be a joke. But it's possible. More than possible. We always used something, didn't we? I thought we did. But we did have some moments of impulsivity. The last time at the lake house. We fucked like rabbits that whole weekend.

Oh my god. This is real.

I'm pregnant.

I stand and take the stick that has essentially turned my life on a dime to Holly, who is sitting outside the door.

"Oh my." Holly covers her mouth with both hands. She looks at me with shock and a twinge of panic. "What are you going to do?"

I sigh. "I have no idea."

✧   ✧   ✧

"GET RID OF it."

I stare at Bain in horror and quickly gape at Mike, who is equally as shocked. "What?"

"You heard me. Call the doctor tomorrow and get rid of it." He is so cold, I can't register where he's coming from.

"Bain, I don't know if that's the best answer right now." I try to be calm but his suggestion is offensive.

"Look, Diesel, this is an accident. Your job is at a dance club. People look to you to be present and accounted for. You can't do that with a kid! Are you kidding? Does Elliot know? I'm assuming it's Elliot's, right?"

"Are you really asking me if this baby is Elliot's?" My

anger surfaces, which is so much easier to handle then the embarrassment and shame of five minutes ago. "And you have no business suggesting how I should be managing this situation."

"She's right, Bain." Mike quickly jumps in and I am happy he's defending me. "She's an adult. She can make whatever decision she wants."

Bain looks at Mike as if he's presented the biggest of betrayals. "Are you serious about this? Do you know what a child entails?" He looks from Mike to me and turns his back to both of us. "This means your life completely changes, Diesel. Everything you have here will no longer be."

"Bain, I need your help and your support in this. Can't we talk about some way to work this out?"

"What do you want to work out?" He is bristling with anger. "You are knocked up by some guy who won't give you or any of us the time of day and you want to *work it out?* Tell me what there is to work out!"

I can't look at him because I know on one level, he's right. What am I going to do? Have the baby of a man who thinks I'm a whore and proceed with my life as it was? Go through nine months a walking walrus to have my baby go to the hands of someone else? Get an abortion? I can't even fathom going through that procedure. Option number three is crossed off the list.

"I'll go to the doctor and see what they say. Okay?" I offer quietly.

Bain looks at me with brooding anger, turns abruptly and stomps out of the room, slamming the door as he exits.

I look at Mike, who shrugs in exasperation. "I'm sorry,

Diesel."

I nod in appreciation for his kindness. I walk the same path Bain had just taken in his hasty exit and I can feel his anger still hanging in the air.

✧   ✧   ✧

THREE DAYS LATER, I return from the doctor's office with numerous pamphlets, a script for prenatal vitamins, and one ultrasound of my baby. *My baby.* I've decided, after numerous hours leading up to this appointment, that I want to keep the baby. I have enough money to take care of a baby. I can still manage Eden without engaging in the actual shows.

I walk to Bain and Mike's apartment and knock on the door. Mike opens up and ushers me inside. I sneak him a peek at the ultrasound and he visibly melts. Over the past few days, Mike and I have bonded over our latest addition. He's excited and quietly told me he's always wanted kids. I feel bad knowing he is at odds with Bain. I'm not sure how much they've talked about it but they are clearly on opposite sides of the fence.

"Well?" Bain's arms are crossed as he looks at us huddled in the doorway. "What are you doing?"

I inhale a stabilizing breath. "I'm keeping the baby, Bain." I stand as tall as I possibly can.

"You're fucking crazy," he spits, and turns on his heel. "Whatever. Do what you want," he yells over his shoulder, waving his hands in resignation.

His dismissal hurts and quickly evolves into fully blown anger. *For all the shit we've gone through with you, you can't be the slightest bit supportive of me in this moment.* Against better judgment, I storm down the hall after him.

Mike is on my heels, offering various pleas. "Diesel, let him go. Don't do this. Now is not the time."

I find him in the living room drinking a beer, flopped on the couch like a frat boy awaiting the next round of online gaming to begin.

On the way here, I planned to have a calm, rational conversation with him. That plan just flew out the window. "What the fuck is your issue?"

He laughs sarcastically. "What's my issue? What the fuck is *your* issue?" He stands and moves directly in front of me. "We had a deal, Diesel. We would run this place and live our lives here and now you want to undermine all of that with a baby?"

"I'm undermining what we have because I want to have a baby? I can still do my job, Bain. I don't need to be present at the shows." I can't help the forcefulness of my tone. *What is his issue?*

He runs his hands over his face and through his hair as he paces in front of me. "You should have known better. I can't believe you would have been this stupid."

His words hit me like a train. "I'm stupid because I accidently got pregnant? Because I decided to go out on a limb and enjoy my life for a few months?"

"Pretty much." He looks at me as if he could pass me dead on the street and not care who I was. I suck in a breath. He raises his eyebrows with his hands held out in a silent *what-the-fuck-did-you-expect.*

That's it! I've had more than enough of the men I love shitting all over me. The gig is up and this bitch is pissed.

"Well, if that's the case, then I guess I am." I hear Mike gasp behind me. "I'm a fucking idiot really, if you think about it. I left my life in England for your brother, for you, really, because you couldn't get your shit together. Because you got your ass handed to you because you couldn't deal with everything you had going on and it almost killed you. I supported all your ventures and goals and experimentations and journeys without question. You did whatever you wanted, took whatever you wanted, and fucked whoever you wanted. I allowed you to push limits and try new things and to take the reins with the club. And despite all of that, loving you, caring for you, and helping you through some really dark times, I'm an idiot for having a baby? Yes, Bain, I'm an idiot, not for wanting this baby, but for thinking that you and I actually had a relationship where tough things could happen and we would support each other." Before he can respond, I walk to the door. "I can manage my responsibilities remotely, which is what I will do. You are in charge of what you've always done. I'll deal with this on my own." I slam the door behind me for emphasis.

Climbing the stairs to my apartment, I know our anger is displaced, thrown at each other for lack of better receptacles. Regardless, I can't be here. I pick up my phone and call Holly to update her. She is ready to come over and deliver a series of assaults on Bain. I tell her my impromptu plan and she agrees begrudgingly. We hang up and I call the only family I really have any more to break the news.

Three hours later, I am sitting on Natalie and Greggor's couch with my hands in my lap and my head bowed with shame and resignation. Natalie moves next to me and puts her arm around my shoulders. I lean into her and she kisses my head. I melt into unrestrained tears.

"Shhhh," she offers quietly. "We'll work this out." She rocks me gently as if willing the deluge to leave my body.

"Yes, my darling," Greggor says as he rubs a hand up and down my back, "we'll get this figured out."

Through my gasping sobs, I hear him rise from the couch and pick up the phone to begin making plans.

Chapter Thirty-One
ELLIOT

"**W**HAT DO YOU mean she's gone?" I can't help the irritation in my tone. *She's gone?*

"Yeah, man. No one knows where she is. Everyone is really tight-lipped about it." Sam looks at me dispassionately. Since my total meltdown a couple weeks ago, I decided I can't continue the story on Eden. I talked to my boss about transitioning the final piece to Sam. He's reliable and a good writer. He's been to the shows before and can relate on a participant level.

"Well, how are Mike and Bain?" The guilt stabs my gut. Those guys were really good to me and I never went back. They had no warning that Sam was coming in until he showed up this week.

"Okay, I guess. They aren't really offering too much." Sam shrugs and starts to walk away. "I'll just wrap it up and we'll move on to something else."

"Yeah," I say half-heartedly, "move on to something else."

I look back at my desk, suddenly unmotivated to do anything. Without knowing why, I grab my phone. I just have to know.

The profile pic on Eden's site is its signature single word:

Chapter Thirty-Two
DIESEL
OCTOBER

Hi...

WHAT THE HELL IS THIS?

Hello
How are you
I'm fine. You?
Okay, I guess...

Are we looking to win a prize here for most engaging conversation?

What's up?
I want to talk to you

You've already said everything you need to say. There is nothing else I need to hear from you.

What do you want to talk about?
Us

Are you kidding?

What about us?
*I don't know how to fix this. I don't know how else to say I'm

sorry. I miss you.

I don't know that this can be fixed.

I've told you I've accepted your apology and you've explained yourself very clearly. I don't know what else there is to do or say. I'm not going to lie. I miss you too, but things are different now. I've told you that.
I'm dying here. Please, Tess.

How dare you, you son of a bitch!

That's a low blow and you know it.
I don't know what else to do. Please come home.

The tears stab at my eyes as I swallow past the dry lump in my throat. Bain's pleas are enough to gut me. I don't want to miss him, but I do. I want to stop being angry with him, but I can't. We had years of love and trust. Everything was obliterated in single moment. *I'm sorry I'm a bitch right now, but I don't know what else to do.* I punch out the text message, dropping the phone on my bed as soon as I hit send. Before I'm even sure it successfully sent, I'm out of the room.

I am home.

Chapter Thirty-Three
DECEMBER

Eden's Profile Picture:

Chapter Thirty-Four
DIESEL
MARCH

THE PAIN IS overwhelming.

I think of you and want nothing more. Nothing less.

Only you.

I can't touch you. I can't reach you.

I am alone.

The crushing weight of this vice around me steals my motivation, my breath, my being.

I need you to breathe with me. Calm me.

Please.

The pain threatens to drown me again and again in this moment, in this darkness, but I must stay focused.

Focus.

On you. Only you.

I miss you.

I need you.

I love you.

After inhaling a lifesaving breath, I exhale my quiet plea.

"Elliot..."

Chapter Thirty-Five
ELLIOT
JUNE

THE PING FROM a text message pulls me from furious typing.

Hey

Riley's text messages are always a pull on the senses.

What's up?
Just wanted you to check something out
Oh, yeah? What's that?
Look who we just saw.

A picture, fuzzy from the lighting, accompanies the text.

Oh my God. Diesel's profile, smiling at something across a room, lights up the screen of my phone. *Where is she? A restaurant?*

Did she recognize you?
I think so, she came to take our drinks, and then some guy took our order. She's not been over since.
Where are you guys?
Back home.

She's in England? Back in London? My mind is reeling.

To say I haven't thought of her would be a complete lie. I went from being totally pissed to missing her to being overwhelmed with guilt for my behavior. Why is she back in England? She always said she wanted to go back, but the club and Bain kept her here.

Dude, she just got off work and our waiter asked her about picking up her kid

The text hits me like a ton of bricks. A kid? She has a kid? *What the hell?* Is she with someone? Another text from Riley shakes me from my racing thoughts.

Blane just asked our waiter how old her kid is and he says it's three months old. How long ago were you with her?

What? Three months old. So, what was nine months prior to that?

It was when I was at Eden. Yeah, we were together then. *Really* together. But she was also with that guy when I went back home. But she said she wasn't...but I saw the picture...he was in her bed.

I begin pacing my apartment. *No way. This is not real.*

My phone pings again. It's a picture of Diesel holding a little boy with reddish brown hair back in the restaurant. She looks so natural and at ease with him in her arms. I can immediately tell that the baby is not Ben's because he shares the same pale complexion as his mother....and me?

What's happening?

It's the only thing I can text Riley. I don't know what else to do. The panic is worse and I am at a total loss for what to do.

*She forgot something here and ran in to get it. Our waiter took
the kid while she got what she needed. The kid's name is Eli.*

My heart is pounding and all manner of irrational thoughts are coursing through my brain. She was pregnant and she didn't tell me. Is the kid named after me? What if this is just a sick coincidence? This has to be a mistake.

Then it hits me.

You were a mistake, Diesel.

"Oh my God."

I grab my coat and run out to my bike.

TWO HOURS LATER, I am pounding on the door of Eden. It's a Tuesday, there may be people here, but all the doors are locked. No answer. I pound the heavy metal door with both fists. I need to get their attention and I need to do something with these emotions. Bain and Mike have to know what happened, right?

Eventually, the door creeps open and Mike sticks his head out. He immediately registers shock at the sight of me in the doorway. My breath is ragged with adrenaline.

"Elliot," he offers flatly, "how can I help you?"

"Where is she?" I spit.

He looks over his shoulder to ensure we are alone before shaking his head. "Not here, dude."

"She's in England. I know that much, okay? For how long?"

He raises his eyebrows in guarded shock. His face is impassive and I want to punch him, full force.

"She's been there for about a year now." He looks down

and shifts his weight. "Why are you asking me questions you already have answers to?"

"Why did she leave?" I can't respond to him. I don't know why I'm asking what I'm asking. I just need some answers.

"She was heartbroken and felt she couldn't be here anymore." His simple response masks the complexity of the situation.

I feel my throat close. "Was it me?"

"You. And Bain." His tone is suddenly cold. "How two of the men she cares for most in this world can shit the bed within a month of each other, I'll never know, but it happened."

"Is it mine?"

"Is what yours?"

"The ba—"

"What the fuck are you doing here?" Bain's voice booms from inside the building. Mike looks over his shoulder at Bain but does not move from in front of me. I figure now is not the time for being guarded. "I got a text from my friends back home that she is working is a restaurant in Essex and she has a kid."

Both of them stop and stare at me then look at each other. "So...you didn't know?" Bain asks.

"Obviously! I just got this text and left Boston two hours ago to come here and pound on your fucking door and try to get some answers!"

"What did she tell you?" Mike questions, his eyes squinted in confusion.

"Nothing! I know absolutely nothing!" My anger has reached an all-time high as spittle flies from my mouth.

Mike glances at Bain and then pushes the door open, offering me entrance to the empty club. They watch me walk in as if I'm a freak of nature for this level of anger. I pull my hands through my hair trying to gain control.

"When she came to see you at your office, she didn't tell you anything?" The questioning nature of Bain's tone shocks me.

"No," I say, pacing in front of the two of them, "but I didn't really give her the opportunity to say anything. I really flipped on her. I was blazingly mad about the whole situation with Ben."

"Whoa, wait. What 'situation with Ben' are you talking about?" Mike asks.

"I got this text message. They were in bed together, and clearly they had slept together."

Bain and Mike look at each other, amused. Bain stifles a laugh and looks at me as if I am crazy. "You think Diesel and Ben slept together?"

"Didn't you see the picture?" My anger flares with indignation. *Why are they laughing?*

"We saw the picture. I can assure you, Diesel did not sleep with Ben. She was sleeping next to him, but they didn't *sleep* together."

"And exactly how are you so sure of that fact?" I spit.

Bain inhales. "Because Ben used to sleep with me." He makes the statement in such a flat tone that it takes a moment to register. "And I will clarify that by saying Ben and I used to have sex together and we used to sleep next to each other."

I can't stop the gobsmacked gape from taking over my face. "You used to sleep with Ben? You're gay?"

"Uh huh." He stands in front of me with his hands in his pockets.

I shift to Mike, who is smiling in wry amusement. "Yeah, me too."

"Ben and Diesel were really close when he and I were together. They do get along fabulously. The night he was here, Jessica was nosing around. Mike and I do our best to be discreet about our relationship, so Ben went up to Diesel's room. Eventually we found out it was Jessica that sent you the text. She'd been messing around with Cass before Diesel was attacked. Between you choosing Diesel over her and Cass being in jail because of Diesel, she had an ax to grind. Needless to say, she's exiled from Eden for life."

I think back on the day Diesel came to my office. *Elliot, please, I can tell you everything. We just need to be more private.*

Bain and Mike continue to watch me without saying a word. "She was really upset about the picture and didn't know what to do. We told her to tell you about everything. The situation between Mike and me, my history with Ben...everything. We hoped that you would understand about, you know, us." Bain gestures with his shoulder to Mike.

"I kept asking Diesel if you two were together and she would get so mad at me."

"I assure you that Diesel and I have never and will never be together. People assume we are because we spend so much time together, but no, we've never been together romantically. She was married to my brother, Elliot! That's just wrong on so many levels." Bain is light as if a weight has been lifted off his shoulders.

"So, you're not out?" I ask.

"Well," Bain shrugs, "to a point. We try to keep low key. Many people think Diesel and I are together and though it's not right, we don't make any real attempt to correct them. It's more on Diesel's part than my own."

"I don't understand." This is weird. I know his vague responses are meant to keep me at bay.

"Um..." He rubs his hands across the back of his neck and exhales.

"Just tell him, Bain," Mike interjects. "Compared to the damage that's been done already, I don't think it's going to make matters worse."

Bain exchanges a look with Mike, processing the clearance. "Okay." He shrugs before turning to me. "I'm sure Diesel told you that I was wild when I was young. I drank and did a lot of cocaine. When I started exploring sex, I got into some trouble. I was in a bad situation and got really beat up one night, so badly that I was hospitalized in critical condition."

"Holy shit, Bain."

"My parents didn't want anything to do with the fact that I might be gay, so when the police tagged the incident as a hate crime, they went ballistic. Diesel and Jamie were in England at the time. They came home to help me with rehab and iron out what happened and who I was, or rather, am."

The impact of the information is too much. His presentation of this is so calm, it's unreal.

"So, she left England because you were almost killed in a hate crime?"

"Yes." Bain rocks back on his heels, hands still shoved back in his pockets. "She is as loyal as they come, Elliot.

When Jamie died and my family went after her, I knew I had to have her back like she had mine. She wouldn't let my mother and father disrespect me and I couldn't let them do that to her. When they wrote both of us off, it bonded us. I think she is always scared that it will happen again, that I'd be hurt or abused in some way. She would do anything for me, including masquerade as my possible lover to ward off any homophobic assholes."

"But she *did* leave. Why?"

Bain rubs his neck again. His sad sigh expresses more emotion than I was expecting. "Yeah. She ran for the border after she found out she was pregnant. I'll be honest, I was a total dick to her and that really pushed her over the edge. Mike was, as always, the rational one. I blew my stack at her and she was gone. It took me a good six months to get back on her good graces."

Tess is gone. Bain and Mike are together. Bain and Tess weren't talking. She ran because of us. I vowed to protect her after Cass yet I wouldn't hear her explanation. The past ten minutes have been a ride on a sick Tilt-A-Whirl. Everything has shifted, changed. The need to know crashes over me.

"Is it mine?"

"Yeah, dude. Eli is yours." Bain offers.

My head reels from the impact of his words. I can't believe this. I have a son. Diesel is in England with our son. And no one told me anything?

"Why didn't anyone tell me?" I ask softly.

"She wouldn't let us." Bain offers. "We tried, Elliot. She was steadfast in not contacting you. She said you made yourself very clear about maintaining boundaries the last time you talked. She respects boundaries. To be honest, she's only really started talking to me again in the past four months and that was after serious groveling and apologizing on my part."

My mind reels with the destruction I've caused. *We're done, Diesel. You were a mistake. This whole thing was a mistake. Don't text me. Don't email me. Get out!*

I did this. I pushed her away. She fled because I couldn't listen to her when she asked me to.

"So she's really not contacted you at all?" Mike asks, snapping me from my horrid memories.

"No. I've not heard word one from her," I reply. Mike and Bain collectively sigh.

"I don't know what to tell you. She made her decision and she's sticking to it. She's really not talked about coming back at all. We haven't even seen the baby yet. She won't come home with him. We leave in a week to see her." Bain's voices trails off, as if he knows he should not be tell me what he's telling me.

"Do you have a picture of him?"

They both stare at me for a moment. Mike moves first, fishing his phone out of his pocket. He presses the button and his screensaver is a chubby-faced baby with blue eyes and reddish brown hair. I can see my nose and Diesel's smile. A ball of emotion chokes me. I ache for this child I didn't even know existed until three hours ago.

I feel the harsh sting of tears behind my eyes. I can't control the waiver in my voice. "Please tell me where she is."

"I can't do that, bro," Bain says quietly. "If she wanted you to know, she would contact you."

I buckle under the weight of his statement. Leaning over, I put my hands on my knees to catch my breath. After all this, they won't tell me. I didn't know. It's not fair. I deserve to know!

"She's back in Essex and working at Barney's." Mike's tone is clear and direct. I snap my head up at his impromptu disclosure.

"Seriously, Mike? What the fuck!" Bain bellows.

"Look," he offers, "it's bad enough she is gone. Now she's gone with our nephew, too. On top of that, Elliot doesn't get any opportunity to see his son or Diesel when we know full well where they are." Mike raises his hands to Bain. "This whole situation is completely fucked up. Why would he come here if he didn't care? Maybe if they can reconcile something, she'll come back and we'll have some level of normalcy restored to our lives." He looks at me and sighs. "It really sucks without her here."

Bain nods in agreement. "All right, I get all that, but when she finds out, you're taking the blame for telling him. I don't want to get back on her shit list."

"Fine. It's me who told Elliot." His eyes dart from Bain to me with determined eyes. "I told you. Now do something about it."

I look at both of them. "When do you guys leave to visit her?"

"Saturday. We'll be there for two weeks. Greggor and Natalie are there for the month so we are staying with them," Mike offers.

"Can you guys send me your numbers so when we are there we can connect? I deleted all the Eden contacts from my phone when I transferred the story." I'm embarrassed at my admission and my attempt to forget everything that was here.

"You are lucky we are a forgiving group, Elliot." Bain looks at me as he slyly pulls out his phone and calls me.

Chapter Thirty-Six
DIESEL

I BUSY MYSELF with wiping down the bar for the last forty-five minutes of my shift. It's been a steady day and I've had the pleasure of working with Quin all day long. He's a joy on so many levels. He is jovial with patrons, makes me feel like I walk on water, and is a hard worker. I'm glad his band is doing the Essex and London circuit for the next month. Greggor and Natalie are here for his tour about town. I've been so happy to have my family with me.

I'm also excited and nervous for Bain and Mike to come. I can't wait for Eli to meet his uncles. They have been so cute with him over Skype. When they call, I put them on speaker-phone and Eli rolls his head toward the phone. I'm completely convinced he recognizes their voices. I'm happy to be able to continue my work for Eden, and that the guys seem to be getting along with me here. I have fallen in love with being a mom. It seems very natural and I have been blessed with a wonderful, happy, healthy baby boy.

A well-dressed man who saunters up to the bar in front of me snaps me from my reverie.

"Hello, sir. What can I get for you this lovely day?" I say as I slide a coaster in front of him.

"Well, Diesel, I'd like a Stella." His tone is even and calm as he looks at me.

I look at him with shock and dismay. *How does this guy know my name from the club?*

"I'm sorry." I smile at him. "You'll have to refresh my memory, I don't seem to remember you. Let me get you your beer." I turn to the tap, fill the glass, and set it down with an efficiency that I'm hoping will scream *stop talking to me,* but he continues.

"Of course you don't remember me, dear, but I know who you are." He winks at me over the rim of his glass. "You dated my son for a while, didn't you?"

"Sorry. I haven't dated anyone in a very long time." I push my rag across the worn wood in front of him before starting a hasty retreat into the kitchen.

"Diesel, or Tess, is it?" he questions. I stop in my tracks.

"How do you know my name, sir?" I try to purr the words but this guy is freaking me out.

"Elliot told me I'd find you here." He says it simply but the words hit me with a force unlike any other.

"How do you know Elliot?"

"Elliot and I are close. It's good for fathers to be close to their sons."

"You're Elliot's father?" Anxiety creeps across my stomach and up into my chest.

"The one and only. You can call me Charlie," he says calmly. "You have my grandson."

I stare at him, willing my emotions to stay hidden. My heart pounds loudly in my ears and there is a slight tremor in my hands. *This can't be real. This can't have happened. Fuck! I knew that was Riley the other day. He must have called Elliot. Shit!*

"I don't know what you're talking about." The waiver in my voice makes my attempt to be blasé laughable.

"Tess, don't play with me."

His words level me. The tone is calm, controlled, and serene but the words are a jackhammer. My name being said by someone other than Elliot is a jarring force that has me curling my fingers around the edge of the bar for support.

"I'm not here to fight with you. I just want to see him."

"Why?"

"He's my grandson. I'm selfish when it comes to my grandchildren."

"Does he know you're here?"

"No."

"Does he know I'm here?"

"Yes."

"But, he's not here?"

"Not yet."

My throat closes as tears threaten to spill forward. "Excuse me." I choke before stiffly walking into the back.

Through the door, I run directly into Quin. "Whoa," he says, gripping my upper arms. "What's going on?"

I try my best to hold it together and avoid eye contact, knowing the tears are seconds away. I resort to dropping my chin to my chest before croaking, "Elliot's dad is out there." I inhale a shuttering breath. "He wants to see Eli. He told me Elliot knows I'm here and about Eli."

"Fuck." Quin has never been good at talking it out. "Want me to kick his ass out?" Talking he can't do, but defend me, always.

I shake my head, sniffing and blinking back tears. "Not yet. I need a minute."

"You got it." Quin squares his shoulder before stalking out of the kitchen into the bar.

I hustle through the kitchen, offering a polite wave to Gerald, our cook, before diving into the walk in freezer. Pulling the door shut, I sink down onto a crate of chicken fingers.

You're a chicken all right.

The whirl of emotions is enough to choke me. *He's not here. Yet? But he's coming. He knows.* How *does he know?*

Son of a bitch! I rip my cell from my pocket, hoping I get service in the freezer.

Elliot knows about Eli. How?

Bain's reply is immediate.

Ask Mike

What?

A minute later, Mike texts me a novella outlining Elliot's illustrious return to Eden.

The chill of the freezer does nothing to cool me. My skin ripples with gooseflesh but my insides churn with molten emotion. The threatening tears breech their holding when I read that Elliot was borderline meltdown when he confronted them at Eden. Mike's follow up text breaks the levees.

I know you are upset. I promise, this will work out.

The two sentences Mike has chanted to me since I left Eden have been the hope I have hung on to, the balm to my broken heart. Amidst all the conflict with Bain, Mike has remained the steady force for both of us. At first, I thought his promise was pure shit, but, at every turn, Mike was right. Sniffing in a most unladylike manner, I wipe my face with my sleeve.

I'm still mad.
I know. You are allowed to be.
Did you let him see a picture of Eli?
Yes.
Why?
It was the right thing to do.

My gut clenches, the guilt overriding the anger and hurt and fear. I did this. I created this shit storm and it's finally come barreling down on me.

Okay...
Do it your way but he deserves to see him. Elliot was torn up when he was here.

He should be. I was torn up, too. Wiping icy tears from my face, I bolster myself to walk out of the freezer.

I'll see you guys soon.
We love you.

I swallow past the lump in my throat as I walk out into the bar. Quin is hovering a little too close to Charlie, eyeing him like a lion that has zeroed in on a limping gazelle.

I give Quin *the eye*, forcing him to back off so I can stand in front of Charlie.

"Well, Tess, I'm surprised. I thought you might have skipped town on me, too."

I glare at his dig with narrowed eyes.

"When is he scheduled to come back?"

Charlie shrugs as he finishes his beer. He sighs loudly before saying, "Don't know."

If that's not a bold-faced lie, I don't know what is.

"Look, Tess, I'm not here to cause a scene or fight with you. Elliot told me what happened and how he shit all over you. Incidentally, he feels like a real fuck-up about it. I just want to pay you a visit and ask to see my grandson." He's so calm and seems so kind. I can see where Elliot gets it.

"I don't know." It's all I can manage to stammer out.

"I'm sure it's a shock to you that I'm here. But when he told me what happened and where you were, I had to make the attempt to see you."

I lean on the bar in front of him, looking at him, trying to assess what he really wants out of this. He puts the beer down, folding his hands passively, looking at me with kindness and the slightest hint of mischief. I turn my head to look out the window, hoping some epiphany will come to me from the street. Nothing. *Damn.*

"Like I said, I don't want trouble." His voice snaps me from my thoughts. "I would just like to see him." He takes a pull from his beer and peers over the rim of the glass with raised eyebrows.

"How long are you going to be here?" I ask him quietly.

"As long as it takes," he replies.

I inhale deeply. *I can't believe I'm doing this.* "You don't take him anywhere. You see him with me present." I need to set the limits of this interaction.

"I understand."

I look at the clock. It's three thirty-five. "I pick him up at four. I'll bring him back here and you can see him then."

"Brilliant." He holds his glass up in cheers and takes a drink.

As I take off my apron and hand it to Quin, I thrust my chin in Charlie's direction. "Please attend to him while I am gone." Quin looks at me with quiet shock. "I'll be back shortly."

"You got it," he grunts, glaring at Elliot's father.

Without any more contemplation, I leave the bar to pick up my son.

✧   ✧   ✧

THE NEXT DAY I am back at the bar, happily running the lunchtime rush with Quin. We are busy and I'm pleased to say the day is dwindling away. It's one day closer to Bain and Mike's visit. They are all prepped to stay with Greggor and Natalie in their house, since I have little space as well as a baby who still won't sleep through the night.

I was pleased with the interaction between Charlie and Eli. He was so kind with my son. He never admonished me or said anything negative about whatever he knows about Elliot and me. We exchanged phone numbers. He agreed all too easily to keep the visit a secret from Elliot. Unfortunately, the happy feelings I have when I think about their interaction are short-lived, cut off by the repetitive circle of words in my head.

"He's not here?"

"Not yet."

Since Charlie's visit, I've been thinking about Elliot constantly. Who am I kidding? I'm reminded of him every day when I look at Eli. He's a carbon copy of his father, with the exception of my mouth. He knows I'm back in Essex. The thought unnerves me. What if he comes to see me? What do I do? I can't really hide anymore. I would have thought if he knew about Eli he would have made some effort to contact me. He's the one who told me to fuck off. I certainly was not going to walk back into that lion's den again. It took me long enough to pull myself out last time.

I do miss him, though. It seems like so long ago that he was in my life but if I think too much about him, it burns with the same intensity. So much left undone. I still can't fathom that he wouldn't at least talk to me. No closure, no nothing. Not that I would ever really put up with any of that to begin with. I never would consider staying with someone who would verbally castigate me like that without hearing both sides of the story. If you disagree on the points made, that's one thing. But to reign supreme over both parties and not engage in an open discussion, that's oppressive. I don't do oppressive.

"Hey, Diesel!" Quin snaps me back into Barney's. "Can you take some time to do the inventory since you'll be gone for a couple days?" He smiles as he punts his least favorite responsibility to me.

I laugh. I love this man so much. He's still so much a twelve-year-old to me. "Of course I'll do it." I walk toward him. "I don't want you to mess it up and have Richard riding you because we ran out of cheese."

"Yeah, Dick on my ass was never something I was fond of." He says slyly.

I laugh and slap him on the arm. He swats me with the towel he had hanging on his shoulder. "You, on the other hand, might really enjoy that. And I'd be just the man to help you."

"Easy, Quin. I'll nail you for sexual harassment," I admonish.

"You can nail me, all right! Ohhh!" He howls and rolls his hips. The few old regulars at the bar howl and pound the bar.

I roll my eyes and head to the kitchen to finish my final tasks before leaving.

✧　✧　✧

"DIESEL, LOVE?" RICHARD finds me in the back office, ordering the last of the supplies. "Why are you still here?"

"I'm just leaving," I say as I review the final counts and hit enter with more flourish than necessary.

"Ah, very good. Thanks for doing that for Quin. He's my nephew but he can be a real fuck-up sometimes."

"Yes, he can be," I say solemnly. "I blame the genetics."

Richard laughs as he puts an arm around me and squeezes me. "Okay, girl, get out of here. I don't want to see your face for two weeks. Have fun and enjoy yourself."

"Will do, but I want to bring Mike and Bain here. I want them to see where all the magic happens."

"Of course, darling. I'll be glad to see you when you do." He looks at me fondly and I am overwhelmed at his affection for me. "Now go. Get out of here." He pushes me toward the front of the bar.

I punch my time card and grab my bag. Natalie has picked Eli up so I have some freedom with getting home and running some last-minute errands.

I step out into the cool evening and inhale the smell of the town. Even though my job is not stressful in the conventional sense, it's busy and it's nice to know I won't have to tend to thirsty men for several days. I head down the street, focused on jumping into my favorite bookstore for a little decompression before heading home. *Yes, browse through some books with a tea and just let the day melt away.*

The town is quiet with reserved *hellos* and tipped hats as I walk down the street. I am distracted by the sound of scuffling behind me. *"Excuse me!"* I hear a woman exclaim. *"Watch yourself!"* a kid yells. I look over my shoulder briefly to gain some idea of who or what is happening. No one is really close to me but I make the quick move to cut across the street. *Better safe than sorry.* I duck into The Book Rack and leave the day's tension at the door.

Thirty-five minutes later, I've purchased my tea, a book for myself, a map of London for the guys, and a book for Eli. It was a childhood favorite of mine. I've been resigned to establish my child a library at a very young age. Pleased with my purchases, I head out the door into the early dusk of evening.

I look down the street and try to assess the quickest way to get back. I'm still learning all the side streets and don't want to take anything too off the mark since it is getting dark. This is a safe town, but I am alone.

"Tess?"

I am snapped from my mental mapmaking, frozen in place. I recognize his voice instantly. I close my eyes and will my heart to stop pounding. My scalp prickles and I inhale slowly in an effort to steady my breath.

He's standing on the sidewalk. I look down at him from

my place on the stoop of the bookstore. Elevated above him, I feel minimally powerful. *If I'm bigger than you, you can't hurt me.*

He breaks our eye contact and looks to his feet as he shifts his weight. "Tess," he says uncomfortably. "Say something." He looks to me again, imploring my response.

I cross my arms over my chest. "Hello, Elliot." My tone is cold, despondent. It shocks me that I could sound so harsh to this man but on a different level, I couldn't be more pleased with myself.

He sags slightly. "Can we talk?"

"What do you want to say?" I don't move from my spot on the stoop.

"Not here, Tess, please." He is calm but emotional. He holds a hand out as if to encourage me to step down.

He runs his hand down his face, squeezing his eyes into his palms. "Tess, I want to see to you. Please, can we talk about what happened?"

"I think you made yourself completely clear already." My hurt bubbles up as if released from a blocked sewer pipe. "I was a 'mistake,' if I remember correctly. Why, after all this time, do you want to talk about a mistake? I certainly don't!"

I quickly step down and move past him, toward my apartment. He makes a move to touch me, but I am able to avoid the contact by edging farther out. I glare at him with disbelief that he would make such an attempt. He holds his hands up for a brief moment as I continue toward home, acutely aware he is on my heels.

"I know about Mike and Bain," he says quietly.

What? I stop in my tracks and he literally runs into me, pushing me forward slightly.

I look at him while we right ourselves from our brief collision. "Tell me, exactly, what it is that you know about them?" My eyes narrow at him. I'm not letting him have anything, he has to give me all the goods in this exchange.

He looks around uncomfortably and puts his hands in his pockets. "I know they are together. That's they've been together for years. I know that you and Jamie left here because Bain was almost killed in a hate crime. They told me about Ben, also." His eyes are locked to the ground until they come up to meet mine as he finishes.

My heart is pounding and I feel the emotion creeping up into my chest. The notion that someone knows about Mike and Bain scares me. I know we live in a different world now but the horrors of Bain's assault still flash vivid in my mind.

"When did you find out?"

"Three days ago."

"Well, now you know. I expect you to be discreet about your newfound knowledge. Mike and Bain deserve their privacy."

I turn and begin walking down the street. I don't hear him behind me and it crushes me. For as angry as I am, I want, no, I need him to fight for me.

"Is he mine?" I barely hear him but the question sparks a fire I can't contain.

I turn and stare at him. "Is he yours?" Rage flares though my entire body. "Is he yours!" I yell and take two powerful steps toward him, our chests nearly touching. "You tell me you know about Ben and you have the audacity to ask me if he's yours!"

He says nothing in response. His eyes search my face with some unnamed emotion "Have you seen him?" I ask as calmly as I can.

He says nothing.

"Have you seen a picture of him!" I demand.

"Yes."

I can't believe this.

"So you're telling me that you've talked to Mike and Bain, seen a picture of Eli, came all this way and you still have to question if he's yours?" I can't contain myself. The anger from a year ago resurfaces like hot lava. "He looks exactly like you Elliot! I wake up to a mini Elliot every fucking day!" I put my hand on my head and pivot in place. "Of course he's yours! Despite whatever you think of me, I'm not a whore." I pace back and forth in front of him. "Why the fuck are you here, Elliot? What do you want?"

He pauses for a long time. Longer than I would like. I wait impatiently with my hand on my hip, seething with anger. If we weren't in public, I might not have to fight the sudden inclination to introduce my knee to his crotch.

"I want to see him," he finally says.

I scoff. "Why? Why do you want to see him?"

"Because...he's my son." He chokes on his words and I know he is on the verge of tears. The sound of his voice rips a vicious tear from my throat to my stomach. "Tess, I didn't know any of this. I'm so sorry."

I close my eyes to brace myself against the anger, longing, and confusion coursing through my body. I hate him for being here, for hurting me, for casting me aside for nothing. *He's my son.* The sound resonates in my heart. All the pain is consumed by his apology and my desire for him to be in my life again.

Tess.... My name spoken in his voice is the panacea to my bruised and war-torn heart.

"Please, Tess, can I see him?"

"I have to think about it," I squeak the words out and can see his wounded look. Tears threaten to break free and I quickly look down. "This is a lot and I need to think about some things first." He flattens his mouth into a thin line and nods in understanding. "How long are you here for?"

"Couple weeks. I'm staying with my father," he offers, choking back his emotion.

Seeing him so broken causes my throat to close. I don't want to hurt him. I just don't think he should be saddled with responsibilities he didn't ask for. I ache for nothing more than to hold him and tell him this will all be okay...

He pushes his hand roughly over his face before looking at me with bloodshot eyes. "I'll do anything, Tess. Anything you want me to."

I believe him. He is genuine and clearly stands before me a raw man.

"Give me a little bit of time and I'll be in touch with you." I offer. "I have to get going."

"Right. Do you want me to walk you to your place?"

"No, Elliot, that's not a good idea." I say it with little conviction. I know if walked me to my apartment, he'd come up and this would continue for God knows how long.

He shakes his head. "I'll hear from you, then?"

"Yes. I'll text you."

"Thank you, Tess."

I shake my head and turn to start my walk home. My chest stirs and the tears that were held back so strongly a few moments ago are now too heavy to contain. They stream down my face with a force that soaks my hands and my shirt. I rush into my apartment, nose running, breath ragged, and close myself behind the door with the full force of my body. I lose the ability to hold myself up and slide down onto the foyer floor as I succumb to the gravity of what just occurred on Ostram Street.

✧   ✧   ✧

THE NEXT DAY, Mike and Bain arrive. I meet them in the airport and instantly demand to know how and when the interaction with Elliot took place. Both are upset that I'm not more, how should we say, pleased to see them. They take turns placating me and assure me that all things will work out in time.

The sight of them with Eli completely eradicates my bad mood. I understand they did what they did out of love for me and truly, they didn't know he would come here. Mike is so hands-on with Eli, it makes me laugh. He's feeding him, changing his diaper, burping him, running to him at the slightest noise on the monitor. Bain has taken more time to warm up, afraid he'll break him or make him cry. Watching Bain and Mike work together to manage Eli is a real treat. Mike is so patient with both of them. It truly makes me consider coming back to the States. *They would do well with Eli together.*

After our first evening, Bain catches me on the porch enjoying the cool evening air.

"So." He looks at his beer, attempting to be nonchalant. "This whole mother thing is working out for you?"

I laugh. "Well Bain, when you find out you're having a baby, the whole mother thing becomes necessary."

"Yeah, you're right about that." He pauses and I can tell he wants to say something.

"Come on." I turn to him, resting one elbow on the railing. "Out with it. What do you want to say?"

He smiles as he continues to examine his beer. "I know I've told you this before, but I'm so sorry for how I acted when you came to us with this. I was a total asshole about you having a baby." He gestures to the house. "You do this so beautifully. Seeing you with him, you're so natural. It amazes me."

"Thank you." I am humbled by his apology. "It's always a work in progress but I think I manage well."

"You do." He turns to me. "What's the deal with Elliot?"

It's the first time his name has been spoken since I berated both of them at the airport.

"Well, he found me after work, told me that he knew about you and Mike, and he wants to see Eli." I've replayed the events on Ostram Street a million times in my head since. "He said he'll do anything."

"Are you going to let him?"

"I don't have a choice, do I?"

Bain nods, considering the options.

"What do I gain by not allowing him to see Eli? I gain the heinous bitch award, that's it. It's bad enough I didn't try to tell him myself, I just uprooted everything and moved to a different country. That's pretty extreme and more than a bit awful. Normal people just change their cell number."

"Well, you left the States for numerous reasons, myself included. I can understand why you didn't seek him out. I wish you would have told us how he flipped. We would have set him straight right away."

"I was worried what you would do, Bain. I didn't want the situation to get out of control."

"Deese, you have to trust that I'm more grown up now. I can handle myself. I know I put you and Jamie through hell for years, but I think I have a good thing going now."

"I know," I sigh. "It's just, I love you so much and I worry."

"Well, back at ya." He pulls at his beer. "For what it's worth, I agree that you should let Elliot see him. He's amazing. I never knew babies could be so...what's the word....cool? They both deserve the opportunity to see each other." He looks over the landscape. I am in awe of his introspection.

"Yeah, you're right."

Bain throws an arm around me and kisses my head as he holds me close. From the upstairs window, I hear Eli stir, crying out softly as he wakes from his nap. We look at each other and I sigh before turning to the sliding glass door. Before I reach the handle, I see Mike is sprinting to the stairs, ready to tackle whatever my baby needs. Bain and I look at each other in shock and amusement.

"Don't get any ideas, Deese," Bain offers as he slugs the last of his beer. "He's all mine."

Chapter Thirty-Seven
ELLIOT

I GRIP THE wheel of my father's car as I drive toward Natalie and Greggor's house. *I'm going to meet my son. I'm going to meet my son.* I keep saying the words to myself but I feel disconnected. I can't believe I have a son.

Tess texted me yesterday and gave me the address and time to come over to meet Eli. She was brief on the message and didn't offer more than the necessary information. I am terribly anxious. *What if he hates me? What if I pick him up and he cries?*

This is the ultimate blind date, which is really weird. I have no clue what to expect.

I have an impression to make, so I'm shaved up. My jeans and shirt are casual but looking well. I got an arrangement of flowers for her. Dad approved of my idea for flowers instantly. I think it's a nice way to start over.

I pull up outside of the house and quickly straighten myself before walking to the front door. I shake out my hands to try alleviating the tremors before I ring the doorbell.

To my surprise, Bain answers the door. "Hello, stranger." He looks at the flowers and what I imagine is disappointment on my face. "Come on in." He gestures for me to walk into the house. "Mike and I were just leaving for a while." Bain offers before handing me off to Greggor, who's sitting in a living room chair.

I nod to both of them and they are gone.

I turn to Greggor, who surveys me with some emotion I can't name, which immediately makes me nervous. After a moment, he sighs and stands, offering me his hand. I take it and he grips me just a little too hard. I immediately flash back to the first time I met Greggor and his lovingly aggressive hold on Tess.

"I'm sorry Elliot," he offers quietly, "but she's not here."

My stomach falls to the floor. "Oh," is the only thing I can think to say.

"She went back and forth for a while about what to do. I think she's confused and a little afraid."

"I see." I say, as I hand the flowers to Greggor. "Can you put these in a vase so she can have them when she comes home?"

"Sure," he says as he takes the flowers and rests a hand on my shoulder. He offers a reassuring squeeze before walking into the kitchen.

I am dumbstruck. *She doesn't want to see me? She can't see me? I don't understand.*

The cooing of a baby down the hall distracts me. My palms begin to sweat and my scalp pricks. Natalie comes into the living area holding Eli, who is awake and wordlessly chattering to her. She looks up at me with a loving smile, as if none of the past year has mattered.

"Hello, dear," she offers as she comes in close and kisses me on the cheek. "Here he is." Her excitement is infectious and, without realizing it, I'm smiling like a total goofball about this little person. Tess was right. He looks exactly like me. I am shocked and suddenly in love with this boy who I've known for all of one minute.

"Do you want to hold him?" Natalie offers. She reads the anxiety on my face and follows up with, "How about you sit on the couch? That's usually easiest to start."

I sit on the couch. Natalie lays Eli in my arms. Once her hands are free, she props my arm with a pillow and sits next to me, facing Eli.

He looks at me and I have no idea what to say to him. *What do I do now?*

"I have no idea what to do."

Natalie smiles warmly. "It's okay. At this stage of the game, we are all still figuring him out. Diesel is really the only one who knows him inside and out. We just smile and offer things and eventually we figure it out."

"Oh, okay," I say. I can smile at him, which I do. I am silently pleased that he's not screaming and I've not hurt him so far.

"Natalie, where is she?" I ask. I need to know why she's not here.

"She wouldn't tell anyone where she was going. Not even Mike and Bain. She gave them explicit instructions to go sightseeing. I can reach her by cell phone."

"She didn't want to see me?" I ask softly, looking at my son, who now has heavy eyelids.

"I don't know if it's that she didn't want to see you, Elliot. I think it might be more that she couldn't see you."

I take a minute to register the cryptic statement. "So, she

wants to see me?" I ask.

"I think she knows what seeing you will do, and has done, to her. She's maintained a steady course since she's been here and I think she feels a little overwhelmed."

"I don't want to overwhelm her. I just want to talk to her." I look at Eli, now sleeping in my arms. "Was everything okay with the pregnancy?" I'm not sure why I want to know but the words tumble from my mouth.

"She was beautiful the entire time, Elliot. Ever present and focused on bringing him into the world healthy and strong. Even when she was in labor, she was so poised. She never screamed, or yelled, or was rude to anyone. She didn't want any drugs, even though it was physically draining on her. She was focused on her breathing and, of course, seeing Eli."

I nod, secretly wishing I could have seen her. Held her hand. Coached her in some way.

"Was she alone?" My question is raspy; the thought of her being alone punches me in the gut.

"No, I was with her the whole time. She didn't want a bunch of people in the room. During the hours she was in labor, it was mostly her and I. She would let Greggor go in and out but toward the end, as she was getting ready to push, it was only me."

"I'm sure she found great comfort in you being there." I offer her a half smile.

"I'm not sure about that, Elliot. She didn't really talk too much." Natalie hesitates and looks at me. "I'm not even sure if she remembers this, but she did call for you."

"What?" Emotion pricks me on all levels, in my throat, at my eyes, my collapsing chest.

She nods. "She called for you, quietly, maybe twice. Just saying your name. It was as if she was willing you to be present."

I picture her lying in a hospital bed, hair messed and swollen belly, mouthing my name. I try to choke the sob but I can't. I can't cover my face because I'm holding my son. Natalie swoops her arm around me, pulling me into her neck. I can't hold on any longer. The knowledge of how poorly I misjudged her, the hell I put us both though for no reason, the thought that she was alone during her pregnancy and labor, and now this. *She called for me? She wanted me? Does she still want me? It was only three months ago.*

Natalie releases me and motions for me to stand. We walk over to a small crib, and I lay Eli down. He stirs but then resumes his steady sleep. Natalie rubs my back and rests her head on my arm.

"He's amazing. Isn't he?" she says.

"Yeah," I agree through a watery voice. "I think he gets it from his mother."

ELI SLEEPS FOR about an hour, in which time Natalie shows me pictures and gives me a brief tour of the house. When Eli wakes, I feed him a bottle and Natalie walks me through the mechanics of changing a diaper. I am secretly glad he doesn't pee on me and completely overjoyed she didn't have him circumcised. He quickly falls back asleep again and Natalie grabs the baby monitor as we walk to the porch to have tea. We exchange pleasantries about Eli but I find it hard not to ask about Tess.

"Do you think she'll come around?"

Greggor and Natalie look at each other. "I think she was really hurt, Elliot," Natalie offers. "She hadn't let someone in for so long until you came along. She risked exposing Mike and Bain and herself for you. She told me that you two were never apart after she was attacked. We talked then about how she felt about you. Hell, Elliot, the first time we met you, she was flustered by you simply making her some eggs."

I am shocked. This woman who is so strong and independent was flustered by eggs? I am embarrassed that Natalie knows all of these things, but then I remember that Natalie is really the only mother figure Tess has.

"She's a powerhouse, Elliot. No one is denying that. But she's also a woman. I think people forget that aspect of her often." Natalie reflects for a moment. "I think Diesel forgets that also. She doesn't always allow herself to be swept away by emotion because she's been in such control for so long. But you showed up and you made her eggs and she liked it."

"So, I should make her eggs?"

Natalie laughs. "You could, if you could get close to her, or you can do what you did before."

"What's that?"

"Be present and be yourself, Elliot. That's how you two connected in the first place, right?"

I think about Natalie's observations as I drive home. Now that I've seen him, I know I'll never be the same. I have a son. I hope Tess responds to the note I felt compelled to write her before I left. I also hope she doesn't feel the need to completely avoid me in the future.

Chapter Thirty-Eight
DIESEL

I DID NOT think Elliot would spend so long with Eli. Natalie texted me three hours after I left to tell me he was gone. I pull myself from the recess of the British Museum and head for the underground.

All day long, I've wondered what was going on at home. I can't believe he was there for three hours. I thought it would be an hour at most.

I come into the house and hear my baby boy giggling with Greggor. I greet them both, picking up Eli and kissing Greggor on the cheek. Surprisingly, he says nothing to me about the interaction with Elliot. He just smiles kindly and turns into the house. In the kitchen, Natalie busies herself with making dinner. I settle into one of the barstools and look at her.

"Well?"

Natalie looks at me as if she hasn't realized I've come into the room. She raises her eyebrows to me and points to the kitchen table with the knife she is using to chop peppers. I look and see an enormous bouquet of flowers and a note. I stare at them for a moment and look back to Natalie.

"Darling, they are not for me." She smirks at herself and

resumes her chopping.

I rest Eli on my hip as I walk toward the flowers. They are beautiful, a mix of wildflowers in bright and vibrant colors. I pick up the note – a piece of paper folded in half with Elliot's handwriting on it. I hold the note up and look at Natalie over my shoulder in silent questioning.

"He came in with the flowers," she says. "He wrote the note before he left."

I look at the paper. "What does it say?" I ask her.

"Well, that I don't know, darling," she says. "My name isn't Tess, now, is it?"

I look at her, trying to find any word to say in response, but I fail. I stare at my name scrawled in his handwriting. Natalie finishes her task and walks over to me. "Take some time and read it, love. He sat here for ages writing it." She takes Eli from my arms and walks out of the kitchen.

I set the note down on the table and stare at it for a moment before I sit down. I have no idea what it will say but I have to read it eventually, right?

I suck in a deep breath and open the note.

Tess,

Thank you for letting me meet Eli. He's amazing and I'm so happy to have been able to spend some time with him. I would like to ask your permission to see him again while I am here. I would also like my father to meet him, if that is all right with you. Please let me know so we can make plans.

I brought you these flowers because I thought you'd be here – but you weren't. Tess, I don't know why you couldn't be here today. I don't know how to say I'm sorry for what I've done but I am, I really am. Please talk to me, Tess.

I've missed you. It hurts to miss you this much. I don't want to miss you anymore.

Please call me.

Yours – Elliot

I read and re-read the note, trying to think of the sound of his voice saying the words to me. My heart hurts again and my throat closes with the threat of tears. I don't know if I can do this. Can I avoid him until he goes back to the States? Will he come back here to stay if he knows Eli and I are here? Can I push down these thoughts? These feelings? It took me so long to decide whether to be here or not when he visited. After I saw him on the street, all I could do was think about him. All I wanted was him. For him to tell me he was sorry. To beg for my forgiveness. For him to forgive me. To kiss me. To touch me. To tell me this would all work itself out. But if we reconcile, it could all fall to pieces as quickly as the last time. I don't think I can go through that pain again. I have finally gotten some semblance of stability back. I can't risk breaking down again, not when I have Eli to care for. But I miss him. What's worse, risking the possibility that love could fall apart all over again, or living with a fractured soul denied the opportunity to mend with its mate?

Sitting in front of the beautiful flowers, I drop my head into the crux of my arm and vent the mourning of a confused and broken heart.

✧ ✧ ✧

MIKE AND BAIN come back to find me pink and tear-stained. I show them the note and they tell me about the brief five minutes that they saw Elliot this morning.

"I don't see what the harm in seeing him is, Deese," Mike offers. "What is the worst that could happen?"

"I don't know." I sigh and look out the window.

"Yes you do," Bain says to me with a warm gaze. "You could be vulnerable to him again and that scares the shit out of you." He raises his eyes to me. "You see him, you want him, he has the power to level you like last time. You don't want that possibility, so you hide." He holds his hands up. "It's a simple equation."

This is really the root of all my issues. With Eden, with Bain, with life in general. I don't want to be vulnerable. Ever. I don't want someone to have the upper hand and have any ability to undermine me in any circumstance. It's about control, pure and simple. I don't have control when I'm with Elliot. Worse than that, I let him in and he ran roughshod all over me. I don't want that to happen again.

"It's very scary," I say quietly as I pick at the placemat.

"Well, no shit. That's what life is. It's a series of ups and downs and good and bad." He stares at me. "You need to learn to pull in the people who love you to help feel more stable when you have to be vulnerable." He pauses. "You make a lousy island. You support everyone else but can't bring yourself to ask for anyone to help you when you know you need it."

I can't look at him. I know he's right. I do half this shit to myself.

He slams his fist on the table, making Mike and I jump. He grabs Elliot's note and holds it up.

"If you don't see him, I'll make you see him. It's obvious to everyone he still has feelings for you. You need to figure out if you have feelings for him in return."

"This could all be because he's shocked about Eli. He may not have those feelings for me anymore." I say it so quickly I realize that this is the heart of the issue.

"So, you do want him?" Bain counters. "And are you are afraid he's only here for Eli?"

I hate Bain so much in this moment. *How did this man get so insightful all of a sudden?* I bury my face in my hands, completely unable to look at him.

"He didn't bring these flowers for Eli. He didn't write Eli's name on this note."

"I know."

"I don't care how you do it. Call him. Text him. Tell him to come over." There's no room for countering Bain's statement.

I nod and swallow down my anxiety. "You'll be here with me?"

"Of course, Deese." He takes my hands in his and stares at me with loving blue eyes. "We'll always be here."

THE NEXT DAY, Natalie and Greggor are in full party mode. The dining room table is filled with meats, cheeses, and everything under the sun. I text Elliot and asked he and his father to an afternoon and dinner at their home. He quickly agreed and then confirmed I would be present as well. I told him Mike and Bain would be here, with Quin and some other family members.

Now I am waiting. Anxiously.

Eli has slept the majority of the morning, which has given

me copious amounts of time to obsess over my hair, my outfit and how to dress his adorable little body, as well.

At two o'clock, I position myself on the deck and make every attempt to look nonchalant. I am failing miserably.

Mike comes to stand next to me, taking inventory of my overall presentation. "You look really good, doll." He smiles warmly at me. "Are you nervous?"

"Severely." I laugh anxiously and pat my skirt down.

"It will be great. You do look amazing. He'd be a fool to let you walk away a second time."

"What if I'm the fool, Mike?"

"You aren't, Diesel. You deserve to let this one come to fruition." He says as he rubs my upper arm. "Okay?"

I smile at him. "Okay."

"They're here!" Natalie yells from the kitchen. I take a stabilizing breath and walk into the house.

I can hear Greggor and Natalie greeting Mr. Archer and Elliot warmly. They exchange pleasantries as Elliot introduces his father to everyone as they make their way to the open kitchen area. Greggor walks in first, checking out the bottle of wine Mr. Archer has brought to the festivities. The two chirp animatedly about local vineyards and how well the wine will compliment the meal. Mr. Archer sees me hovering by the table. He smiles warmly and walks to me.

"Hello, Tess." He offers his hand for me to shake. "It's good to meet you." He offers me a sly wink. He didn't tell Elliot he came to see me!

"Hello, Mr. Archer. It's nice to meet you." I reply.

"Please, Tess, call me Charlie. There is no need to be so formal." He holds my gaze, waiting for my response. I offer a curt nod and a tight smile. He mimics my actions before releasing my hand and turning back to Greggor, who has broken out the bottle opener and started pouring drinks.

I look anxiously around the room and notice that Elliot, Bain, Mike, and Quin never came into the house completely. I walk across the room and peer through the door. The four are hanging together by the door, enrapt in some private conversation. Elliot is the only one with his back to me. Quin catches me out of the corner of his eye.

"Hey, there," he says, pushing his chin toward me.

The remaining three quickly stop their discussion. Mike, Bain, and Quin are the only faces I can see but I know they are exchanging glances with Elliot. Elliot pivots and turns to me, holding yet another bouquet of flowers.

"Hello," he offers.

"Hi." My response is breathy and quiet.

We stare at each other for what feels like an eternity in awkward silence.

As if on cue, Mike, Bain, and Quin offer shouts of "Right, then!" and "We'll be on the porch!" and "Where's that wine?" The three beat a hasty exit out the front door that would rival a Three Stooges exit.

"You look really great," Elliot says, walking toward me, holding the flowers out.

"Thanks, you look well also," I offer. "These are beautiful, thank you. The ones you left yesterday were great also. You didn't have to bring more."

"I didn't get to put those in your hand. That's the best part of giving flowers, seeing the reaction," he says.

My heart simpers. *How can he be so damn romantic!* "Oh, I see." It's all I can say.

"Thank you for texting me, Tess. I am so happy you contacted me. I really wish you would have been here yesterday." His tone is quiet but urgent, as if he's practiced what he wanted to say.

"I know. I wanted to be here too, but, I decided not to."

"Why? Please tell me why you couldn't be here." He's moved so close, I can smell him. His hand hovers over my arm as if he wants to touch me, but I am a hot surface. My knees quiver at the anticipation of his touch. I long for him in a very deep place within me. He runs a hand though his hair, closing his eyes. "Why can't you be around me?"

"I want to be." I pause, swallowing the burgeoning tears. "But, Elliot, it hurts so much to be near you. I loved you and you were so angry with me. You told me not to contact you, and then I was pregnant and you told me I was a mistake and I didn't want you to think the baby was a mistake, also. So I had to make this life for myself where you weren't here but there was a piece of you constantly reminding me of how I felt." The words are quick. I'm convinced my pounding heart is visible though my shirt. I can't bear to look at him. "Being near you...it brings all those feelings back. And it hurts, Elliot. It hurts very badly."

He steps closer, searching my face with anguished eyes. "I don't know how else to say I'm sorry. This entire situation is maddening. There is so much I don't know that I deserve to know. About you. About Eli." He pushes my hair away from my face and lifts my chin up so I meet his eyes. "Please talk to me." His eyes show deep hurt and I know these past few days have been difficult for him also.

I shake my head. "Okay, but you've got to give me some time. I need to ease into all of this again."

"Understood." He releases my chin and takes the smallest step back. I have every urge to reach out and pull him near me again. "I really want to kiss you right now." He says with a slight smile.

My breath hitches. "I know." I wipe the tears from my face. I can't believe how much I've cried over the past few days. I thought I got all this stuff out already. I am embarrassed and feel like a baby.

"Do you?" His question is genuine.

"Elliot." I push out a breathy laugh. "I may be all over the map with you right now, but I still find you very attractive. That's what got us into this mess in the first place." I've always prided myself on being honest, but in this moment, I'm not sure if it's appropriate.

Elliot raises his eyebrows. "You being attracted to me was what got us into this mess? I think me forgetting my boundaries as a journalist got us into this mess. I was nothing but honest when I told you I wanted you the instant I saw you at Rosie's."

His admission shakes me to the core, amplifying my desire to ravage him in the foyer. "I see." I can't look at him or this will get very out of control. I motion to the interior of the house. "We should get in there, don't you think?"

Elliot looks down the hallway. "I think we are fine here, don't you?"

"Elliot, I can't do all of this right now. Let's have the afternoon and go from there, okay?" I have to set some kind of pace for this or we'll be having sex in the bathroom in ten minutes. Damn, he is so good-looking! I take a defensive step backwards, toward the kitchen.

He nods in reluctant agreement and takes my hand, kissing it gently. "I'm so happy to see you, Tess."

I smile at him and let the words wash over me. "It's good to see you too, Elliot."

✧   ✧   ✧

THE AFTERNOON PROGRESSES without a hitch. The food, conversation, and wine are plentiful and satisfying. Eli has been the prize for the entire day, being passed from hand to hand, and loving every minute of it. At seven, he starts to get cranky and I know it's time for bed. He fusses in Bain's arms and I'm not sure who is more uncomfortable.

"Here, Bain. I've got him." I pick him up, rescuing Bain from the throes of a full-blown cry. "If you will excuse me," I say to the crowd, "I'll put him to bed."

Elliot stands immediately. "Can I come with you?" The room is silent, holding its collective breath in wait for my answer.

I swallow my shock. Why am I so surprised? I shouldn't be. He's been amazing with him all day. "Of course." I think I see even the wall sag with relief. Greggor breaks the silence with the solicitation of more wine.

We climb the stairs as I coo at my fussy little boy. In his room, I show Elliot where his nightclothes are. He again changes Eli's diaper and gets him in his pajamas. He sits on the floor next to the glider and watches me as I feed and rock our son to sleep.

"He fell asleep really fast," Elliot whispers. Standing up next to me, we look at Eli sleeping in his crib.

"He had a busy day," I offer. "Being passed around, he didn't get a whole lot of time to nap."

We are silent for a moment, watching our son.

"Tess." Elliot breaks the silence. "Natalie told me you called for me when you were in labor."

My cheeks flair. I didn't even think she heard me. I was so overwhelmed in that moment. She told him? NATALIE! Ugh! That woman! I love her, but really! "Um, yeah, I did."

"Why?" He's turned to me, hip leaning on the crib.

"I don't know, Elliot. Because you're his father. Because I wanted you to comfort me. Because you helped me get pregnant so I wanted you to be up for nineteen hours straight with me." I snort at the memory. Nineteen hours of labor for a nine pound baby with no drugs. I'm either part horse or a complete masochist.

He shakes his head. "Did you video it?"

"Eww! No!" I lightly smack his arm. "It's really not all that attractive. There's a lot of blood and...fluids. Besides, I don't need my crotch vomiting this one on video for all time." I jerk my thumb toward Eli.

He laughs me. "Okay, good point. So that was not your favorite part?"

"What? Of pregnancy? No, not even close. It's strange, though. Labor is the worst part of the whole deal but it yields such an amazing outcome. It was worth it to finally see his face and hear him cry."

I see Elliot considering my admission.

"To be honest, my favorite part was carrying him. Knowing that I had the ability to help him develop well by what I ate. I stayed active and exercised throughout to make labor easier. I listened to great music during my pregnancy, knowing that he would hear it. I told him how much I loved him every day. I was so proud to be the vessel that held him safe for ten months."

Elliot's breath hitches and his arm snakes around my waist before I know it. I feel my legs quiver in response to his breath on my neck. "You're amazing."

"Thanks." My voice wavers and I can't stop staring at his lips.

"Tess, when we were talking this afternoon...you said you loved me."

"Yes, I did." My heart is pounding. Desire courses through my body.

"What do you think about loving me now?"

What? "What do you mean, Elliot? Like you want to have sex now or you want to know if I love you?"

He considers the question for a moment. "Both."

I pull out of his hold and step back. "We're not having sex, Elliot. We haven't seen each other in a year, after you told me in no uncertain terms to fuck off. Now you think I'm going to sleep with you?" I have to try very hard to keep my tone low. I can't believe this is our conversation in our son's nursery, while he's sleeping in his crib.

"Okay." he holds his hands up. "I understand. So, does that also mean you don't love me anymore?"

Oh, there it is. The million-dollar question. *I think about you all the time. I long for you. I secretly hope to see you on the street on a daily basis. I touch myself and I think of you. I imagine us back in New York. I want you to make me eggs. I want to go on sex runs with you. I want our life the way it was before all of this happened, because, now it feels...different.*

"I don't know, Elliot. This is so confusing."

"Did you love me?" His tone reveals that he is afraid of

the answer.

"I think so."

I see him sag with relief. "Tess, please let me touch you." He's begging. Isn't this what I wanted? For him to feel so bad that he begged for me?

He holds his hand out to me. It takes every fiber of my being to stay rooted where I am.

"I can't Elliot. Not right now, at least."

He audibly exhales and closes his extended hand in a fist. He flops in the glider in the room and runs his hand over this chin and mouth as if in deep contemplation.

"I don't think I ever fell out of love with you, Tess. I just pushed it aside. After I got word you left Eden, I was a mess. I knew it was somehow because of me and couldn't make it right. I didn't even know about Ben or anything." He stands quickly and paces the nursery. I stand immobilized by his confession with my arms handing at my side. "I tried to date other girls and they paled in comparison to you. No one talked to me the way you did. No one was as confident, smart, or sexy as you are. They were all compared to you and none of them came close." He abruptly stops inches from my face. "Did you find that, Tess? That no one compared to you and me?"

"I didn't and haven't dated anyone since you, Elliot—lest you forget I was a walking Volkswagen for ten months." I lean into him. "It's not a real big secret that not too many guys find pregnant, unattached women super attractive. But good for you for getting back out there."

My anger resurfaced, I flip the monitor switch on and walk out of the room. I think the only thing keeping this conversation from becoming a screaming match is the eleven pounds of new life sleeping soundly three feet from us.

"I didn't sleep with anyone, Tess. Shit!" I can hear the panic in his voice. "I couldn't. Not with you on my mind."

I lead us down the stairway on the far end of the hallway, which takes us back down to the foyer. Better the foyer than dropping back into the kitchen where we can perform after-dinner drama for the entire family.

He's running his hands though his hair. "How the fuck do we go from being so awesome to back here again?" The frustration in his voice is evident and I feel guilty because this volley was completely mine.

"Hey, guys?" Bain says the words as he walks into the foyer. He must have heard us and wanted to give us fair warning. He holds his hands up as if he's being held at gunpoint. "Elliot, your dad is asking to head out. I told him I'd come get you."

"Right, thanks Bain."

Bain all but runs back to the living room.

"Look." Elliot grabs my upper arms, forcing me to look at him again. "I'm saying you have been on my mind since you left. *Only* you, Tess. I know what I said when you came into my office. It was heinous and so over the top, I don't even know where it came from now. But I thought you'd cheated on me. That burned me to the core, Tess. Despite that, I couldn't stop thinking about you. I still think about you...all the time. I want us back." He sighs and pulls me in, kissing me hard. He stops only when we hear Greggor and Charlie coming down the hallway. We stare at each other in our collective breathlessness.

"Quin has a show tomorrow. Bain and Mike are going.

Will you come?" His change of topic shocks me. *You say all that to me and now you want to go to a show?*

I glance at Greggor and Charlie, now in the foyer with us, "I have to make sure someone can watch Eli." I sigh, clearly he does not understand the level of responsibility associated with procreation. "If I can get a sitter, I'll meet you at the show tomorrow."

He nods, slowly releasing my arms. "Good."

Greggor and Charlie share a goofy grin. As we say our goodbyes, Charlie kisses me on the cheek, wishes me a warm farewell, and compliments my good-looking son. Elliot leans in and kisses me on the cheek. "Don't be using your charms on old men, Tess, especially not my dad." It's a whisper that only I can hear.

"I'll see you, not your dad, tomorrow." *Easy, Archer. I know where you're coming from.*

He smiles at me. "Tomorrow." He turns and walks into the night.

✧　✧　✧

THE NEXT DAY, the house is a ghost town. Mike, Bain, and Quin are nowhere to be found. Greggor and Natalie are out visiting friends. It's just Eli and I at home watching *Breaking Dawn, Part 2*. The twist gets him every time. Who am I to deny my only child this one true joy in life?

I call our sitter to confirm she can come over this evening to watch Eli. I'm not sure when Natalie and Greggor are coming back. I vaguely recall them saying this morning that they would meet us at the show.

At one o'clock, I text Elliot to figure out how tonight is

going to play out. *Why yes, I do need to make all attempts to control this uncontrollable situation.*

What time are you going to be at the show?

His return text is immediate.

I'll be there at 8. Quin starts at 9. I thought I'd get there early and have a drink before the festivities. When are you coming?

Hmmm...do I go early?

I'll have to check with M & B and see what their schedule is like. I'll let you know

I refuse to be an island per Bain's instruction. I need my boys on this one. Drinking and Elliot in a dark bar with music. That's a recipe for Tess to lose her pants...quick. *Note to self: don't wear a dress tonight.*

My email pings with a text from Bain. *What?*

Hey, what time are we going tonight?
I was going to ask you. Elliot just texted me, he'll be there around 8. What do you think? What should I wear?
8 is good. We'll be back to N&G's around 6. I think you should wear something slutty. No underwear.
You're a pig. I'll see you at 6.

If I arrive with Bain and Mike, that will be good. I text Elliot back.

Hey E – we'll be there around the same time as you. See you then.
Brilliant T – can't wait to see you.

I roll my eyes. Flirty Elliot always makes me smile.

✧ ✧ ✧

BY FIVE O'CLOCK, the sitter arrives for Eli and I jump into a steamy shower, taking extra care to shave—though even the act of doing that has me conflicted. I have to get the guys at Natalie and Greggor's and then get us to the bar so the process of getting ready has to start early. I stand in front of my closet and stare at the possibilities. What sort of vibe do I want to put off tonight? I could play up the *I'm hard to get* angle, which I'm not really. He knows this. Do I want to look demure and romantic? In a bar? No, thank you. How about sexy in a nonchalant way? I pull on my favorite pair of white jeans that hug me in all the right places and a navy blue cami. The outfit is topped off with saucy wedges and a little necklace with an anchor charm. *Ahoy Sailor!* I do my hair and makeup and am pretty pleased with the overall look.

As I grab my bag, I glance at myself in one of the hallway mirrors. A ripple of doubt runs through me. This is the first time since Eli that I've really dressed up to go out.

I grab my phone and snap a quick picture of myself.

*Does this outfit scream "bereft woman with illegitimate child"
or "damn – that girl's got it going on!"**

I attach the picture, hit *send*, and then anxiously play with my hair until I hear Holly's return text.

*You look amazing. I'd fuck you. Go out and have a great time.**

I snort a laugh. She really is pretty awesome.

*You know how to make a lady feel adored.**
*Just doing my job! Let me know how it goes!**

I breathe a sigh of relief and head for the door. My phone pings again.

BTW – your baby boy is completely legit....love you.

I smile lovingly at the message.

Love you, too. Thanks!

✧   ✧   ✧

BY EIGHT FORTY-FIVE, the bar is packed. Quin's band is sharing the night with open mike karaoke and I harass him about not being able to differentiate between the two. Quin has rewarded my innocent teasing by encouraging random guys in the bar to buy me drinks. I'm grateful Quin is with me until his set begins, when I'm left to fend for myself. Before I left, Mike texted me and told me Elliot would pick up he and Bain since they are in the same area. It saved me gas but it also meant walking in here solo.

I'm leaning up against the bar with Quin's latest sucker who is working all the moves, when I see the trifecta enter the room. Elliot walks in first, flanked by Mike and Bain. All of them look mouth-watering as they immediately catch the attention of several girls hanging at the high tables. It appears as though they've dressed Elliot this evening as well, in jeans, white shirt, and navy blazer. I've always been so impressed with Mike and Bain's style. They look exceptionally handsome this evening, easily sliding into 'do-able' category for any woman here. My thought is immediately confirmed by a tight blonde walking up to Bain and lightly running her hand across his chest as she sashays in the opposite direction. I snicker as he follows her with his eyes. All the years of passing as straight have made him very good at playing the part.

Watching them survey the room from behind my glass, I'm very grateful I've gone for casual but sexy. As I take in Elliot, a very stupid part of me immediately focuses on the obvious. *We match! Damn, you are a total dork!* My self-castigation lasts for a brief moment before Elliot sees me in the presence of the guy handing me yet another martini. He moves quickly toward me, glaring at Mr. Opportunity and putting his arm between us. He leans against the bar, his back to the potential suitor.

"Tess." He takes my hand and lifts it to his mouth.

"Hey, I think I got this one bro," Mr. Opportunity says to Elliot.

"No, friend, you've got that wrong," he says over his shoulder, not looking at the guy. "I've had this one for a while." He's staring at me intensely as he gently lays his lips on the back of my hand.

I look at him with amusement. With my hand still held to his lips, I force myself to look away and focus on Mr. Opportunity. "Sorry, buddy. Thanks for the drink."

He walks away from the bar muttering something offensive I'm sure, but I can't hear him and don't particularly care at this moment.

Bain and Mike move in, order drinks and banter with some of the ladies that have honed in on them.

Elliot leans into me. "Have you been here long?"

I shrug. "Maybe twenty minutes." I lean into his ear. "You know how I feel about being late." My martini consumption is making me brave and I regret the words the instant they have flown from my mouth. It's wrong to be flirtatious when I'm still so up in the air about all of this.

He inhales sharply and looks at me with his head cocked to one side.

"Does this mean you've decided we are okay?"

I shake my head. "No Elliot. I'm merely telling you my feelings about your tardiness." I have to pace myself with these drinks. Not drinking for a year and no dinner does not mix well with martini number two.

He looks wounded for a moment and pulls his lips into a fine line. "You're a vicious tease." He looks at me, eyes dancing devilishly. "Let's have some fun. Like we used to."

A wave of comforting familiarity comes over me as I remember the early days of hanging out and just being ourselves. We immediately fall into our former selves, toasting each other with shots and enjoying the controlled chaos of the bar. Quin's band is hot tonight and we are all enjoying his lyrical mastery. The night is progressing with ease. Elliot and I continue to stay close to each other, lightly touching at times but not engaging in overt flirtation. I want more from him but I'm not willing to push the limit when the night has been so good.

After one of the karaoke sets has ended, saving us all from making serious attempts to hurt ourselves, Quin hops back on stage and eyes me with a wolfish stare.

"Where is my Tess?" He questions loudly in to the mike.

I shake my head because I know he knows exactly where I am, yet another opportunity to draw attention my way. Suddenly, one of his band mates turns a spotlight on me. Like cockroaches, Elliot, Mike, and Bain scatter. *Jerks!*

"I'm right here, Quin. Right where you left me." I can't help my earsplitting grin. I do love this little banter before he asks me to sing with him. I walk away from the bar into the open area in front of the stage.

"Good," Quin says before looking into the crowd. "Has everyone had a chance to meet Tess?" The crowd responds with catcalls and drunken whoops. I raise my hand in acknowledgement.

"I have a treat for you, Tess," Quin coos into the microphone. "I think you'll see there are some additions to my group tonight." The spotlight shifts from me to...Bain? He's sitting at an upright piano on stage. *What?*

I look at Bain with confused amusement. He winks at me as I hold my hands up in a what-the-hell gesture.

"Okay, Tess," Quin says. "Here we go."

The stage goes black for a moment until I see a light warm around Quin wailing out a guitar riff I know all too well.

I only have the thought for a moment before the microphone is lit and from the surrounding darkness, I see Elliot step into the light.

"You cannot quit me so quickly...There's no hope in you for me... No corner you could squeeze me...but I got all the time for you, love..."

I look at him, my mouth slowly dropping open, as he belts out Dave Matthew's Band's *The Space Between*. He's staring at me intensely. It's as if no one else exists in the bar.

He's singing. To me.

"We're strange allies with warring hearts..."

What? He's singing to me. He's singing what I consider one of the best love songs ever written.

"The Space Between... the bullets in our firefight...is where I'll be hiding, waiting for you..."

I am transfixed, rooted in place by his voice, his passion, and this act. He moves off the stage toward me, singing soulfully and proud. As Bain, Mike and Quin offer up the background vocals, I'm barely distracted from the man who is now directly in front of me.

"Take my hand 'cause we're walking out of here... Oh, right out of here... Love is all we need."

The song ends with a blinding flourish. The crowd erupts into cheers and applause and I realize that tears have been streaming down my face. He sang, for me?

He looks at me with playful adoration. He wipes my cheeks. "I love you, Tess," he says into the microphone, "whenever you are ready and for as long as it takes."

His honesty breaks me in half. My wounded heart swells with the possibility that this could be real again.

Real. Open. True.

I nod at him for lack of discernible words and attempt a smile through the emotional onslaught. I am vulnerable and I am his.

"Yeah?" He says into the microphone.

I nod again.

"Yeah!" He drops the microphone and grabs me, full force, kissing me with unapologetic passion as the club erupts around us.

I am released for a brief moment as his picks up the microphone. "I must take a minute to thank my blokes for helping me win back my girl." Elliot gestures to the stage where Mike, Bain, and Quin have gathered and take an overly dramatic bow.

They conspired to do this? For me? For Elliot to do this for me?

In this moment, I am shocked, awed, and overwhelmed with feeling utterly adored and loved.

Epilogue

TE$$

THREE MONTHS AFTER the serenade in the club, Elliot and I have made our home in the lake house. We have both been granted the benefit of working remotely, so we decided to collectively live away from Boston and Eden. His success with the Eden blog has afforded him a new position in his company as the New York correspondent. Elliot checks out new and upcoming clubs, highlights current flights of fancy, and makes sure readers don't forget about the oldies but goodies still lurking in the recesses of certain alleyways.

I'm able to travel back and forth to Eden and continue to the management of upkeep and daily functioning while Bain and Mike have taken over all the creative aspects of the club. With Eli in tow, I use my old apartment as a functional office and play space for Eli on the days I need to be physically present. It always astounds me that the instant Eli is in the building, Mike is on him. I think he's trying to soften Bain to the idea of adopting. Unfortunately, I'm not sure how well he's doing with his campaign. Last week I walked into a conversation that ended with Bain saying, "How about we just keep trying to get pregnant and see what happens."

Though Elliot and I had nights where Eli has slept soundly to reunite after our time apart, this weekend we are completely baby free. Natalie and Greggor have come home and they want to see their grandson. A whole weekend without our son seems strange yet oddly exhilarating. An entire weekend of just Elliot and me? Well, that's a dream I thought would never come true again. So, today I made sure that I had all the necessary things to keep us from needing to leave the house. Food, water, and, entertainment in the form of some of the sexiest pieces of lace I've ever put on my body.

I hear the garage door open and close, signaling that Elliot is home and Eli is safely sequestered, and quickly sit on top of the kitchen counter, legs spread as they dangle over the corner. My hands rest between my knees, spilling my breasts over the top of the sheer demi bra that could not shield anyone's eyes from seeing every blessed curve I have to offer. Part of the reason for buying this little flimsy number is the rip-ability rating I think it will receive. Yes, Elliot could destroy this flimsy number in a second, and that makes me hotter than hell in July.

My man stops in his tracks the instant he is through the door and stares at me with a dark passion I've not seen in a very long time. The flowers in his hand slip as he moves his eyes over every inch of my body.

"Baby," he says as he starts to walk toward me, "you are all manner of sins right now." He places the flowers on the counter next to me before running his hands over my body. "You are beyond beautiful."

"Thank you." I smile, satisfied that I can easily see how turned on he is through his jeans. "Dinner's just about ready."

"How much time?" His eyebrow quirks upward.

"We have about an hour," I offer, looking over at the oven before back at him.

He blows out a breath before grabbing me off the counter, wrapping up my legs and torso to carry me up the stairs. "Dinner may have to wait a little longer."

I laugh at his quick pace up the stairs and unapologetic rush onto the bed. Before I can blink, his lips are on mine, kissing me with the fervor of a man possessed.

Our mouths exploring each other, our synced breath, and his weight on my body all stoke the fire that ignites every fiber of my being. I am his in every way: mind, heart, body, and soul.

And I know, without a doubt, that he is mine. Smiling in the bliss this man has created, I wrap my arms around him a little tighter, hugging him against me.

"Baby," he breathes softly, "are you okay?"

"Oh, yes. I am beyond okay." I nuzzle along his neck before lightly kissing the beautiful juncture of his jaw and throat. "I'm in Heaven."

Piper Malone became passionate about writing in her early years and has always found comfort and belonging in the beautifully crafted words of authors she adores. Enchanted by the connection of pen to paper, Piper is never without a journal to capture her thoughts and musings. An insatiable adventurer, Piper rarely passes on the chance to try something new but also enjoys the simple pleasures of a glass of wine, dark chocolate and a good book. She lives in Pennsylvania with her husband and son.

For the latest information on book releases, upcoming events, and social media links, please visit Piper at
www.pipermalone.net

More from Piper Malone:
Tied: Book One, The Reign Series

Coming Soon:
Bound: Book Two, The Reign Series
Genesis: The Prequel to Diesel